MISSION ROAD

ALSO BY RICK RIORDAN

MISSION ROAD

RICK RIORDAN

BANTAM BOOKS

MISSION ROAD
A Bantam Book / July 2005

Published by
Bantam Dell
A Division of Random House, Inc.
New York, New York

Library of Congress Cataloging-in-Publication Data

Riordan, Rick.
　Mission road / Rick Riordan.
　　p.　cm.
　ISBN 0-553-80185-6
　1. Navarre, Tres (Fictitious character)—Fiction. 2. Private investigators—
Texas—San Antonio—Fiction. 3. Married women—Crimes against—Fiction.
4. Policewomen—Crimes against—Fiction. 5. Fugitives from justice—Fiction.
6. Police murders—Fiction. I. Title.

PS3568.I5866M577 2005
813'.54—dc22

2005046404

Printed in the United States of America
Published simultaneously in Canada

www.bantamdell.com

10　9　8　7　6　5　4　3　2　1
BVG

To Jim and Ben Glusing, for
many years of friendship
and support

MISSION ROAD

CHAPTER 1

ANA HAD TO GET THE BABY OUT OF THE HOUSE. Things were about to get ugly.

She called Ralph's sister, told her one of them would drop off Lucia in ten minutes.

She packed a bag of diapers, bottles, extra clothes, Lucia's favorite blanket and stuffed beagle.

In the kitchen high chair, Lucia was finger-painting her tray with yams, her meaty little hands coated with orange goo. She'd managed to get some in the black tufts of her hair.

Ana stared at the mess on her daughter's bib and realized she was thinking about blood-splatter patterns.

Looking at her own daughter, and thinking about the homicide case.

Ana had to end this. Tonight, before she lost her nerve.

She zipped the travel bag, unlocked the high chair tray and immediately got yams on the sleeve of her blazer.

"Damn it," she muttered.

She hadn't bothered changing from work. She'd only taken time to empty her shoulder holster and lock the service-issue Glock in the hallway closet where it always went the moment she got home.

She was trying to figure out how to get the baby cleaned up without ruining her clothes when Ralph stormed into the kitchen.

He'd showered and put on his old traveling outfit—black jeans, steel-tipped boots, crisp white linen guayabera, black leather jacket. His newly braided ponytail curled over one shoulder.

He clunked a Magnum clip next to the baby's sippy-cup and started loading his .357.

"What are you doing?" Ana demanded.

He gave her that high-voltage look which had been bothering her for weeks.

Since laser surgery, Ralph had set aside his thick round glasses for contact lenses. There was no longer any shield between his ferocity and the rest of the world. His stare reminded her too much of the people she worked with—cops and killers.

She wasn't afraid of him. She'd never been afraid of him. But tension from their earlier argument hung in the air like the smell of burnt fuses.

He finished loading the gun, hooked it inside his pants—a makeshift holster rigged from a coat hanger. "Johnny Shoes has a lead for me. I'll drop Lucia on the way."

Johnny Zapata.

That's how desperate they'd become: begging for help from a drug lord who literally cut his enemies to pieces.

"Ralph, the last time you saw Zapata—"

"I'll be fine."

"He tried to kill you."

"You want to give me a better lead?"

He must've known she was holding back. She'd asked for time alone tonight. She only did that when she needed to make an important decision. And this time, their lives hung in the balance.

"I can't," Ana told him.

"You know who killed Frankie, don't you?"

"I've already told you more than I should."

He considered that, his eyes boring into her. "Yeah. Maybe you did."

"Ah-ba." Lucia held up her gooey hands to her father. "Ah-ba."

Ralph unfastened the seat strap and lifted the baby out of the yam disaster area. Her fingers made streaks of orange on his white guayabera, but Ralph didn't seem to care. He kissed the baby's messy cheek, put her over his shoulder. Lucia made a high-pitched squeal of delight and kicked her bunny feet against Daddy's belly.

Ana's heart felt sore.

Lucia never acted so happy when Ana picked her up.

Career necessity. Lieutenant Hernandez hadn't put his butt on the line recommending her for sergeant so she could take six months off to change diapers. Still, the first year of Lucia's life, mother and daughter had spent most of their time telling each other goodbye.

"Hey, Sergeant." Ralph held out his hand, his tone so fierce he might've been issuing a challenge. "It'll be okay. *Tú eres mi amor por vida.*"

She wanted to cry, she loved him so much.

Two years ago at their wedding, her police friends had given her horrible looks. Hernandez had pulled her aside, eyes flooded with concern, fingers like talons on her forearm: *Ana, how can you love this guy? He's a goddamn killer.*

But they didn't know Ralph. He loved her the way he did everything else—with absolute intensity. Since the day he'd decided he wanted Ana, she never stood a chance. He had boiled over her like a wildfire.

She laced her fingers with his.

She couldn't let anything happen to him. She should never have opened that cold case file.

"Zapata will have proof," Ralph promised. "Anybody does, it's him. And he's going to give it to me. Believe that, okay?"

She knew what Ralph was capable of. Which was exactly why she didn't dare tell him everything she knew.

He gave her hand a squeeze, kissed her lightly. His whiskers were rough. He smelled of patchouli.

Ralph cradled the baby against one shoulder and slung the travel bag over the other. He stuffed an extra clip of ammunition in his pocket.

The kitchen door swung shut behind him, winter air gusting into the room.

Ana listened to his footsteps crunch down the gravel walkway. He was calling Lucia his little *niña*, singing her a Spanish carol, "Los Animales," as he strapped her into the car seat.

His headlights swept across the kitchen, illuminating the Christmas *ristra* and the empty high chair, then disappeared down Ruiz Street.

• • •

ANA SAT IN THE LIVING ROOM, trying to formulate a plan.

He would be here in fifteen minutes.

There had to be a way—something to make him come clean. Their earlier conversation gave her little hope he would listen to reason, but she had to try. She owed him that much.

On the coffee table, a photograph of her mother stared back at her—Lucia DeLeon Sr., twenty-nine years old, in dress uniform, 1975, the day she received the Medal of Valor.

Her mother's face was a patchwork of yellow bruises, her arm in a sling, but her posture radiated quiet confidence, black eyebrows knit as if she didn't quite understand all the fuss. She'd saved three officers' lives, become the first female cop in SAPD history to use deadly force. What was the big deal?

Ana liked to remember her mother that way—self-assured, indomitable, always firm and fair. But over the years, the photograph had lost some of its magic. It could no longer quite exorcise that other memory—her mother fifteen years older, slumped in bed with the drapes drawn, a glass of wine at her lips, skin sickly blue in the light of an afternoon soap opera.

Come back when you don't feel like preaching, mijita.

Ana put her face in her hands. A sob was building in her chest, but she couldn't give in to that. She had to think.

If her mother—the Lucia DeLeon of 1975—had been handed Ana's problem, what would she have done?

Ana pulled her laptop out of her briefcase. She booted it up, typed in her password. She reviewed her case notes, the crime scene photos. Poor-quality scans of pre-digital black-and-whites, but Ana could still get the feel. She'd been to the scene many times.

Ana imagined herself as the killer.

It was a little before 10:00 P.M., midsummer, on the rural South Side. She was standing on the shoulder of Mission Road, arguing with the young man she was about to murder.

A warm rain had just pushed through, leaving the air like steam engine smoke, scented with wild garlic. In the woods, cicadas chirred.

Ana and the young man had both pulled over their cars—possibly a prearranged rendezvous, though why the young man would've agreed to it, Ana didn't know. There was nothing for miles except barbed wire fence, railroad tracks and old mission lands overgrown with cactus and chinaberry.

The road was an ancient trail connecting the five Spanish missions of San Antonio. It was also a popular dumping ground for corpses—isolated and dark, yet easy to get to. Homicide department trivia: The first recorded murder along Mission Road had been in 1732. According to the diary of a Franciscan friar, a Coahuiltecan Indian girl was found strangled in the fields of maize. Not much had changed over the centuries.

On the night Ana was thinking about, the victim was a young Anglo, six-one, thickset, dressed in khakis and a white linen shirt. He wore a platinum Rolex that would still be on his wrist when the police found his body. He had shoulder-length blond hair, parted in the middle, feathered in that unfortunate Eighties style. He was handsome enough, the way a young bull groomed for auction is handsome, but his expression was arrogant—a natural disdain that came from being born rich, well-connected, absolutely untouchable.

She and the victim argued. There was probably name-calling. Some pushing. At some point—and this was critical—he grabbed her arm. When she yanked away, his fingernails drew blood. He turned away, probably thinking the fight was over. He started back to his car—a silver Mercedes convertible just a few yards away.

But the fight was not over for her. She grasped the murder weapon—a blunt object, shorter than a baseball bat. She imagined herself striking from behind, cracking the side of the young man's skull. He went down, crumpling before her, but she wasn't satisfied. Rage took over.

Afterward, she left him there—she made no attempt to hide his body or move his car. She would've known damn well who the victim's father was, what kind of hell would break loose when the body was found. She knew what would happen to her if she was ever discovered. She simply drove away, and her secret had stayed hidden for eighteen years.

Ana could slip into the killer's skin so easily it frightened her. But then, she knew him well. His size, his strength, his motive, the way he would've lost control. Everything fit.

But how could she make an arrest?

Light flooded the living room windows.

A car pulled into the drive—familiar headlights, ten minutes early.

Ana wasn't ready. She glanced at the hallway closet, where her gun was locked, but he was already coming up the front steps.

Don't panic, she told herself. *It won't come to that.*

The doorbell rang.

Ana had a sudden desire to bolt out the back, run to the neighbors.

But no. She was in control. She'd asked for this meeting. She had faced down desperate men before.

She walked to the front door to greet him.

• • •

HE HAD BEEN IDLING A FEW blocks away in a *taquería* parking lot, getting up his nerve, replaying the argument with Ana over and over.

She was so goddamn stubborn. He'd put the obvious answer right in front of her, given her overwhelming evidence, and still she refused to believe.

He tried to think of an alternative to what he was about to do.

There wasn't one.

He loaded the .357 Magnum, put the car into drive.

He wasn't worried about neighbors. Ana DeLeon's house fronted Rosedale Park. On either side were vacant lease properties—not unusual for the West Side. The only neighbors were the ones in back, an elderly couple across the alley.

If things went right, it wouldn't matter if he was seen. Her husband, Ralph Arguello, was a reliably volatile son-of-a-bitch. Ralph would start the fight. If things went wrong . . . no. He wouldn't let things go wrong.

He pulled into the driveway. He could see Ana through the living room window.

He walked toward the porch, the cold air stinging his eyes. The butt of the unfamiliar gun chafed against his hipbone.

She met him at the door.

As always, the sight of her stirred an unpleasant mix of feelings—resentment, longing, grief. She was the closest thing he had to family. She was also his deepest war wound—a scar that wouldn't heal.

Her short black hair was disheveled; there was a long smear of baby food on her sleeve. The top button of her blouse was undone. Her collarbone made a smooth shadow against her skin. A beautiful woman, but she had interrogator's eyes—dark as magnets.

"Well?" she asked.

"I have an answer for you." His voice sounded strangely dry, even to him. "May I come in?"

•   •   •

ONCE HE WAS INSIDE, SHE DID a good job of acting calm, but he knew her too well. Her shoulders were tense. Her fingertips tapped against her thumbs.

"Make yourself comfortable," she called from the kitchen. "You want a soda?"

He stared at the photograph of Lucia on the living room table. He was always amazed how strongly Ana resembled her mother.

Next to the photo was Ana's laptop—crime scene images frozen on the screen.

"Where's Ralph?" he asked.

"Out. Was that a no on the soda?"

"Out?" He tried to keep his voice level. "You were supposed to keep him here. This is a conversation about him."

"We got Sprite, Diet Coke—"

"Ana, goddamn it. You're out of time."

She popped a can of Sprite. "This conversation isn't about Ralph. It's about you."

"Me?"

She leaned against the kitchen doorway. "I can't let you skate."

He could feel the situation unraveling. This was not the way it was supposed to happen. Ralph was the enemy. Ana had to realize that. Ralph was supposed to be here, to be provoked into showing how violent he was, how capable of murder.

Carefully, he said, "You're not serious."

"You left a trail." Ana's voice was heavy with anger, as if he had let her down. "You were sloppy. How could you think I wouldn't find you?"

Her expression stirred bad memories—memories he couldn't tolerate.

"You have any idea what you're saying?" he asked. "*Me,* for Christ's sake?"

She nodded to the computer. "Read my notes."

He glanced at the morgue photo on the screen. He touched the keyboard, brought up a minimized document—Ana's draft report on the investigation.

It didn't take long to see that she'd done her homework. Every mistake he'd made, then and now—neatly documented.

He felt claustrophobic, dizzy, like he was waking up inside a coffin.

The irony was horrible. Yet she'd done good detective work, maybe even enough to convict.

"Ralph Arguello is poison," he managed. "You don't know who your friends are anymore."

"I'm telling you first because a confession would be easier. We can get you some kind of deal. Protection. Otherwise, once word gets out, you're a dead man."

His jaw tightened. She wasn't going to change her mind. She would risk a confrontation, her career, everything, rather than see something happen to that goddamn criminal she'd married.

He put his hand at his waist, felt the butt of the .357 under his coat. "You're right."

"Give me a statement, then."

"I'm a dead man." He brought out the gun. "If word gets out."

Her face paled. "You won't shoot me. I'm going to call now. We'll get you a lawyer."

She walked to the hallway phone—tension still in her shoulders, but damn, she was keeping it together well.

The thing was: She might be right. He wasn't sure he could hurt her. Her, of all people.

She picked up the receiver.

"Put it down," he ordered.

"I'm calling dispatch."

Eighteen years of fear, shame and anger boiled to the surface—eighteen years of living with that worthless kid's blood on his conscience.

Ana would never understand what had happened that night. He had sworn to die rather than let the truth come out.

"Put the phone down," he pleaded.

"No choice." She started to dial.

The first shot surprised him almost as much as it did her. The bullet tore through her pants leg. She dropped her Sprite and stood there, stunned, as a line of blood trickled down her ankle. Sprite gurgled from the overturned can on the hardwood floor.

She stared at him, silently saying his name.

11

"I'm sorry," he told her. And he meant it. Goddamn it, he had never wanted this.

Ana reached for her own weapon, but of course her shoulder holster was empty.

She did not believe in guns around the baby. This house was a sanctuary.

Which may have been why his second shot, leveled at her chest, rang out so alarmingly loud.

CHAPTER 2

MONDAY MORNING I GOT A PAYING CLIENT.

Wednesday afternoon I killed him.

Friday evening I buried him.

The Tres Navarre Detective Agency is a full-service operation. Did I mention that?

My girlfriend, Maia Lee, drove me home from the funeral. We cruised down Commerce in her BMW, discussing the likelihood of my PI license being revoked. Maia thought the odds were high. Being a lawyer, she probably knew what she was talking about.

"The criminal charges don't worry me," she said. "The DA didn't sound serious about filing."

"That's because he wanted your phone number."

"But the licensing board . . . I mean, killing clients—"

"Generally frowned upon."

"Tres Navarre: impeccable judge of character."

"Oh, shut up."

The guy I'd killed, Dr. Allen Vale, had asked me to find his estranged wife. He said he needed to work out an inheritance problem with her. He hadn't seen her in five years. They'd never gotten an official divorce. No hard feelings. The relationship was old history. He just needed to sort out a few legalities.

He wore a tailored suit. He laughed at my jokes. He paid cash in advance.

I took the job.

Two days later I located his wife, living in San Antonio under an assumed name. I met Dr. Vale at my office and gave him her new identity and address. He thanked me, calmly walked out to his car, loaded a shotgun and drove away. That's when I realized I'd made a mistake.

I called the police, sure. But I also grabbed my father's old .38 and followed Vale straight to his estranged wife's house.

She was standing in her front yard watering her Mexican marigolds. She dropped the hose when she saw Vale trudging toward her with the shotgun.

No police in sight.

I had the choice of either stopping Vale or watching him murder his wife. I yelled at him to drop the gun. He turned on me and fired.

Three minutes later the police surrounded the house.

They found me standing next to Allen Vale's Infiniti, a dinner-plate-size shotgun hole in the driver's side door, two feet to my left. The good doctor was sprawled on the lawn with an entrance wound through the middle of his silk tie, his estranged wife on her knees, her face chalky with terror, her forgotten garden hose spraying blood and marigold petals down the sidewalk.

Maia had asked me why I wanted to go to the memorial service and face Vale's family. I told her closure. That was a lie. The truth was probably closer to Catholic guilt. I was raised to believe repentance is not enough. One must emotionally flag-ellate oneself as much as possible.

Maia reached across the car seat and squeezed my hand. "You did what you had to."

"Would *you* have shot him?"

She drove another block before answering. "I would've talked to the wife before giving her away. I think I would've seen through the client's bullshit at the first meeting."

"Thanks. I feel better."

"You're a guy. What's obvious to me isn't to you."

"A woman who collects assault rifles is lecturing me on sensitivity."

Maia called me a few endearing pet names in Mandarin. In the years we'd been together, I'd learned all kinds of helpful Chinese phrases like *Idiot white boy* and *My father told me not to date barbarians.*

We drove over the Market Street Bridge. Below, the River-walk's fifty-foot cypress trees blazed with Christmas lights like frozen fireworks.

In the multicolored glow, Maia looked unusually pensive.

She was beautiful in funeral black. Her dark ponytail al-most disappeared against the linen dress. Her caramel skin was smooth, radiating such obvious health that she might've been mistaken for twenty-five rather than forty-five.

There was something timeless about her—a kind of fierce

resilience that might've been carved from jade. Before losing everything to the Communists, her ancestors had been warlords of Guangzhou Province. I had no doubt Maia would've made them proud.

She didn't seem to notice the holiday lights or the traffic. Her eyes stayed fixed on some point a thousand miles away.

"What're you thinking?" I asked.

"Nothing," she said, a little too quickly.

She turned on South Alamo, headed into Southtown.

First Friday. The usual hordes were out in force for the monthly gallery openings. Cars circled for parking. Drunk socialites and *Nuevo* Bohemians wandered the streets. It was as if God had upended all the chic restaurants and coffeehouses in town, mixed the patrons thoroughly in alcohol sauce, and dumped them into my neighborhood to find their way home.

Maia parked at the hydrant on the corner of Pecan, in front of my two-story Victorian.

A lady in a mink coat was throwing up in my front yard. She'd set her wineglass on top of my business sign:

TRES NAVARRE DETECTIVE AGENCY
Professional Investigations
(This is not an art gallery)

As our headlights illuminated her fur jacket, the lady turned and scowled at us. She staggered off like a sick bear, leaving her wineglass and a steaming puddle.

"Ah, the romance of San Antonio," said Maia.

"Stay the night," I said. "It gets better."

"I have to get back to Austin."

I took her hand, felt the tension in her fingers. "Tomorrow's Saturday. Live dangerous. Sam would love to see you."

She gave me a look I couldn't quite read. "I have to catch up with work. I've been busy bailing out my no-good boyfriend."

"Men," I said.

She leaned in closer. "Some of them, anyway."

We kissed. ·

I tried my best to convince her that one night together really wouldn't hurt.

She pulled away. "Tres . . ."

"What is it?"

She dabbed her lipstick. "Nothing."

"Something's wrong."

"I have to go—"

"Maia?"

"—if I want to get home before midnight."

We sat there with the car idling. A group of drunk art gallery patrons parted around us.

"Multiple choice," I offered. "Work or personal?"

Maia's eyes betrayed a glint of desperation—like a cage door was closing on her. "I'll call you, okay?"

It wasn't okay. Even *I* was sensitive enough to see that. But I also knew better than to press her.

I kissed her one last time. We said an uneasy good night.

Maia's BMW pulled away down South Alamo. I fought an urge to follow her—an instinct almost as strong as when I'd grabbed my father's gun and tailed Dr. Vale.

"Hey," a passerby called to me. "Gotta restroom in there?"

He was an art gallery cowboy—grizzled ponytail and black

denim, too much New Mexican jewelry. Judging from his slurred words, he was about three beers shy of a keg.

"I got a restroom," I admitted. "Last visitor who used it, I just got back from his funeral."

The cowboy laughed.

I stared at him.

He muttered something about not needing to pee that bad and stumbled off down the street.

I glanced at my business sign, wondering how much longer it would be there if my license got revoked. The art patrons might have the last laugh. By the next First Friday, this place *might* be a gallery.

I headed up the sidewalk, feeling like I was still walking behind somebody's coffin.

•   •   •

SAM BARRERA AND OUR HOUSEKEEPER, MRS. Loomis, were playing Hearts in the living room.

When I'd moved in last summer, I promised my accountant the whole first floor of the house would be used for business. The residential space would be confined to upstairs. Unfortunately, Sam and Mrs. Loomis did a lot more residing here than I did business.

Slowly but surely, my waiting room had reverted to living room. Mrs. Loomis' crystal knickknacks multiplied like Jesus' loaves. My carefully placed stack of *Detective Industry Today* got shoved aside for Sam's medication tray. Framed photos of the Barrera family proliferated on the walls, with sticky note names and arrows next to all the faces so Sam could remember who was who. A crochet basket lived on my desk, right next to the skip-trace files.

All I needed now were lace doilies on the sofa and I'd be trapped in my grandmother's house forever.

Sam and Mrs. Loomis had taken over the coffee table for their card game.

Sam wore pleated slacks, a dress shirt and a blue tie. His FBI standard-issue shoulder holster was fitted with a black plastic water gun.

The gun was a compromise.

I'd learned the hard way that when Sam got up in the morning, he wouldn't rest until he found a firearm. I could take them away, lock them up, whatever. He would tear the house apart looking. If he didn't find one, he would wander around irritated all day. He'd try to sneak out and drive to the gun shop.

Finally Mrs. Loomis suggested the water gun, which was a dead ringer for Sam's old service pistol except for the bright orange plastic muzzle.

Sam was happy. Mrs. Loomis was happy. Sam could now shoot my cat as much as he wanted and Robert Johnson got nothing worse than a wet butt. Domestic harmony reigned.

"Who's winning?" I asked.

"Special Agent Barrera," Mrs. Loomis grumbled. "Five dollars and counting."

"Go easy on her, Sam," I said.

Sam looked at me innocently. He stuffed a roll of quarters into his pants pocket. "Hell, Fred. I never play for cash."

My name isn't Fred, but that never bothered Sam much.

In the last six months, he'd put on weight. He looked more robust and relaxed than he'd ever looked during his prime. Living at the Southtown office obviously agreed with him.

Of course, it should. He'd grown up in this house.

Through an odd series of circumstances, I'd become Sam's caretaker and tenant when his memory started going. He didn't want to give up the family home. He couldn't maintain it by himself. I needed a cheap place to live and work.

Sam being a legendary former FBI agent and my biggest rival in the local PI market, I figured I was doing myself a favor by helping him retire. Every so often, I trotted him out to meet clients for "high-level consultations." Sam loved it. So did the clients, as long as I didn't mention Sam's mental condition.

"How was the funeral?" Mrs. Loomis asked.

"The sermon was short." I sank into an armchair. "Good appetizers. Closed casket. Nobody assaulted me."

She nodded approvingly.

Sam laid his cards on the table. "I win."

"Agent Barrera," Mrs. Loomis chided. "I haven't even bid yet."

"Can't beat the master." Sam plucked another quarter from her change dish.

Mrs. Loomis sighed and reshuffled the cards.

She was by far the best assisted-living nurse we'd had. She got room and board, so she worked cheap. Being the widow of a cop, she was unfazed by the grittier aspects of my work. Sam and I provided her with company and a purpose. In return, she scolded Sam into taking his meds and kept him from interrogating the mailman at water-gun-point.

Out on South Alamo, Friday night traffic built to a dangerous hum. Somewhere, a glass bottle shattered against asphalt.

I needed to get up, change out of my funeral suit. But whenever I stopped moving, numbness set in. I started thinking about the .38 caliber hole I'd put in Dr. Vale's chest.

What bothered me most wasn't my remorse. It was that my remorse seemed . . . intellectual. Detached.

I was stunned at how easy it had been to kill a man. I was horrified by the elation I'd felt afterward, when I realized the doctor's shot had missed me.

I was alive. He was dead. *Damn right.*

Perhaps Maia Lee had seen the wildness in my eyes when she'd met me at the police station. Maybe that's what was bothering her.

My finger curled, remembering the weight of the .38 trigger.

Years ago, I'd asked a homicidal friend if stepping over the moral line got easier each time you killed a man.

He'd laughed. *Only moral line is your own skin,* vato.

That friend now had a wife and kid.

He'd stopped hanging around me because I was a bad influence.

In the kitchen, by the back door, Robert Johnson licked a tuna can. A moth with smoking wings fluttered around the lightbulb.

"Tres?" Mrs. Loomis asked. "Would you like to play?"

When I tried to speak, I realized I'd been clenching my jaw.

"Thanks," I said. "But I should—"

Bang.

The back door rattled.

Robert Johnson evaporated from the doormat, abandoning his tuna can.

"Not again," Mrs. Loomis muttered.

We were used to unwelcome visitors on the weekends— stray partiers looking for art, free food and beer, not necessarily in that order. Most came to the front door, but some wandered in from the backyard.

"I'll deal with 'em," Sam said, going for his water gun.

Then a familiar face appeared at the kitchen window—the friend I'd just been thinking about.

"Keep playing," I told Sam. "I'll take care of it."

I walked into the kitchen, closing the living room door behind me. I went to the back door and let in Ralph Arguello.

"*Vato* . . ." His voice faltered.

He had blood on his hands. There were speckles of it on his forearms, a large red explosion drying on the belly of his white guayabera.

I don't remember exactly what I said. Something intelligent like "Oh, shit."

Ralph pushed past me, collapsed in a chair. He dropped a gun on the breakfast table. His regular .357. At least, it used to be his regular .357 until he got married and swore never to use it again.

Mrs. Loomis called, "Tres? Are you all right?"

Ralph locked eyes with me. His expression was a few volts shy of a stripped power line.

"I'm fine," I called. "Just an old friend."

"Zapata set me up," Ralph croaked. "Two of them. I got one in the gut. The other—"

"Slow down," I said. "Any of that blood yours?"

"No. No, I don't think so."

I drew the shades. I ripped a roll of paper towels off the dispenser and soaked them in hot water.

"Shit, Ralph. Johnny Shoes? What were you thinking?"

"Had to talk to him . . . Supposed to be a goddamn talk."

"We'll call Ana."

"No!" He snatched a steaming wad of paper towels from me and pressed his face into them. "It was self-defense, *vato*.

But Ana can't . . . she can't see me like this. You gotta let me rest here—just for a little while."

Several reasons to say *hell, no* occurred to me.

If Ralph had acted in self-defense, he needed to come clean with the police immediately. He would already be in deep crap for leaving the scene. Besides, I was in enough trouble with the SAPD.

Still, something in his voice made me hesitate.

The kitchen door creaked open. Sam stuck his head in.

He didn't look surprised to see a blood-splattered man sitting at our kitchen table.

"Who shot this agent?" he asked.

Ralph and I exchanged looks.

"It was an ambush," I told Sam. "Our CI gave us bad information."

"I hate when that happens," Sam said. "You need an ambulance, son?"

"I'm okay," said Ralph, a little shaky, but catching on fast. "Thanks, Mr. Barrera."

"Special Agent Barrera," Sam corrected.

"Sorry, sir."

"Sam," I said, "we don't want to upset Mrs. Loomis, seeing an agent in this condition. You think you could convince her to take you to the store for some Metamucil or something?"

Sam nodded grimly. "I'm on the case."

• • •

I WRAPPED RALPH'S BLOOD-SOAKED SHIRT and .357 in a plastic garbage bag and stuffed them behind the loose plywood wall in the laundry room. I told myself I could retrieve them as soon as Ralph calmed down enough to call the police.

I reparked his Lincoln Continental so it wasn't blocking the entire alley. I didn't realize there was blood on the steering wheel until it was all over my hands. Feeling nauseous, I washed off with the backyard hose.

I thought about Ralph appearing at my door—the first time I'd seen him in five months. I should've resented him showing up like this, after he'd become a family man and let our friendship waste away. I should've been angry that he was bringing me so much trouble.

But the truth was I was too dazed to be angry. Not because he'd shot somebody. He'd killed men before. But I'd known Ralph Arguello since high school, and I couldn't recall any time when he'd looked so shaken, or come to me for help. It was always the other way around.

I also understood why Ralph didn't want his wife, Ana DeLeon, to know anything. Their marriage two years ago had caused a huge scandal in the SAPD, especially since she'd just become the first woman ever to make sergeant in homicide. Officially, there had been no problem with Ana marrying Ralph. He had no criminal record. Unofficially, everybody knew he deserved one.

For years, Ralph had monopolized the pawnshop business in town. It was common knowledge that he moved stolen goods. He wasn't above violence to protect and expand his territory. In fact, the main reason Johnny Zapata hated Ralph was that Ralph wouldn't sell his properties, which Zapata wanted to use to front his own smuggling operations. Zapata wasn't used to having people tell him no, and Ralph had been telling him to go screw himself for years.

Ralph had promised Ana he'd go clean when they got married. He'd dropped out of the street scene, turned over his shops to his managers, become a stay-at-home dad. These days, the most dangerous thing he did was trading on eBay.

Until tonight.

•   •   •

BY THE TIME RALPH CAME OUT of the bathroom, showered and dressed in a spare set of Sam's clothes, I was sitting in the rocking chair of my upstairs bedroom, Robert Johnson purring like a low-rider engine in my lap.

The cat made a chirping sound and leapt to the floor as soon as he saw Ralph. He padded over and began rubbing against Ralph's legs.

Ralph is allergic to cats. Cats, of course, know this. They think he's the best thing since flaked tuna.

"So what happened?" I asked Ralph. "Exactly."

He faced the mirror, buttoned Sam's linen shirt. "I needed information."

"You must've needed it pretty bad."

He rolled the cuffs. His unbraided hair made a wet black fan across the baggy shoulders of the shirt.

I'd always thought of Ralph and Sam as about the same size—both heavyset men, both with a juggernaut aura that came from their reputations. But Sam's clothes were much too big on Ralph. The gray slacks sagged. The cuffs crumpled around his bare feet, as if Ralph had shrunk in the shower. I realized he would've done better in my clothes. It hadn't even occurred to me that they might fit.

"I've been accused of something," he said finally. "Ana . . . she found out about it. I need to clear myself. Zapata was my best lead."

"What's the crime?"

25

He stared at the mirror. "I told Zapata I'd meet him at Jarrasco's tonight, down on South Flores—"

"I know where Jarrasco's is."

"He wasn't there. Two guys intercepted me. Big *cholo* with red hair. I didn't know him. A thinner guy I recognized, one of Zapata's enforcers. They lured me out back. I was stupid as shit. The big one pinned me. Thin guy brought out a hunting knife. You know Zapata . . . what he likes his guys to do with knives. I got one arm free, got to my gun. I don't know—I didn't have a choice. I shot the thin guy in the gut, point-blank. The big one released me from shock, I guess. I ran."

His hands were trembling on top of the dresser.

"You sure he's dead?" I said.

Ralph nodded. "Cops'll be after me."

"It was self-defense, like you said." I tried to sound reassuring. "Shooting one of Zapata's goons—shit, police'll probably give you a medal."

"I'm not talking about for that."

Without the glasses, Ralph's eyes were unnerving—hot and raw, like holes in the ozone.

"This crime you're accused of," I said, "the one you don't want to tell me about . . . the police have any evidence?"

"I shouldn't be here, *vato*. Shouldn't get you involved."

"Don't worry. Whatever's wrong—"

The doorbell rang downstairs.

Ralph looked at the bedroom window, but there was nothing to see on this side of the house—just the old fire escape ladder, the backyard, the alley.

"Sam and Mrs. Loomis?" Ralph asked.

I shook my head. "Too soon. I'll check it out."

"It's the police."

"It isn't the police. Just sit tight. Watch my cat."

"That fire escape work?"

"Ralph—"

"I haven't told you everything, *vato*. If it's the police, I can't surrender."

The doorbell rang again.

Robert Johnson said, "Murrrp?"

I scooped him off the floor, handed him to Ralph. "You guys make nice. Don't do anything stupid."

At the bottom of the stairs, I remembered the gun box in my dresser drawer. Ralph knew I kept it there. He knew the combination. My dad's .38 had been confiscated after the Vale shooting, but I still had a .22. I didn't want it in Ralph's hands, the way he was acting.

Unfortunately, I couldn't turn back. One of my homicide department admirers was glaring at me through the glass panel of the front door, waiting to be let in.

•   •   •

"OPEN," DETECTIVE KELSEY GRUNTED AT ME through the screen door. "Now."

For Kelsey, this was downright civil. That made me nervous.

Kelsey was an ex-SWAT member with a face like a battering ram. He wore a cheap blue suit with an American flag on the lapel. His eyes were marksman eyes. Everything he examined was either a potential kill or useless. He'd also been Ana DeLeon's partner until she got promoted over him and became his supervisor.

Alone, Kelsey wouldn't have bothered me. But the head of homicide, Lieutenant Herberto "Etch" Hernandez, was standing behind him, flanked by a couple of uniforms.

I let them in.

Kelsey took a seat on the sofa. Lieutenant Hernandez drifted toward the fireplace and studied the labeled photos of Sam Barrera's family. The uniforms stayed by the front door and glared at me.

"Look," I said, "if this is about the Vale shooting . . ."

Kelsey picked up one of Mrs. Loomis' glass knickknacks, turned it so it magnified the knife scars on his fingers. "You watch TV in the last hour, Navarre? Listen to the radio?"

Somewhere down in my gut, a lead-weighted fishing hook made a tiny splash.

I was used to cops being mad at me, but there was something different about the level of anger here—a barely restrained thirst for violence so strong I could feel it arcing between the four men.

"I've been busy," I managed.

Lieutenant Hernandez turned toward me. His Armani suit was immaculate as always, his ash-gray hair combed and gelled. He exuded such power and style he could've passed for an investment banker, but tonight his face was gaunt, grief-stricken. "Mr. Navarre, we're looking for your friend Ralph Arguello. We're hoping you can tell us where he is."

Four sets of cop eyes drilled into me.

"You work with his wife," I said. "If Ana doesn't know—"

"Navarre." Kelsey's voice tightened. "Just under an hour ago, at her home, Sergeant DeLeon was shot twice. Once in the leg. Once in the chest. She's at Brooke Army Medical Center, dying."

Everything came into sharper focus—the bristle on Kelsey's chin, Hernandez's cologne, the sounds of traffic outside.

"She's comatose," Kelsey said. "Chances are she won't last the night."

"Ralph . . . doesn't know?"

"We'd love to inform him," Hernandez said evenly. "He's nowhere to be found."

I stared at the glass apple rotating in Kelsey's fingers.

"Mr. Navarre," Hernandez said, "Sergeant DeLeon was about to press charges in a reopened murder investigation—a cold case from eighteen years ago. Does the name Franklin White mean anything to you?"

The room started spinning faster than the glass apple.

I got unsteadily to my feet.

"Mr. Navarre?" Hernandez said.

"Would you gentlemen excuse me? I have a number that might help . . . up in my bedroom." I staggered toward the stairs. "I'll get it, soon as I finish throwing up."

"I'll come with you," Kelsey said.

"I'll manage. Unless you want to watch me hug the toilet."

Kelsey and Hernandez exchanged looks. Apparently I looked as bad as I felt.

"Two minutes, Mr. Navarre," Hernandez told me.

"Lieutenant—" Kelsey protested.

Hernandez held up his hand. "And Mr. Navarre, this phone number better be *very* helpful."

•　•　•

I OPENED THE BEDROOM DOOR AND found myself staring down the barrel of my own .22.

"Kelsey's voice," Ralph muttered, pulling me into the room. "Is Ana with him?"

29

I swallowed the dryness out of my throat. I told him what the cops had said.

Ralph backed into the bed and sat down hard.

Robert Johnson, never good with empathy, materialized in his lap and rubbed against the gun, demanding attention.

I figured we had about one minute before Detective Kelsey came looking for me.

Ralph's fingers whitened on the pistol grip.

"Ralph, give me the gun," I said.

He stared at the .22.

"*Ralph,*" I said sharply.

He gave me a look I knew well—Sam Barrera, 7:00 A.M. every morning—a blank slate into which I would have to pour all the names and geography and relationships he'd forgotten overnight.

"I have to see her." His voice was ragged with grief.

"If you give yourself up—"

"I told you, *vato,* I can't. They'll take me in. They'll never catch the right guy."

"Four cops downstairs, Ralph. Give me the goddamn gun."

We had about thirty seconds now, tops.

Ralph's eyes were molten glass. "I didn't shoot Ana."

"I know that."

And I did know. There wasn't a single doubt in my mind.

But I also knew—given Ralph's mental state and the mood of the cops—that if I let Ralph go downstairs, somebody was going to die.

"They mentioned Frankie White," I said.

Ralph nodded, unsurprised. "So you understand why I can't give myself up."

"Aw, Ralph—shit."

"That fire escape work?"

Kelsey's voice from downstairs: "Navarre?"

"We can't just run," I told Ralph.

"There is no 'we,' *vato*. I'm going out that window. I'm going to find the guy who shot my wife. Somebody's going to pay."

So simple. So incredibly insane.

The cat stared at me, his eyes half closed, purring contentedly from his allergic friend's lap. Robert Johnson's motto: Never abandon a friend as long as you know you're bad for him.

Footsteps started up the stairs.

Out of time. No options. When in doubt, listen to the cat.

I slid open the window. "I'm driving."

God or the devil was with us. We were a block away in Ralph's Lincoln Continental before we heard the sirens.

NOVEMBER 24, 1965

IF SHE'D LEFT FIVE MINUTES EARLIER, she wouldn't have been his first victim.

But she stayed for one last drink, trying to drown the bitterness of her day.

Above the bar, a black-and-white television played something she'd never seen before—a "Vietnam report." Ninety thousand American troops had just arrived in this place, halfway around the world. The reporter didn't explain why.

Around her, working-class *cholos* showed off for her sake—talking loud, drinking too much, swatting each other with pool cues. The men all looked the same to her with their blue work shirts and their hair like polished wood. They smelled of mechanic's grease and unfiltered Mexican cigarettes. Their eyes hovered over her like mosquitoes—always there, taking bites when she wasn't looking.

She shouldn't have been in the bar. She was old enough to drink, but just barely. She was out of place in her college clothes—her wool skirt and pantyhose, her white blouse. She nursed her fourth beer, thinking about her professor, getting angrier as she got drunker.

That's when the gringo came in.

Conversation in the barroom died.

The newcomer looked even more out of place than she. He wore a beige Italian suit, a loosened silk tie, a felt hat cocked back on his forehead. A blond Sinatra, she thought—someone straight out of her parents' record collection.

The regular *cholos* studied him apprehensively, then went back to their conversations. The way they turned from him, making an effort to pretend he was invisible, made her wonder if the gringo had been here before.

He walked to the bar, ignoring the uneasy stir he'd caused. Men moved out of his way.

He gave no indication of having seen her, but he slid onto a bar stool next to her, placed his hat on the counter. He shook loose a Pall Mall, offered her one.

"I don't smoke," she told him.

She did, of course. She wasn't sure why she'd lied.

He lit his cigarette.

"You drink," he noticed. Then to the bartender: *"Jorge, dos cervezas, por favor."*

The bartender didn't look surprised to be called by name. He dipped his head deferentially, brought out two ice-cold Lone Stars.

"No thanks," she said.

The gringo finally looked at her, and she caught her breath. His eyes were startlingly blue, beautiful and distant like stained glass.

"Lady comes to a bar," he said. "If she isn't here to smoke or drink, there's only one other possibility."

She braced for the inevitable proposition, but he surprised her.

"You got a problem," he said, "and you need somebody to talk to."

She studied his face.

How old was he? Mid-thirties, at least. As old as her professor. But so different. He had an aura about him, as if he owned this bar and everyone in it. He was important. Powerful. No man in the bar dared look him in the eye.

He pulled a clip of money from his jacket pocket—a thick wad of twenties—peeled one off carelessly and tucked it under the beer glass.

She couldn't help feeling impressed. She felt like she was caught in a riptide. An irresistible force was surging around her legs, pulling her toward deeper water.

"You want to tell me about it?" he asked.

"I don't even know you."

He grinned. "We can fix that."

•   •   •

HIS CAR WAS A NEW MERCEDES 230SL, a hardtop two-seater gleaming white. Red leather interior, radio, air-conditioning. The dashboard glowed like hot caramel. She'd never seen a car like this, much less driven in one.

They glided along the dark streets, cutting through neighborhoods she knew well, but from inside the Mercedes everything looked different—insubstantial. She felt as if they could go anywhere. They could turn and drive straight through her old high school and they'd pass through it like a mirage. Nothing could stop them.

"Where are we going?" she asked him.

She tried to sound suspicious. She knew she shouldn't have gotten into a stranger's car any more than she should've gone to that bar. But something about this rich gringo . . . He treated her presence as a given. As if she deserved to be next to him. As if there were nothing strange about the two of them riding through the South Side in a car that cost more than the houses they were passing.

"You're the boss," he told her. "I don't know this area. Show me around."

That threw her off guard. *She was the boss.*

She guided him past the drugstore her grandfather had started in the thirties, the shack where Mrs. Longoria sold tortillas off the griddle, the homes of her childhood friends. She told him stories—her first broken arm from that tree, her first boyfriend lived there. They passed within a block of her house, but she didn't show him where she lived. He didn't ask.

"Where would you go for a quiet talk?" he asked.

Her heart trembled. This was dangerous. Her parents, her friends would not approve. They were always protecting her, reminding her how fragile she was, how unpractical her dreams were.

"I'll show you," she decided.

She directed him down South Alamo, then onto a stretch of dark rural road where her friends and she used to stargaze. It was a desolate spot—perfect for ghost stories and underage drinking. At night, the fields and woods were so black she always felt she was at the edge of an enormous sea.

The gringo pulled his Mercedes next to a stand of live oaks and cut the headlights.

"Perfect," he said.

An orange November moon shone through the tree branches, making shadow scars across his face.

"What's your name?" she asked.

"Guy. Guy White."

He said it as if it were a private joke—as if, with his luminous car, his Nordic features, his milky clothes, he were *the* gringo. The essence of everything her life was not, would never be.

"They want me to become a secretary," she told him, blurting it out.

"Who does?"

"My college advisor. He wouldn't write a recommendation for UT. He said I should stick with typing. Stenography at best. Because I'm a woman."

"You don't like that."

"I can do better. I want to study law."

"A lawyer." He smiled. "Perfect."

His tone made her angry. He said it like he was watching the end of a movie—some momentary amusement that would mean nothing tomorrow.

"I can do anything," she insisted.

"Can you?" He rested a hand on her shoulder.

Outside, the darkness seemed closer, thicker. Tangled in the live oak branches, the moon looked like a blind man's eye, webbed with cataracts.

Why had she brought him here?

Even as a child, this road had scared her. Walking to church as a little girl, she'd imagined hearing whispers in the wind through the grass. Her father had kept his eyes on the ground, picking up grim pieces of history to show her— arrowheads a thousand years old, a lead musket ball from Santa Anna's army, tiny flecks of stone her father said were fossilized scales of prehistoric fish, back when Texas was an ocean for dinosaurs. The place was layered with ghosts, yet it electrified her. It made her feel alive.

She brushed the gringo's hand away. "Take me back, please."

"I could help you," he said. "I could do so much for you."

He stroked a wisp of hair behind her ear, and she noticed the pale skin on his finger, where a ring would be worn.

"You're married," she said.

"Yes," he agreed. "We're expecting our first baby."

"What are you *doing* here?" She scooted to the edge of the seat, pushed his hand away again. "I want to leave. Now."

"You said you could do anything," he chided. "Show me. What are you going to do about me?"

She yanked at the door handle. It was locked.

He slid next to her, blocking her fists as she tried to pummel him. The car was too cramped. She tried to kick him, but he pressed against her, a wave of cologne and muscle and white cloth, pushing her down, pinning her arms.

He was strong—much stronger than she'd realized. She screamed, but there was no one to hear. The car windows were well insulated. Nothing that happened in this expensive box of leather and glass would register in the outside world.

She struggled as he straddled her, pushed back her wrists.

"Do something," White coaxed. "You won't get anywhere if you can't even fight me."

Above her, the moon shone through the window. She wanted it to eclipse, to hide her in darkness, but it kept glowing through the car window, watching as she withered inside.

CHAPTER 3

MAIA LEE ARRIVED AT SAPD HOMICIDE SATURDAY MORNING, JUST IN time to watch two detectives and a uniformed cop subduing one of Santa's elves.

"Serial murderer-rapist," Lieutenant Hernandez explained, ushering her past. "Seven warrants in Missouri. Department store actually did a background check for once."

The elf was doing pretty well for himself. His green felt sleeves were torn and his green tights were rolled up to his knees. A broken plastic handcuff dangled off one wrist. The uniformed cop had his legs and the detectives had his arms, but the elf was still managing to scream obscenities, spit, occasionally bite.

His mean little eyes locked onto Maia as she passed, but

she'd been ogled by too many incarcerated sociopaths to feel bothered. She had worse problems.

She followed Hernandez through the cubicle jungle.

"Sergeant DeLeon's office." Hernandez pointed toward a glass door at the back of the room. "Quietest place to talk."

Inside, a big Anglo detective was sitting at the desk, flipping through files.

Before Maia could go in, Hernandez caught her arm. "I won't be going in, Miss Lee. But just so you know, I've already done as much for you as I can."

Hernandez had aged in the last few years.

Maia had met him several times before, thanks to Tres' incredible luck getting tangled in murder cases. She liked the lieutenant's calm manner, his quiet professionalism. He was one of those men who had never been a father, but had clearly missed his calling.

He was still handsome, impeccably dressed, but his hair had turned the color of wet porcelain. He'd lost too much weight. The lines had deepened around his eyes.

People didn't age incrementally, Maia decided. They went along fine for years, then hit some invisible dip and *boom*: a decade caught up with them overnight.

"I'm not asking for help," she said. "Just an open mind until we locate Tres."

"That may be difficult. Your boyfriend—"

"My client."

"—your *client* made the wrong choice at exactly the wrong time. My best sergeant is in the hospital dying. The prime suspect is on the loose. Navarre is aiding and abetting."

"Supposition. You never saw them together."

A shout went up across the room. One of the detectives got a pointy-toed elf shoe in his face. His gun rattled loose in his shoulder holster.

"Miss Lee," Hernandez continued, "you know Sam Barrera, the old man—"

"I know Sam."

"He wasn't easy to interview. Kept talking about a man with a bloody shirt in the kitchen. Kept asking if 'the agent' was okay. Finally we showed him some photographs. He ID'd Ralph Arguello."

"You're proceeding on the testimony of an Alzheimer's sufferer?"

"It was enough for a warrant, Miss Lee. We searched your friend's house, found a .357 and a bloody shirt stashed behind the laundry room wall. By lunchtime, forensics will have those items matched to Ralph Arguello."

Maia bit back a curse. She wanted to strangle Tres, which in itself was not an unusual feeling, but damn it. Damn it.

She felt her blood pressure rising. A black oily ball started rolling around in her stomach.

Not now, she told herself.

The last few days, it had gotten worse. It struck at the most inconvenient times—left her curled on the bathroom floor or hunched over the steering wheel on the side of the highway. The doctors had promised her it would not get this bad so soon.

"Miss Lee?" Hernandez said.

"I'm fine."

"You don't look fine," Hernandez said. "Do you want some water?"

"No . . . thank you."

In Ana DeLeon's office, the big Anglo detective was still sitting behind the desk, poring through paperwork. He had a buzz of rust brown hair, a rumpled dress shirt, a brutish face. Queasily, Maia tried to remember where she'd met him before.

"Kelsey," Hernandez offered. "Lead investigator on the shooting."

Maia willed herself to stay upright. "Ana's old partner."

"Yes." Hernandez said it without enthusiasm. "He's a good cop."

"He hates Tres."

Hernandez held her eyes, trying to send a message she couldn't decipher. "As I said, Miss Lee, the help I can offer in this situation is limited."

"You run the department."

"For three more weeks. I retire at the end of December. In the meantime, the brass want this case resolved decisively. An officer has been shot. It's a miracle she lived the night and not at all certain she'll survive. Ralph Arguello is our prime suspect. Your friend Mr. Navarre just threw himself into our line of fire."

"You're telling me not to expect justice?"

"I'm telling you nothing of the sort, Miss Lee. Just listen to Kelsey. Take his warning seriously. And realize that whatever breathing room I can give you, I already have."

Hernandez turned and made his way through the rows of cubicles.

The rabid elf, now on the ground with a cop foot against his neck, spat at the lieutenant's polished black shoes as he passed.

•　•　•

EXCEPT FOR THE MAJOR EYESORE NAMED Detective Kelsey, Sergeant Ana DeLeon's office was a nice workspace. Mahogany desk. Two cushy chairs. Walls painted a cool shade of avocado. Her corkboard was pleasantly cluttered with family photos, department memos and silver *milagro* prayer charms.

Definitely a woman's office.

Maia was impressed it could maintain that aura considering the amount of testosterone that must burn through here every day.

Kelsey sat behind DeLeon's desk with his feet propped up. He had files stacked high all around him, desk drawers overturned on the carpet nearby. He was reading through a homicide casebook. The fingers on both his hands were laced with faded white scars, as if he'd long ago lost a fight with a wildcat. "Sit down, Miss Lee."

"Making yourself at home?"

Kelsey raised an eyebrow. "I'm doing my job."

Maia nodded toward the stacks of files. "What were you searching for?"

"Just being thorough."

"*Very* thorough, it looks like."

Kelsey flipped a page in the homicide book. He chose a photo and slid it across the desk. "Franklin Muriel White. Nineteen eighty-seven. Twenty-one years old when he got turned into that."

The photo was a black-and-white autopsy head shot. The face, badly mutilated, had once belonged to a blond Anglo. Beyond that, Maia couldn't tell much. Savage blows had destroyed the features. Maia had seen worse, but not many times.

"A tire iron," Kelsey told her. "First hit laid him out cold. Back of the head, just above the left ear. Probably would've been enough to kill him. The other six to the face—those were just dessert."

Kelsey watched her for a reaction. His eyes reminded Maia of a rich man's son she'd once defended in court—a boy who liked to set sleeping derelicts on fire.

"Eighteen years ago," she said. "What were the leads?"

"Forensics got a DNA sample—blood under the victim's fingernails. Probably the killer's. Unfortunately all they had in '87 was RFLP testing. You needed a big sample to work with. There wasn't enough blood."

"And now you've got PCR," Maia said. "So as time permits, you rotate your detectives through the cold case squad looking for old evidence in storage that you can retest."

"Hernandez tell you that?"

"It's standard practice, Detective. Every department in the country is doing the same thing. Why *this* case, and why did it get DeLeon shot?"

Kelsey studied her impassively, then tossed her another piece of paper from the murder book—an old-fashioned carbon copy of a patrol officer's report.

A brief handwritten paragraph described the first response to a motorist's 911 about a body on the side of a rural South Side road, just after 10:00 P.M., July 14, 1987.

At the bottom, the signatures of the first two officers at the scene: Herberto Hernandez, Lucia DeLeon.

Maia looked up. "Ana's mother?"

"First female class of cadets," Kelsey said. "Twenty-seven years on the force. There's a plaque with her name in the main hallway."

"Hernandez was her partner. That's why he's distancing himself from the case?"

Kelsey seemed to think about that. He looked like he was about to say something, then changed his mind.

"Ten days ago," he told her, "Ana was rotated to cold case duty. She could've picked any file she wanted, but she saw her mom's name on that report . . . sentimental bullshit. She decided to poke around in it. Hernandez and I both warned her she'd get more than she bargained for."

"Meaning?"

Kelsey creaked back in the chair. "Ana started asking around, found out Franklin White had been arguing with a young . . . ah, business associate right before he got whacked. Wasn't common knowledge, but the two guys had acquired some pawnshops together. This friend was the front man, Franklin was the money. The friend stood to gain if he could get Franklin out of the picture. Franklin got whacked. Within six months, his former business associate was the number one owner of pawnshops in San Antonio."

"Ralph Arguello."

"Jackpot."

Maia felt her dizziness getting worse. She'd be damned if she'd give Kelsey the satisfaction of seeing her pass out. "If that's true—"

"If?"

"Why didn't anybody put Arguello and the victim together sooner?"

"He and White were real careful not to advertise their business relationship. Still, Arguello was one bold SOB, starting his career by whacking Franklin White. Dangerous game, considering Franklin's dad."

"Who's his dad?"

Kelsey stared at her. "I forgot you're an out-of-towner.

Maybe this doesn't mean anything to you. Franklin's dad is Guy White."

Maia's heart fluttered. She had a flashback to several years ago—Tres taking her on a case to a mansion where even the butler carried a gun.

"Guy White," she said, "the most powerful mobster in South Texas."

"Please, Miss Lee. *Private businessman*. Mr. White donates to orphanages and shit. Just because his enemies for the last thirty years have all turned up in the river—"

"Guy White's son was beaten to death in 1987 . . . his only child?"

"Only son. Got a younger daughter, but Frankie was the golden boy."

"And the case was never solved."

Kelsey smiled. "Well, see, you got a mob boss with lots of enemies. Somebody whacks his son. You think the detectives at the time were going to bend over backward trying to figure out what happened? Best guess, White's big rival in town, Johnny Zapata, ordered the hit. Zapata controlled most of the Latino side of town. White was muscling in. Anyway, White blamed Zapata for the hit. After Frankie died, San Antonio saw its biggest gang war ever. The homicide rate spiked by thirty-five percent. If you're the police, you're not going to go out of your way to find another scapegoat for Frankie's murder. Unless, of course, you're Ana DeLeon, and you can't stand loose ends . . ."

"The DNA under the victim's fingernails?"

"Results came back two days ago. Positive on Ralph Arguello. Ninety-nine point nine percent."

Maia looked around the room for something to concentrate on besides Kelsey's smirk.

She hated hopeless cases.

For years, she'd known that Ralph Arguello was bad news. She had never understood how a woman like Ana DeLeon could get involved with him. And she'd been secretly relieved when Tres and he had started to drift apart.

She focused on DeLeon's corkboard—a picture of Ralph and Ana with their baby girl standing in front of a bronze elephant at the zoo.

She felt horrible for that poor child. Her mother dying in the hospital. Her father a fugitive.

But she couldn't get drawn into that.

She didn't care why Ralph Arguello had bludgeoned a mobster's son eighteen years ago.

The question was how to extract Tres—how to get him untangled when the fool kept throwing himself into the most dangerous situations he could find, to help a friend who shouldn't have been his friend in the first place.

"Miss Lee?" Kelsey asked.

On the corkboard just above Kelsey's head was another photo, circa the Seventies, of a woman in patrol uniform, obviously DeLeon's mother, Lucia. She was standing next to another patrolman—a much younger Lieutenant Hernandez.

Maia hated this town. Everything was connected. Everybody was somebody's cousin or childhood friend. A city of a million-plus people, and they still operated like a little country town.

There was a sticky note attached to the photo—the name *White,* then *Timing is wrong,* and a few more words Maia couldn't read from where she sat.

Why hadn't Kelsey taken that note down?

"Miss Lee?" he asked again. "Are you going to help us out?"

The back of Maia's neck tingled. She suddenly doubted Kelsey had even seen the note. He wouldn't bother looking at DeLeon's family pictures. It would not occur to him that anything of value could be there. *Sentimental bullshit.*

She forced her eyes back to him. "How is it that you expect me to help?"

"Obvious, isn't it? Convince your boyfriend to bring in Arguello."

"Assuming I know how to reach him."

"Navarre called you. He got you here."

"He called from a pay phone."

"And you made arrangements to talk again. Let's not play games. We've known about the DNA for two days. Lieutenant Hernandez ordered us not to act on it until Ana had time to do the right thing, turn over her case notes to me so I could make an arrest on her husband. Obviously, Ana didn't cooperate. She must've told Arguello, and Arguello shot her. If it was up to me, we wouldn't be doing him or Navarre any more favors, but Hernandez has told me to offer you a deal."

"What kind of deal?"

Before he could respond, a detective with a bleeding cut over his eye came to the door. "Yo, Kelsey, a little help, man."

Kelsey scowled. "What, still the elf?"

The other detective turned pink around the ears. He was mid-twenties—young for homicide detail. He was the one Maia had noticed with the loose holster. It was still loose. "Hey, man. We figured we had him secure."

Kelsey sneered. "A roomful of cops, and you can't lock down a damn elf?"

"He's on speed or something. We mentioned sending him back to Missouri and he went ape-shit on us. I know you were in SWAT and all . . ."

The young detective's eyes were pleading. His voice verged on panic, which played Kelsey just the right way.

Kelsey smiled like a sadist anticipating a bar fight. "Miss Lee, if you'll excuse me."

The moment he was out of the room, Maia moved around DeLeon's desk and read the note on her corkboard.

White——Timing is wrong.
Santos—ME——retired
2107 Dunbar
864-9719

Maia simply could have memorized the information—she was good at that—but some instinct made her peel the note off the board, along with the photo of Lucia DeLeon and Etch Hernandez.

This is crazy, she decided.

But she slipped the photo and the note into her coat pocket. She moved another picture to cover the blank space— the photo of Ralph and Ana and their baby at the zoo.

Another wave of nausea swept over her, leaving her shivering and weak-kneed against the sergeant's desk.

Last night, she had come so close to telling Tres what was wrong with her. Now he was on the run, protecting a murderer.

Damn him.

She should've left Tres where she found him, tending bar in Berkeley. The most impetuous thing she'd ever done: slipping a business card across the bar to a guy she barely knew, just because he had beautiful green eyes and a smile that doubled her heart rate.

You might make a good investigator, she'd told him. *Give me a call.*

Fifteen years later, her judgment was still rotten. She'd quit her job in San Francisco, moved to Austin to be closer to him, left everything behind. She would do anything to help him. But when it came to making responsible choices, he was hopeless.

Ralph Arguello embodied everything Maia resented about Tres' hometown—dangerous, suffocating roots that had been pulling Tres away from Maia as long as they'd known each other. She'd almost lost him once before, when he'd first moved back to Texas. Now, when she needed his full attention more than ever . . .

If she'd told him the truth last night, what would he have done?

An explosion of voices from the cubicle area brought her back to the present.

"Hell—he's got my—"

"Damn it!"

Sounds of scuffling, something heavy thrown against a cubicle wall. Then a bruised and bloody elf, now armed with the young detective's Glock, burst into the office, Kelsey and two other detectives close behind.

Maia's reflexes were slow. Before she knew what was happening, the elf was behind her, his arm clamped around her waist, the gun at her throat.

"Back off!" the elf screamed at the cops. "Back the hell *off!*"

The elf's breath was sour and warm against her cheek. The

muzzle of the Glock dug under her jaw. But at that moment, Maia was more scared of Kelsey. He had his pistol trained on the suspect, just an inch to the right of Maia's ear. She saw no thought of negotiation in his eyes. No concern for her safety. He was hesitating only because he wanted a nice clean shot.

Maia grabbed the elf's arm around her waist. She dug her thumb into the acupressure point at his wrist.

He screamed, his muscles loosening from the shock to his nervous system.

She drove her elbow into his ribs. He buckled forward and she rammed his head into the desk. He crumpled to the floor, the gun clattering onto the carpet.

The cops went slack-jawed.

"Gentlemen," she said shakily. "If you'll excuse me . . ."

They parted for her like a bead curtain.

Halfway through the homicide division, Kelsey caught up with her. *"Counselor."*

His face was a beautiful shade of pomegranate. "What was—how did you . . ."

She took a shaky breath. "We have no further business, Detective. If I communicate with my client, I will advise him of our conversation."

Kelsey looked at her as if reappraising her value. He rubbed the old scars on his fingers. "I didn't tell you the deal, Miss Lee. Forty-eight hours."

"Until?"

"Until the DNA test results from the Franklin White case are made public. Until we release the fact that Ana got shot because she was about to name her husband as prime suspect."

"You wouldn't."

50

His expression stayed deadly serious. "This time Monday morning, Counselor. Navarre has that long to bring me Ralph Arguello. After that, believe me, I won't have to worry about bringing Arguello to justice, or anybody who's helping him. Guy White will take care of our problem for us."

CHAPTER 4

RALPH AND I SPENT A COLD SLEEPLESS NIGHT WITH SOME transients under a bridge on West Main.

The homeless guys decorated a Christmas tree with beer cans. They roasted pecans over a trash can fire, tried to remember the words to "We Three Kings" and kept asking Ralph if he had the DTs because of the way he was shaking.

I tried talking to him about Ana and the Frankie White case. I told him Ana would be okay. We had other options besides running from the police.

I might as well have been talking to the transients' shopping cart.

Ralph stared into the flames, every once in a while muttering the Rosary in Spanish, as if trying to draw ghosts out of the heat.

• • •

THE FIRST TIME I'D MET RALPH was also my first real experience with Frankie White. We were all juniors at Alamo Heights High School. Ralph got jumped by three Anglo linebackers outside a convenience store because he'd flirted with one of their girl-friends. I was on the football team, too, but I never liked unfair fights. I jumped in on Ralph's side. He and I kicked some ass. One of the linebackers happened to be an overgrown blond preppie named Frankie White.

In typical Ralph fashion, he became friends with both Frankie and me after the fight. I was never sure what Ralph saw in Frankie, but I understood Frankie's fascination with Ralph. Ralph was completely unintimidated by Frankie's mobster family ties. No one in San Antonio had ever had the guts to punch Frankie in the face.

Several months later, Ralph invited Frankie and me to dinner at his house for the first time.

The Arguello family lived in a crumbling white adobe cottage on the wrong side of McCullough, ten feet from the train tracks. The skeet club's shooting range was behind the back fence.

The tiny rooms were packed with a horde of smaller Arguello siblings, cousins and nephews whose names I could never keep straight. The extended family, Ralph informed me, lived with Mama Arguello full-time. Most had dead or missing or apathetic parents.

Frankie White gave me an amused look, like, *Can you believe this shit?*

Sleeping bags filled the living room. Three dogs lounged on the sofa. The walls were cluttered with family photos and crucifixes and portraits of saints. No air-conditioning. A hundred degrees inside, with a limp breeze pushing the pale yellow curtains. Ralph's mother stood at the stove, making tortillas by hand and cooking them on a hot plate. She kissed me, though she didn't know me. She smelled of gladiolas and cornmeal.

If it had been me, at age seventeen, I would've been embarrassed by the house, my mother, the way the kids clamored over Ralph and demanded piggyback rides and quarters and arm-wrestling rematches. Especially with Frankie White there, who lived in a mansion and drove his own Mercedes. But Ralph didn't care. He grinned at the kids, laughed, joked around. He seemed as confident as he had when Frankie and the other linebackers tried to assault him. Nothing fazed him.

At least, not until we went into the backyard to set the picnic table and found his latest stepfather (the sixth) trying to kiss Ralph's fourteen-year-old cousin. Apparently, it had happened before, because Ralph's voice turned to ice. "I warned you, *pendejo*."

Twelve minutes later, Ralph dumped the battered stepfather half-conscious into the curbside trash can, tossed his suitcase next to him and called a taxi.

Frankie beamed like a kid at his first R-rated movie. "That was hella cool, Arguello."

Ralph said nothing.

Back inside, his mother screamed, cried, made excuses for the bum she'd married, but Ralph just held her while she pummeled his chest. "He's no good for you, Mama. I'll look after you."

When she argued money, Ralph produced six hundred-dollar bills for the week's expenses, more cash than I'd ever seen. He told the younger kids to go back outside and set the table. He grounded his fourteen-year-old cousin to the bedroom.

By the time dinner was ready, the family's happy chaos seemed to be restored. We ate homemade *carne guisada* tacos and drank Big Red while fireflies blinked across the lawn. Gunshots crackled in the summer air. Every so often a train rumbled by and made the ground shake.

Frankie White enjoyed himself immensely. He kept glancing at the bedroom window, where the fourteen-year-old cousin was watching him.

Ralph's mother was the only one who didn't cheer up. She stared at the citronella candle on the table as if she wished the flame would freeze, just once, into a shape she could hold.

That night under the Main Street Bridge, years later, staring at the trash can fire, Ralph reminded me of his mother for the first time.

• • •

IN THE MORNING, WE CHANGED INTO clothes from a Goodwill donation box.

We'd already ditched Ralph's car in an H.E.B. grocery store parking lot, so we hot-wired the Chevy Impala of a former client I didn't like very much. Then we headed downtown with my .22 pistol, six dollars and thirty-two cents between us, and very little hope of living through the weekend.

I'd managed to grab my cell phone before leaving the house, but we decided to use a pay phone on the corner of South Saint Mary's instead. I doubted SAPD could triangulate a mobile call.

According to Ana they couldn't even figure out their own e-mail system. But there was no point taking chances.

I called Maia's number. She was already in town. If possible, she sounded even angrier than she had the night before, when I called to let her know I was a fugitive from justice.

As she told me about her conversation with Detective Kelsey and the note she'd found on Ana's bulletin board, a pickup full of immigrant laborers cruised past on Houston Street. The driver slowed to see if we wanted work. Ralph shook his head. The truck drove on.

"Tres?" Maia prompted.

"I heard you."

"You're protecting a murderer. Turn him in."

I pinched the collar of my Goodwill ski jacket, tried to pretend the smell of mildew wasn't coming from me. "The lead on the ME . . . 'timing.' What does that mean?"

"I don't know," she said wearily. "It doesn't matter. DNA is one of the few things you can't argue with. That's all they'll need to convict."

Something in her voice worried me. Aside from the anxiety and the anger, she sounded . . . sick. The way she sounded whenever she was forced to face her phobia about boats and deep water.

"Are you okay?"

"Of course I'm not," she said. "You're running from the law."

"Look, Maia . . . Ana didn't believe the DNA results. You could retrace her steps, find out where she was going with the investigation."

"Where she was . . . Tres, I just told you—"

"Ralph would never shoot his wife. Which means somebody else did."

"He's standing right there, isn't he?"

"Yeah."

"You want me to call the police for you?"

"No."

"Tres—"

"I'll call you tonight. Take care of yourself. I love you."

I hung up and tried not to look at Ralph.

"She wants you to sell me out," he said. "I don't blame her."

"They have DNA on you for Frankie's murder."

"I know."

"What do you mean, *you know*?"

"Ana told me. She's my wife, *vato*."

"She was about to name you prime suspect."

"*Chíngate*. Ana didn't believe I killed Frankie. I gave her a DNA sample myself 'cause I knew it wouldn't match up. Somebody in the department framed me."

"Conspiracy theory. Great defense."

Rage sparked in his eyes. "Ana trusted me, *vato*. You got to do the same."

A few blocks over, a cop siren sounded. Probably it had nothing to do with us, but it got my blood pumping.

"Come on," I said.

Ralph didn't move. "You think I'm crazy enough to kill Guy White's son?"

"Maia talked to Kelsey. He said Frankie gave you the money for the pawnshops. You never told me that."

"Mr. White *knew* we were doing business. It was his idea. We had a deal."

"What kind of deal?"

Ralph shifted his weight to his back foot, like he was

getting ready for a punch. "All I'm saying—if Mr. White thought I'd killed his son, I wouldn't still be breathing."

The siren got louder, maybe a block away now.

Ralph wasn't telling me something, but I didn't have time to figure out what.

I grabbed his arm and pulled him across the street. "Forty-eight hours, Ralph. Then Kelsey makes the DNA test public. After that, I wouldn't count on Mr. White's good graces."

We took the steps down to the Riverwalk, ducked under the Commerce Street Bridge. A siren echoed off the sides of the buildings. Tires slashed across the asphalt above.

As the noise faded, Ralph sat on the edge of the cistern that fed into the river.

I'd always found it odd that these little fountains had been installed under the bridges—in the darkest grimy places where tourists were least likely to stop.

"The whole SAPD hates my guts," Ralph said. "You know that, *vato*. Ever since I married Ana, any one of them would love to frame me."

I wanted to tell Ralph he was wrong. No cop would do that.

The trouble was I knew how the cops felt about him. I'd seen it in their eyes last night.

Ralph cupped his hand under the stone lion's mouth. "Let's say a cop killed Frankie."

"Ralph—"

"Just *listen, vato*. Last night, Ana knew. She *knew* who did it, but she didn't want to tell me. She'd already warned me about the DNA match. She was risking her job just doing that. Why would she not tell me who the killer was?"

"She was afraid of what you'd do."

"Maybe," Ralph conceded. "But I think she was having trouble turning in a fellow officer. That wouldn't be easy for her. She'd need a lot of time to think about it. She'd try confronting the guy first, giving him a chance to come clean. I know she would."

"Ralph, that's so damn hypothetical—"

"She'd been working on the case for weeks. If she was getting close to discovering this guy, he could've found out. He could've gotten into the evidence room and tampered with the DNA. All he'd have to do is get some of my blood, and I've been served warrants for DNA for other shit before. They probably got a sample of mine still sitting down there."

"They're supposed to destroy stuff like that."

Ralph laughed. "Yeah, right. Next you're gonna tell me the evidence is too secure to get access. That's a joke. Some of the stories Ana tells me—they had a vial of poison go missing a week ago. From an old murder case. This shit is absolutely undetectable. Really bad news. And it just disappeared. They hushed it up, but if *that* stuff can walk out the door, what's a little DNA sample?"

His eyes glowed with desperation, the kind of look a psychotic gives you when he's explaining the logic that holds together his dreamworld.

"You've been thinking about this," I told him. "You have somebody in mind, don't you?"

"Kelsey," he said instantly. "He hates me. He hates Ana."

I shook my head. As much as I detested Kelsey, it was hard to imagine him as a murderer.

"He started on the force the same year Frankie White died," Ralph said. "I checked on it. First patrol duty, Kelsey had a run-in with Frankie."

"Be hard to find a cop that *hasn't* had a run-in with the Whites."

"Yeah, but you know Kelsey. He holds a grudge. Those scars on his hands, *vato*. You ever wonder where they came from?"

"Ralph . . . we've got to leave the case to Maia. She'll figure out the truth. There's not much we can do from here."

"I want to see Ana."

"You know that's impossible."

"*Vato*, I don't care about me. This was about saving my own ass, then the hell with it. But I gotta make sure Ana is safe. She's all I care about. Her and the baby."

The brittleness in his voice worried me.

I wanted to believe I'd done the right thing, helping him run. I was playing for time, trying to calm him down until I could convince him to accept some kind of surrender deal.

But if Ralph went to jail, if Guy White found out he was a suspect in Frankie's death, I knew damn well there would be no time to prove him innocent. Ralph would never go to trial. He'd be dead before Christmas—shanked, or hanged in a cell, or shot while escaping. Some tidily orchestrated accident.

Maia might be able to find a solution in two days, but she didn't know the city or the local police like I did. And if I showed my face, I'd be arrested.

I needed a cop I could trust—somebody inside the system who could find out what the hell was going on and wouldn't arrest me on sight. Despite the fact that my dad had been Bexar County Sheriff back in the eighties, my list of friends in active law enforcement was regrettably short.

An answer came to me, but I didn't like it.

I stared at the river. Maybe if I jumped in, I could wake myself up. I'd find myself back in Southtown, Sam reading the Saturday morning paper while Mrs. Loomis cooked bacon in the kitchen.

I sighed. "Let's go, *Ralphas.*"

"Where to?"

"Back to the phone. I've got an idea that'll probably get us killed."

•　　•　　•

LARRY DRAPIEWSKI WAS WAITING FOR US at Mi Tierra—an outside table, just like I'd told him.

The shops on the plaza were just opening up, sunlight melting the frost off the windows. Sleepy mariachis tuned guitars by the fountain. Except for pigeons and one tourist family braving the cold, we had the restaurant patio to ourselves.

Larry pointed to the extra breakfast plates he'd ordered.

He kicked out a chair for me. "Wasn't enough you shot a doctor this week, huh? You're riding a shit avalanche, son."

"Good to see you, too, Larry."

Since retiring from the Sheriff's Department, Larry had gone completely gray. He'd gotten a hearing aid, grown a scraggly beard and cultivated a potbelly. He looked like Santa Claus after boot camp.

Ralph sat across from him and spread a napkin in his lap. He started heaping huevos rancheros into a tortilla.

Larry glanced at him with distaste. "Tres, if your father could see you now—"

"Can you help us or not?" I asked. I'd already told him everything over the phone. Some of it he'd already heard from cop friends. None of it seemed to surprise him.

Larry ran his finger around the edge of his Bloody Mary glass. "Your friend here is a killer."

"You can talk to *me*, Drapiewski." Ralph took a bite of eggs. "I speak *inglés*."

Larry's eyes turned steely. I remembered something my dad had said once about Larry Drapiewski being better than a cattle prod when it came to scaring the shit out of suspects.

"Arguello," he said, "if it wasn't Tres asking me this, if I didn't owe his father my life a dozen times over—"

"My wife. Can you get me in to see her or not?"

Larry stared across the plaza, toward the parking garage where we'd come in. "Not possible."

"Your guys work hospital security when an officer is shot," I said.

"We rotate with SAPD. Professional courtesy. The answer is still no."

"Is Ana stabilized?" I asked.

"She's still alive. That's all I know."

"Then she needs protection," Ralph said.

Larry glared at him. "Why do you think the cops are on round-the-clock guard duty, Arguello?"

"And if the guy who shot her is a cop?"

Larry blinked. "You're some piece of work. Why don't you be a man and turn yourself in? You have a daughter to think about."

Ralph started to get up.

I grabbed his arm, pushed him back into his seat. "Larry, promise me you'll keep Ana safe. Promise me the deputies looking after her are good men."

"I'm retired, Tres."

"Every man in the department owes you something."

He sipped his Bloody Mary, checked his watch. His eyes drifted again toward the parking lot. "I'll do what I can. In exchange, Arguello surrenders."

"We're talking about Frankie White's murder," I said. "You know what'll happen to Ralph once word gets out."

"He made that bed."

"He didn't," I said. "You must've heard something about the case back then—some rumor. Something."

"This is crazy, Tres. Don't get sucked into it."

"White's enemies, maybe?"

"Just talk." He checked his watch again. "Zapata—you probably already know that. Or the Zacagni family out of Houston. There was something about a hit man, Titus Roe, maybe hired by the family of one of Frankie's victims."

"What do you mean—Frankie's victims?"

Larry glanced uneasily at Ralph, then back at me. "Hell, Tres . . . You don't know? Forget it. Nobody on the right side of the law is going to help you with this. You've got to surrender."

Something about the way he said it—the way he kept glancing at the parking lot.

I pushed my chair out. "It's time we left," I told Ralph.

"Eat first," Larry said. "I paid for that and you haven't touched it."

"Since when have you worn a hearing aid, Larry?"

Ralph put his hands in his lap. "It's a trap."

There was a glint of movement on the roof of Mi Tierra, just at the corner of the building.

"I'm sorry, Tres," Larry said. "I don't have a choice. Mr. Arguello, put your hands on top of your head, please, very slowly."

"A cross fire," I grumbled. "Damn you, Larry."

"Why don't you use that little two-way radio in your ear," Ralph said evenly. "Tell your friends I got a pistol under my napkin, aimed straight at your dick."

"Shoot," Larry dared him. "Sniper on the parking garage roof will take off your head. Otherwise, put your hands up and we'll wait for the SWAT team to join—"

Ralph overturned the table into Larry's lap.

I rolled to the ground and got up running.

Ralph was way ahead of me. He dove behind the only other occupied table—the family of startled tourists—and burst into the restaurant where the crowd was thicker.

There was no snap of gunfire. No clear shot.

We wove through the dining room, knocking down waiters and kicking over breakfast platters. Larry Drapiewski was yelling and cursing behind us.

I glanced back long enough to see two SWAT guys in full combat gear jump the patio railing. Both were carrying assault rifles.

Nice to feel wanted.

"Not the front," Ralph warned.

He was right. Two uniformed deputies were pushing through the hostess's line, knocking over baskets of pralines.

Fortunately, Ralph and I knew Mi Tierra better than most places on earth. I'd been coming here since age fifteen. I'd retched my first pitcher of margaritas into their men's room toilet.

We burst into the kitchen, ran for the delivery ramp. Cops behind us yelled at the dishwashers: "Get *down!*"

Finally one of the smarter cops yelled it in Spanish, but by the time he got off a shot we were through the service exit.

I didn't notice the uniformed officer outside the door until it was too late.

"*Vato!*" Ralph yelled.

The deputy was waiting to the side of the kitchen entrance, his gun drawn, ready to fire at whoever came through first. That happened to be me.

In a heartbeat, I registered his cocky smile, the gleam in his eyes that told me he intended to shoot first and make up a good story later. I watched him level the gun, then *wham*. I went flying sideways, the air slammed out of me. The pistol cracked.

When I looked up, the deputy was crumpled on the curb. Ralph's knuckles were bleeding. I could hear the other cops still pushing and cursing their way through the kitchen, trying to shove through the mob of upset dishwashers.

"Come on!" Ralph ordered. He yanked me to my feet and ran.

I shook off my daze and followed. When I caught up, Ralph had already stopped a cab and pulled out the driver. I had just enough time to jump in the back before Ralph peeled out, the cabbie screaming and running after us, providing beautiful cover from the cops who were trying to take aim at us.

We heard a lot of sirens, saw a lot of lights, but they were too slow bringing around the helicopter. A critical mistake. We shot under Interstate 10 and into the labyrinth of the West Side, which opened up to embrace us like a mother.

• • • •

EIGHT MINUTES LATER WE WERE SHIVERING in a storm drain off Palo Alto, listening to the police helicopter circle overhead and the sirens wail.

We'd left our cab half submerged in the lake of Our Lady of the Lake University, the car's back end sticking up like the Iwo Jima Monument. The way Ralph and I figured it, SAPD would have to dispatch at least five cops to deal with that new neighborhood conversation piece, which left only two thousand and fifty on the force to search the West Side for us.

Ralph kicked the corrugated metal of the storm drain as if it were Larry Drapiewski's face.

"You saved me back there," I said. "You pushed me out of the way."

The look Ralph gave me was the same he'd given Frankie White, years ago, when Frankie made a comment about Ralph beating up his stepfather. A blank stare—as if I were questioning something that was completely obvious. "What was I supposed to do?"

"You could've gotten yourself killed."

Ralph shrugged.

Despite my gratitude, that made me angry. Here I was trying to save his butt . . . He was the one with the family. He was supposed to know better than to risk himself.

"What did Larry mean," I asked, "about Frankie's victims?"

Ralph wrapped his bleeding knuckles in his shirt. "That was after high school, 'round '86, '87. You seriously never heard?"

I shook my head. Those years had been a daze for me. My father had been murdered in '85. Shortly afterward, I'd fled San Antonio for the Bay Area and tried to sever my Texas roots as much as possible.

"Frankie was getting into trouble," Ralph said. "I mean . . . bad trouble."

Some of my memories about Frankie White started weaving together—the image of him staring at Ralph's fourteen-year-old cousin through the window, other things I hadn't thought about in a long time. I remembered my dad's old stories about Frankie's father, Guy White, and some of the things Guy had done in his youth to prove his power. A few of those exploits had supposedly driven his wife to an early grave.

"Frankie's trouble," I said. "It wouldn't have anything to do with women, would it?"

Ralph nodded. "When it started getting bad . . . I mean, so bad it was affecting his family, Mr. White talked to me about him. You know, helping him settle down. Finding a business he liked."

"Mr. White came to you?"

"Maybe it was a little bit my idea. But Mr. White and I were square, *vato*. After Frankie died, I got nothing out of that. Took me five years to pay back Mr. White for the money Frankie had fronted me, but I did it. I paid off the pawnshops free and clear. I'm not crazy."

I tried to imagine how much trouble Frankie could've been in for Guy White to see Ralph as a moderating influence on his son. It wasn't easy.

The police helicopter made another pass overhead, the rotors' noise making the loose rivets of the storm drain rattle.

Ralph said, "I *am* thinking about her, you know."

"Ana?"

"The baby." Ralph closed his eyes. "Drapiewski said I have a daughter to think about. I been afraid since the day she was born that something in my past would come back to hurt her. Last two years, *vato* . . . I felt like I've been loaned somebody else's life, you know? Never deserved this kind of luck. Best two years I ever had."

I didn't answer right away. I wasn't sure how. He was talking about the two years when I'd been part of his life the least.

"We'll figure out something," I managed. "What about the hit man Drapiewski mentioned? You ever heard of Titus Roe?"

Ralph kicked at a puddle of icy water. "Just stories. None of them good."

"Could we find him?"

"If he's still around. Zapata could point us the right way. They knew each other."

"You already tried Zapata. He baited you."

"I still think he knows something, *vato*. He got the blame for Frankie's death. Suffered bad from that gang war with White. I'm sure he made it his business to find out what really happened to Frankie. If I could just get Zapata alone, corner him for five minutes without him trying to kill my ass—"

"He makes himself hard to find," I reminded Ralph. "We've got no resources. No money. No wheels. And only forty-eight hours."

Ralph checked his watch. "Forty-*three* hours."

The chopper thundered overhead.

I thought about what Larry Drapiewski had said: *Nobody on the right side of the law is going to help you.*

And I got my worst idea yet, which was saying something, considering the banner week I was having.

I locked eyes with Ralph. "We need to find Frankie White's killer. And we can't do it without help."

"There is no help. Not a single person cares enough about who killed Frankie to risk their neck."

"I can think of one person."

Ralph stared at me, slowly getting it. "You're crazy."

"Lots of resources. Plenty of clout. No love for the police."

"And he won't know I need killing for a whole two days."

I spread my hands. The suicidal logic was perfect. "Let's go knock on Guy White's door."

CHAPTER 5

"LIEUTENANT?" MAIA ASKED.

Etch Hernandez stood at the ICU window, fingering some-thing in the pocket of his tailored wool slacks. When he turned, Maia was sorry she'd interrupted him. His face was raw with emotion.

"They said she was a little better." He struggled to get his voice under control. "I was hoping . . ."

He didn't need to finish.

On the other side of the glass, Ana DeLeon lay webbed in tubes and wires. A nurse was changing her IV. Another was frowning at the heart monitor.

To believe there was a human being in the hospital bed, Maia had to concentrate on small details—a glossy black wisp of hair curled against the pillow, a smooth stretch of forearm exposed against the white sheet.

If *this* was better, Ana DeLeon was in bad shape indeed.

"Has she ever regained consciousness?" Maia asked.

The lieutenant shook his head. "The surgery—they said it went well . . ."

The nurses worked grimly, aware of their audience. Their expressions reminded Maia of jurors about to return a verdict.

In a weak show of optimism, someone had placed a picture of Ana's baby on the bed stand. In case Ana woke up, it would be there to comfort her. There were no pictures of Ralph.

Hernandez took his hand out of his pocket. He scooped his cashmere coat off a nearby chair. "I have to go before your friend makes another headline."

"What do you mean?"

He gave her a hard stare. "Assuming that's an honest question? An hour ago, Navarre and Arguello set up a meeting downtown with a retired deputy, Larry Drapiewski. Drapiewski alerted the Sheriff's Department. The hotshots in county SWAT were stupid enough to try setting a trap on their own. Without notifying SAPD."

Maia processed this, trying not to show her anxiety. "Tres and Ralph got away?"

"After threatening Mr. Drapiewski, endangering a restaurant full of tourists, assaulting a deputy and stealing a cab at gunpoint, yes. I've told the sheriff I never want to see his deputies again. That's why I'm here. I'm placing my own men in charge of guarding Sergeant DeLeon."

Which explained, Maia thought, the dour-faced SAPD uniform who had frisked her at the door.

71

Hernandez put on his coat. "Our goodwill toward your boyfriend has pretty much evaporated, Miss Lee. Now if you'll excuse me—"

"Why did you try to warn Ana off the Franklin White case?"

He scowled. "Who says I did?"

"Your good cop. Kelsey."

Hernandez's face darkened. "I'm not sure why he'd . . . I didn't discourage Ana. I only told her it would stir up bad memories. As I said, Miss Lee, on this case, I've tried very hard to distance myself."

"Because you and Lucia were the first people at the scene?"

"Yes. Partly."

"How long did you work with Ana's mother?"

"Twenty years. All of it on patrol. She was the most exceptional officer I've ever known."

"After she died, you sponsored her daughter's career. Tres told me you recommended Ana for the sergeant's position in homicide."

"She was the best person for the job."

"Does Detective Kelsey see it that way?"

The lieutenant stared through the glass at Ana's hospital bed. He radiated worry and frustration, but whatever he wanted to say, he kept it to himself.

Maia wondered what it would be like working for this man.

He reminded Maia of her old law firm mentor, John Terrence, back in the days when she still trusted his sincerity. There was something about him—an air of long-ago heartbreak that sparked a woman's instinct to nurture, to heal. With Hernandez, you'd have to exert a conscious effort *not* to want to please him, not to start treating him like a father figure.

"Ana was . . . *is* a good detective," he said.

"She wasn't going after her husband," Maia said. "She had another lead. Do you know who it was?"

Hernandez pinched the knot of his tie. "Ana was desperate to clear her husband, Miss Lee. Grasping at straws."

"But did she tell you anything?"

"No."

"Case notes?"

"There was nothing in her office. She usually kept everything on her laptop, which she would've carried home with her, but the laptop was not there when we got to the scene. Disappeared, just like Ralph Arguello."

Maia thought about Kelsey riffling through Ana's desk drawers, poring through stacks of case files.

Just being thorough.

"Lieutenant, what happened the night Frankie White died?"

Hernandez watched the nurses. One filled a hypodermic needle. The other was checking something on Ana's chart.

"We found John Doe bodies along Mission Road all the time," he said. "Popular dumping ground for the gangs. Nice rural stretch, heavy ground cover, hardly any streetlights. That night, I knew who the victim was the minute we pulled up. Frankie White used to cruise our beat. I knew his car. Good thing, too, because his face was unrecognizable. When we found him . . . Lucia was the professional. She did everything by the book. She said even Franklin White deserved justice. Me? Honestly, Miss Lee, I wanted to push the body into the bushes, back out and pretend we never saw anything. I knew what kind of hell would break loose when word got out. I knew Lucia and I would be on the hot seat for all kinds of questions because we'd found the body. I didn't care who killed the son-of-a-bitch, as long as he was dead."

"You make it sound personal."

"Miss Lee, I was hoping to make retirement without *some* things coming back to haunt me." Hernandez's gaze was so intensely sad it sent a shiver down Maia's back. "Apparently, God has other plans."

He swept out of the room, the guard in the corridor straightening to attention as he passed.

Alone at the observation window, Maia tried to keep vigil.

That was why she'd come—as if by being close to Ana, Maia could understand what she'd been after, why she'd gotten herself shot.

All Maia felt was growing unease. She felt like she was still back at police headquarters, the rapist elf's arm around her neck, his sour breath on her cheek. She hated feeling helpless.

She took the note from her coat pocket.

She'd already located the medical examiner, Jaime Santos. Two quick calls had done that, but Maia was loath to go. She never liked talking to MEs. Since childhood, she'd had an aversion to people who handled dead bodies.

Bad luck, her father always said. *The worst luck of all.*

Of course, her father had had his own reasons to fear death.

Maia looked at Ana DeLeon. She tried to imagine the sergeant's limp hand writing the words: *Timing is wrong.*

The picture of Ana's baby grinned at her on the bedside table. The heart monitor bleeped, ticking off seconds Maia didn't have to waste.

•   •   •

ETCH HERNANDEZ SAT IN HIS CAR considering what Miss Lee had said.

The lawyer reminded him strongly of Ana, which made him uneasy. He didn't like the doubts she'd raised about Kelsey. He wished she hadn't asked about Lucia. No matter how many years went by, that subject was always painful.

Most of all, he was ashamed she'd caught him at a weak moment. Looking at Ana in that hospital bed had been harder than he'd anticipated.

He had a reputation for being professional—calm and collected. Yet for all the years he'd been climbing the ranks, he still felt like a pretender. At heart, he was still a simple patrol cop. He wanted nothing more than to be back in his unit again, with Lucia DeLeon, drinking bad coffee at three in the morning and watching the moon rise over the South Side barrios.

He closed his eyes and remembered the day he'd come closest to dying. August 10, 1975.

He and Lucia had been patrolling together for almost a year at that point. Etch had been doing his best to hate her.

Lucia had started in '67. She'd spent five years relegated to typical women's jobs—doing body searches on female prisoners, caring for children after domestic disputes. Finally in '72 she'd made enough noise and rattled enough cages to get a regular patrol assignment. The male officers despised her. Many refused to work with her. She spent three years getting bounced from partner to partner, given the worst shifts in the most boring parts of town, but she wouldn't quit. Finally, in '75, she got her wish—a patrol on the near South Side, the Mission area where she'd grown up. Etch was the lucky guy who got her as partner.

He tried his best to ignore her, to say nothing that wasn't absolutely necessary. She never let him get away with it.

"Herberto Hernandez," she mused one night as they were riding the dog watch. "H.H. *Hache, hache*. Too much of a mouthful. I'm gonna call you Etch."

"The hell you will."

Lucia smiled. She loved goading him to talk.

"Etch," she repeated. "Like *hache*, see? It's a good name."

His protests didn't matter. Even his male colleagues picked up the nickname. It fit, they said. He'd been Etch ever since.

Seven months into their partnership, they got a call for backup from the Pig Stand restaurant on South Alamo—two officers on a disturbance call, a fight between a woman and her jilted boyfriend. The officers on the scene were having trouble subduing the male assailant.

The Pig Stand was an old diner even in '75. A slim box of glass and neon and brick, it sat on a triangle of asphalt where South Flores scissored into South Alamo. Its most remarkable feature was the giant concrete pig outside.

The two patrolmen who needed help were Ingram and Halff, old-timers in the department. Hernandez knew damn well they would never have picked a Latino and a Latina to be their backup, but they sure as hell needed help.

Judging from the broken furniture and shattered windows, the fight had started inside and moved out into the parking lot.

Ingram was lying on his back in the diner doorway. Etch didn't know whether he was dead or just unconscious. Halff was on the pavement, being straddled and beaten by the assailant, a long-haired Anglo biker who must've weighed three-fifty. A woman knelt next to him, crying, trying to pull him off the cop. She had a bloody mouth and a black eye and her paisley dress was torn.

The biker was yelling at half-conscious Officer Halff: "I'll do whatever the fuck I want to her! You understand? Whatever the fuck I want!"

Lucia started forward, but Etch said, "Let me handle this."

"Etch—"

"*No.* Stay back. Call for an ambulance."

He didn't wait for her to argue. There was no way he was going to send a woman into a brawl like this.

Etch drew his weapon and approached the biker. He yelled the right commands in just the right tone of voice. He was cool. He'd done this before. He didn't know that the biker was pumped up on Angel Dust, something nobody in San Antonio had seen yet. It wouldn't be common on the streets for another ten years.

The biker reared and charged with such intensity Etch never had time to shoot. He saw a flash of black and he was on the pavement, the barrel of his own gun swimming in front of his face.

"I'll start with you!" the biker yelled, pressing the muzzle against Etch's forehead. "Cops in my business! I'll do you first!"

Etch realized there wasn't going to be any help. There wasn't time. The biker would murder three cops and his girlfriend just because it felt good. Then he would probably shoot himself. Etch knew cops who had died this way. He just never thought he would be one of them.

"Hey, asshole!" Lucia yelled, somewhere off to the left. "Maybe it's because you got no dick."

The biker lurched toward her voice. The pressure of the gun muzzle eased up a little between Etch's eyes. *"What?"*

"You heard me," Lucia called.

Etch could only see her feet behind the patrol car, but he understood what she was doing—crouching for cover, both hands on her weapon, elbows steadied against the hood of the car. Etch wanted to scream *no*. He couldn't allow her to die, too. And yet he was totally powerless.

"I'll kill this motherfucker!" the biker warned.

"Yeah," Lucia said. "Because you got no dick. No wonder your girlfriend left you."

"You bitch!"

"That's right," Lucia coaxed. "I'm the one you should be mad at. I'm laughing at you—a dickless coward who beats up his defenseless girlfriend. How'd you do against *me*, asshole? Come on, show me your gun."

"I'll kill you, you goddamn—"

He took the gun off Etch and pointed it at Lucia, which is what she'd been waiting for.

She shot him through the heart.

A month later, an official hearing cleared Lucia to return to patrol. The brass presented her a medal of bravery for saving three officers' lives. She got an avalanche of press attention. She turned down offers of better assignments and went right back to patrol.

Etch and Lucia started meeting at the Pig Stand for dinner every night before their shift. Surprisingly, the manager was glad to see them. He comped every meal.

The changes between Lucia and Etch were subtle but seismic. She had saved his life.

"Thank you," he told her one night, the first time he'd been able to say it.

Lucia looked up from her plate of onion rings. "No problem, Etch."

He didn't object to the name.

"How did you know the guy would turn the gun on you?" he asked. "How did you know what to say?"

She smiled ruefully. "I've made it a point to understand men."

"Even men like that?"

"Especially men like that."

He sensed more of a story there. He knew she was a single mom, raising a nine-year-old daughter named Ana. Speculation around the department was Lucia had to be lesbian. But Etch wasn't so sure.

He'd never noticed the amber color of her eyes before, the way her short black hair curled behind her ears. She wore no makeup, but she had nice lips, the color of plums. He found himself wondering what she would look like in civilian clothes—a dress, perhaps.

Thirty years later, he could still remember the way she looked that night.

He opened his eyes. He thought again about what Miss Lee had told him.

He'd never trusted any cop the way he trusted Lucia. He sure as hell didn't trust Kelsey to do things right.

He dialed the private number of a detective who owed him a favor—a narcotics guy who would've lost his job in an IA investigation if Etch hadn't withheld some damaging information.

"This is Hernandez," Etch told him. "I need you to do some surveillance for me. Starting now."

•   •   •

MAIA WATCHED RETIRED M.E. JAIME SANTOS play golf for ten minutes before she decided he hated the game.

"You ever try driving with a nine-iron, Miss Lee?" he asked. "Horrible technique."

The old man eyed the golf ball like it had offended him. He tapped it tentatively, holding his club in vein-gnarled hands. He swung. With a crack, the ball sailed toward the tenth hole. It rolled to a stop at the edge of the green.

If the swing gave him any pleasure, Santos didn't show it. He pulled the pin out of the turf like a pest control expert extracting vermin.

Maia said, "Dr. Santos—"

"Call me Jaime."

"—if I could ask you about the case."

Santos' eyes were watery brown.

Despite his sour expression, Maia thought she detected kindness there—deeply submerged, diluted from years of autopsying every type of atrocity man can do to man—but still present.

He glanced at the two caddies—his own, and the one who'd brought Maia out to the course. "Why don't y'all run and get some drinks or something? The young lady and I will walk from here."

"But, sir, your bag—"

"I got a nine-iron," the doctor snapped. "What else do I need?"

He handed them each a twenty. The caddies got in their golf carts and drove away.

Maia and Santos began walking.

A cold drizzle fell.

In the distance, Highway 281 was shrouded with mist. Christmas lights blinked on the smokestacks of the Quarry shopping center.

"So you're Tres Navarre's friend," Santos mused. "Met him a few times. Dark hair? Pain in the ass?"

"That's him."

"He did some work for a friend of mine who was down on his luck. Got the loan sharks off his back. He wouldn't accept any payment."

"That's him, too."

The old man found his golf ball, gazed across the green toward the tenth hole flag. "Thirty years of autopsies, Miss Lee, they all tend to run together. But the Franklin White case . . . like I told the lady cop, that's one you remember."

"You spoke with Sergeant DeLeon?"

Santos studied his putting angle, didn't seem to like it. He nudged the ball a little closer to the hole with his foot. "Seven blows to the head. Six of those to the face. Don't see pure rage like that very often. Mind you, plenty of people were mad at him. That young man made his father look like a gentleman."

"How do you mean?"

Santos gave her a raised eyebrow. "You don't know?"

"I was hoping you could tell me."

Santos gripped his club, faced the ball. "I hate golf. Blood pressure. Had to do something."

"Jaime, about Franklin White?"

Santos sighed. "Back in '87 there was a string of rape-murders on the South Side. Half a dozen young women picked up in bars, driven to secluded spots, raped and strangled. These women, all nineteen, twenty years old. All of them bright college girls, sweet kids. The kind of young women families pin their hopes on. You look at their photos . . ." The old man shook his head sadly, as if he could still see the victims' faces. "Nobody was ever arrested, but they got a sketch of a man seen talking to one of the victims shortly before she disappeared. Young Anglo guy, blond and stocky, looked a lot like Guy White's son."

Maia felt her nausea coming back.

"You all right, Miss Lee?"

"I'm fine."

Santos studied her more carefully. "Let me see your hands."

"Why?"

"Come on now."

Reluctantly, she extended her hands. The old man pressed at her fingers, felt her pulse.

"I'm fine," she said again, pulling away. "Sergeant DeLeon thought you knew something about the Franklin White case. Something important, maybe about the blood under Franklin's fingernails?"

For another moment, the old man stared at her. Then he turned his attention back to the golf ball. "Guy White isn't what he used to be, Miss Lee, but he's still vicious. Maybe more so now that he doesn't have much time."

"What do you mean?"

He shrugged. "You can't be evil as long as Guy White's been evil without it catching up with you. Rots you from the inside. That's my medical opinion." He tapped the ball. "If I were you, I wouldn't stir up the Whites. I see a lot of directions this might go. I don't like any of them, after what happened to the sergeant."

"DeLeon wrote something about the timing being wrong."

"I don't know about that. The timing . . . I told Ana she should ask Mike Flume out at the Pig Stand. He could probably tell you about that, if the old bastard is still alive. Mike vouched for Lucia and Etch Hernandez that night. They had to have a clean alibi, see. All the cops involved did."

"Why?"

Santos pulled back his nine-iron. He hit the ball much too hard and watched it roll past the hole.

"Hell with it," he murmured. "Seemed so important at the time. That's the problem with getting old—you stop caring about secrets. The weapon marks—"

"Detective Kelsey said the murder weapon was a tire iron."

Santos' mouth twitched. "Kelsey knows better. But, yeah. That's the story we decided to go with."

"You lied in the report?"

"I was . . . vague. Had to be, or we would've had a war on our hands. Those marks were consistent with a very specific type of bludgeoning device. Murder weapon was never recovered, mind you, but the match was pretty damn exact. Police nightstick. The type most patrolmen carried back then."

Maia felt as if the rain and the cold were soaking into her bones, turning her to ice water. "Did Kelsey work the scene, too?"

Santos shook his head. "As I recall, he was still on medical leave, but you better believe he scrambled to get an alibi."

"Medical leave."

"Few months before the murder, Kelsey had had a run-in with Frankie White. Frankie was brandishing a knife in a bar on the Riverwalk. Kelsey was a rookie, straight out of the academy. He made the mistake of trying to take Frankie's knife away."

"The scars on Kelsey's hands."

"Almost lost several fingers. Afterward, Guy White took Kelsey apart in front of his superiors. White's lawyers turned the whole incident upside down, claimed Kelsey was responsible for using excessive force. Nearly got Kelsey kicked out of the department." Santos sighed. "There weren't many cops back then who *hadn't* had run-ins with the White family, Miss Lee, but I'd appreciate it if you're more careful with this information than Ana DeLeon was. I don't like young ladies getting shot."

Maia watched the cold rain drifting across the hills. She imagined Frankie White, the blond preppie from 1987, as a rapist-murderer, not so different from the elf who'd attacked her that morning. She imagined the same wild light in Frankie's eyes, the same foul breath. She could easily put herself in the place of those women Frankie had murdered, his hands closing around her throat.

"Thanks, Jaime," she said. "I'll tell Tres you said hello."

"You sure you're feeling all right?"

"I'm fine. Probably just something I ate."

He smiled in a sad way, like he'd just come across a tender love note in the pocket of an autopsy subject. "One more question, Miss Lee, just because you can't fool an old doctor. Does Tres Navarre know you're pregnant?"

CHAPTER 6

REMEMBERING RALPH'S SECOND COUSIN was a stroke of inspiration, if I do say so myself.

Like many San Antonians, Guy White ordered large quantities of tamales for his Christmas celebrations, and Ralph's cousin from Mama's Cocina delivered to all of the biggest accounts. The rich Anglos loved this. It gave them the flavor of a Tejano Christmas without the trouble of actually going to the West Side and mixing with Hispanics.

At any rate, hiding in the back of the cousin's delivery van was the only thing that got us past police surveillance—a black Chevrolet sitting across the street from Guy White's mansion. It had tinted windows and a slapdash stenciling job that read *Lou's Electronics*.

"SAPD?" I murmured to Ralph.

"Nah, they'd blend in better. I'd say federal. Not for us."

He tried to sound confident about it—or as confident as you can be, crammed in between forty-pound canisters of hot tamales.

"FBI," I speculated. "That execution White ordered in Louisiana."

"I'm guessing Secret Service. The counterfeit twenties."

"Ten bucks says FBI."

"You're on."

From the front seat, Ralph's second cousin said nervously, "I'm telling you guys, if you cost me this job—"

"No worries," I told him. "If we get caught, you can say we're tamale-jackers."

I'm not sure that made him feel any better, but he pulled up to the gates of the mansion.

In one of San Antonio's weirder architectural fantasies, the house had been built to resemble a miniature White House. I'd never been clear whether Guy White constructed the place to reflect his name, or bought it that way because it did. Either way, it was a pathetic attempt at grandeur—like a Taj Mahal model on a putt-putt course.

As we waited to be buzzed in, I tried to figure out why the grounds looked so gloomy. Maybe it was the winter fog, or the bare pecan trees. Even the Christmas tree in the windows seemed to glitter halfheartedly.

Then I realized the gardens were dying.

The few times I'd been here before, whatever the season, Guy White had taken meticulous personal pride in his gardens. Now there were no plants to speak of. No winter blooms. Just weeds and yellow grass.

A woman's curt voice came over the intercom. Ralph's cousin nervously announced himself.

The iron gates rolled open.

The back of the van was like a grease sauna. On either side of me, metal canisters cooked their way through my coat sleeves.

"You got a plan what to say, *vato*?" Ralph dabbed the sweat off his forehead.

"Let's play it organic," I said.

"Organic."

"Yeah. You know. 'How 'bout them Spurs? Nice weather. Wanna help us find Frankie's killer?' "

"We're so-o dead."

•   •   •

THE VAN BUMPED UP THE DRIVEWAY.

I looked at Ralph and tried to gauge how he was doing.

Before we hooked up with his cousin, Ralph had called his sister and asked about the baby. His sister was worried out of her mind, frantic about Ana, furious with Ralph for running, but the baby was fine. She told Ralph all this, then demanded to speak to me.

"Stop him," she told me. "He's gonna get himself killed. You gotta stop him, bring him back to his daughter."

I could hear Lucia Jr. in the background, banging on a pot and saying, *Ab, ab, ab.* I said, "I'll do my best."

"You'll *do* it," the sister insisted. "No accident Ralph came to you. You're the one he respects the most. He's told me that a million times. You gotta keep him from going over the edge."

I didn't bother protesting that we'd grown pretty far apart. I just promised again to do everything I could.

"You know why he got involved with the Whites, don't you? You understand why he *had* to help Frankie?"

Before I could ask what she meant, the police came on the line and tried to negotiate with me. I hung up.

The call energized Ralph. He didn't seem as depressed. He talked more. But there was also a new restlessness in his manner—a three-espresso buzz. I recognized it, unfortunately. It was the way Ralph acted when he was anticipating a fight.

He looked at me like he was following my thoughts. "My sister wanted you to hold my leash?"

"I guess."

"She never figured I'd be the one with the wife and kid. She always figured I'd live that shit through you. You know?"

I wasn't sure I wanted to know.

The tamale truck slowed.

I hazarded a look out the front windshield, but Ralph's cousin immediately hissed, "Get down!"

My brief glimpse was enough to show me why.

Ahead of us, where the driveway divided, an angry-looking blond woman and an Anglo man in a brown leather jacket stood waiting for us with all the seriousness of Nazis at a checkpoint.

•　　•　　•

"YOU'RE NEW," THE WOMAN SNAPPED.

"Y-yes, ma'am." Ralph's cousin's voice wobbled.

Withering silence.

I made myself small behind a column of tamale canisters.

"Deliveries don't come through the front," the woman said. "Why do you look so nervous?"

Her voice didn't match the glimpse I'd gotten of her.

She'd looked young, like a pissed-off sorority girl, but she sounded like my third-grade teacher Mrs. Ziegler, with the steel-gray beehive and the paddle hanging from the chalkboard.

"S-sorry, ma'am," Ralph's cousin said. "I just don't want to mess up this job."

Footsteps crunched in the gravel—the leather jacket goon, making his way around to the back of the van.

I got my spiel ready, should he open the doors. I hoped I'd have time to smile and say *"Would you like a free sample?"* before he shot us.

Finally, the woman's voice: "Around to the right. The kitchen entrance is marked. You *can* read?"

"Yes, ma'am," Ralph's cousin exhaled. "Thank you."

We lurched into drive.

I tried not to worry about the woman's tone—suspicious, almost taunting. Why had she let us go so easily?

Ralph's cousin rolled up his window.

"Good job, *ese*," Ralph told him.

"Shit, man." His cousin was sweating as much as we were. "Did you see that lady's eyes? I think she was going to gut me."

"She couldn't be older than college age," I said.

The cousin glanced back at me. "College for what? Ax murderers?"

The back lawn was the size of a football field and just about as busy. Workers were draping garlands on the bandstand gazebo, erecting a large white tent pavilion next to the swimming pool, setting up buffet tables and covering them in plastic to protect against the weather. At the far edge of the property, where the ground sloped down to a stand of live oaks along the banks of Olmos Creek, electricians were stringing the entire forest with Christmas lights.

"Intimate party tonight," Ralph guessed.

"For a thousand friends," I agreed.

The cousin parked the van. Seconds later, he opened our doors.

"Clear," he reported unconvincingly.

Ralph and I climbed out, half baked in grease. Ralph's jacket steamed in the cold air.

"Two cans of pork." The cousin shoved canisters at me. "Ralph, you take the two venison. I'm gone. Don't tell me how your visit turns out."

"Thanks, *ese*," Ralph said.

"Relatives," the cousin grumbled.

By the time we'd lugged our tamales to the service entrance, the cousin's van had disappeared around the drive.

Inside, Guy White's kitchen was a cavern of white marble and chrome, bigger than any apartment I'd ever lived in. The counters overflowed with gourmet food, catering trays, grocery bags, vases of flowers. I was too busy getting the crap burned out of my hands to notice much else about my surroundings until I found a free space to park my tamales.

"Damn." Ralph rubbed his red hands. "Now what?"

A female voice behind us said, "Now, you explain."

We turned.

Standing in an interior doorway, the angry young blonde was pointing a nine-millimeter pistol at my head.

· · ·

SHE ESCORTED US INTO THE MAIN foyer, to the base of the presidential staircase, where her leather-jacketed friend was waiting.

The guy wore khakis and a button-down with the brown leather jacket. With stiff blond hair, athletic build, he might've been straight off any college football team, but I had the creepiest feeling I'd met him before. Then it struck me: He looked like Frankie White. If Frankie had been resurrected a little slimmer, a little more handsome, still alive and in his twenties.

He even had the same cruel grin.

He did a thorough job frisking us. If I'd been wearing a wire, he would've found it. If I'd had a nail file concealed in any crevice of my body, he would've found it.

He took my .22 and cell phone, Ralph's wallet. He turned out the pockets of our Goodwill jackets.

He raised an eyebrow when he read Ralph's ID. "Ralph Arguello. I heard about you."

"All true," Ralph said.

The guy snorted. "I heard you'd gone soft and Johnny Zapata was taking over your business."

He shoved Ralph against the wall and frisked him a second time.

"No wallet on the other one," he told the blonde, digging his gun into my ribs. "Think he's a cop?"

The woman appraised me coldly.

She had a tan much too good for the middle of winter, mussed-up shoulder-length hair the color of wet sand, a spray of freckles over her nose, black cargo pants and a black turtleneck sweater. She might've been any college kid just back from a week in Cozumel, except for her eyes.

She was too young to have eyes like that—startlingly blue and hard as glacier core.

"You're not a cop if you're with Arguello," she decided. "Who are you?"

"Tres Navarre."

Her eyes narrowed.

An uncomfortable sense of recognition prickled behind my ears. "Do I know you?"

She studied me about the length of time it would take to empty a clip into my chest. Then she glanced at her large friend. "Alex, put them in the wine cellar. I've got to think about this."

Alex scowled. "I don't take orders from you, Mad—"

"Just *do* it for once!"

"If Mr. White says to, sure."

She glared at him.

I hated to interrupt their lovefest, but I said, "Alex is right. We need to talk to Mr. White."

"No, you don't," the woman snapped. "Mr. White isn't taking visitors."

"He will for this," Ralph said. "It's about Frankie."

Alex and the woman both froze. Eighteen years since the murder, the name Franklin White was still good for a hell of a shock wave.

The young woman was the first to react. She walked over to Ralph and punched him in the gut.

It was a professional punch—her whole body weight behind it, straight from the waist. Ralph doubled over with a grunt.

"You do *not* mention that name." Her voice was steel. "Nobody is going to do that to the old man again."

"Do *what* again?" I asked.

She whirled toward me, but Ralph said, "Listen, *chica*."

He was clutching his stomach, trying to ignore Alex's gun

at his head. "My wife is a homicide cop. She was about to nail Frankie's killer when she got shot. I'm going to find the bastard who shot her. Mr. White's gonna help, because the shooter's the same person who killed his son."

"Mr. White doesn't want to talk to you."

"That's not your decision to make," I said. "Is it?"

Her kick was even faster than her punch.

I thought I was ready for it. I was no stranger to martial arts.

She launched a side-strike and I caught her ankle. I pulled her off balance, but instead of landing on her butt like a good opponent she pivoted in midair, connected her other foot with my face and turned her fall into a roll.

At least, that's what Ralph told me later.

At the time, I was too busy staggering, admiring the floating yellow spots and tasting blood in my mouth.

The young woman got to her feet. She picked her gun up off the carpet.

"Forget the wine cellar," she growled. "These two get dealt with right here."

"Frankie's killer's gonna get away for good," Ralph told her. "That what Mr. White wants?"

The woman raised her nine-millimeter. It was a newer model Beretta, a 9000S with a compact barrel and a discreet black finish. I imagined it would make an elegant hole in my chest.

A man's voice said, "Madeleine."

The young woman's face filled with bitterness, as if she'd just been caught sneaking out after curfew.

At the top of the stairwell, leaning heavily on a cane,

looking infinitely older and frailer than when I'd seen him last, stood a white-haired man. He wore a burgundy Turkish bathrobe. His face was the color of milk.

"What is this," Guy White murmured, "about my son?"

• • •

WE WERE THROWN DOWN ON THE carpet of Mr. White's study. Persian weave. Silk. I'd had my face slammed against worse.

"Enough, Madeleine," Mr. White said.

The demon girl's foot eased off my back. She yanked me to kneeling position, dragged me backward and shoved me into a plush armchair. Next to me, Ralph got a similar treatment from Alex the goon.

Guy White stood in front of us, staring out his library windows.

His back lawn spread to the horizon. The workers were everywhere, setting up the tent and the banquet tables and the Christmas decorations on the denuded grass.

"It's been a long time, gentlemen." Mr. White turned.

He had once been a handsome man—tan, blue eyes, trim figure. He loved spending time in his garden. He boasted of never being sick. At forty, he'd looked twenty-five. At sixty-two, when I'd last seen him, he could've passed for fifty. A local *curandero* once assured me *Señor* White had made a pact with the devil for eternal youth.

Now, as he was approaching seventy, it looked like the devil had decided to collect.

His gaze was as fierce as I remembered, but the skin under his eyes was translucent. His lips were colorless. He reminded me of a corpse with a light inside.

"Lymphoma," he said, answering the question I didn't dare ask. "I don't make many public appearances these days. Not to worry, however. My doctors are quite optimistic."

His eyes glittered as if this were deeply humorous. "Now, gentlemen, enlighten me. What do you claim to know about my son's murder?"

"Sir," Madeleine protested.

White held up his hand.

He gave me a smile that might've been mistaken as kind, if you weren't used to dealing with reptiles. "You must excuse Madeleine. She believes I'm easily taken advantage of. A dying man, still doting over a dead, worthless son."

"Sir, I never—"

"You'd never say so to my face," he agreed. "You don't need to."

Alex cleared his throat. "I tried to tell her, Mr. W. I thought you should make the call."

"Your sensitivity to my wishes is appreciated, Alex Cole."

"Sir," Madeleine said, now gritting her teeth, "the last private investigator—"

"Yes, my dear. The last private investigator took my money, taxed my health, played my hopes for nothing. But you paid him accordingly, did you not?"

White offered me another cold smile.

I wondered what lake that PI was floating at the bottom of.

"I understand from the news you are both wanted men," White told us casually. "Shot your wife, did you, Mr. Arguello?"

"No, *patrón*," Ralph replied. "I didn't."

Mr. White gave him a sympathetic look. "You put me in an

awkward situation. I have my annual Christmas party tonight. I must keep up appearances, you know. Show my, ah, business associates I'm still alive. On top of this, I have the Secret Service hovering outside my house."

"Secret Service?" I asked.

Ralph looked at me. "You owe me ten bucks."

"My point, gentlemen," White said, his voice a little frostier, "is that I have enough to worry about. Why should I not, as a law-abiding citizen, turn you in to the police?"

"We were friends of Frankie's," Ralph said. "You know that."

White studied us. What Ralph said was technically true. In my case, "friends" was pushing it, but I tried to look, well . . . friendly.

"My wife," Ralph said, "Ana DeLeon—"

"The homicide detective," White said.

"—she was reopening Frankie's murder case."

White tugged the cuff of his Turkish bathrobe. "I knew nothing of this."

"Ana had a fresh lead. She was getting ready to make an arrest when somebody shot her."

"The police say *you* shot her."

" 'Course they do." Ralph's voice was raw. "The police hate my guts. They didn't want Ana reopening your son's murder case, 'cause they hate *your* guts, too. But Ana was my wife. I'd never shoot her. The person who shot her was the suspect. Frankie's killer."

Ralph's gaze was so steady even I was impressed.

Guy White cupped his hand, as if to gather the pale winter light coming through the window. "What do you propose?"

"Sir, no," Madeleine protested.

"I need to find this guy to clear myself," Ralph told Guy White. "You want to find him, too. We have a common goal."

Madeleine exhaled. "Sir, they have *nothing* to offer you. We've tried . . . *you've* tried for eighteen years. If there was a way—"

"All we need is some discreet help," I put in. "Wheels. Clothes. Firepower. Your leverage to open a few doors. What have you got to lose?"

White pondered this. His face gleamed from the tiny effort of speaking with us. He looked impossibly ancient, nothing like the man I remembered. "Mr. Navarre, do you truly believe you can find my son's killer?"

"I believe I have no choice."

White's eyes betrayed nothing. "I've been keeping tabs on you. You're good. Probably better than you realize. I've heard you can find anyone."

"This is bullshit," Madeleine spat.

I wondered how Madeleine had kept her job and her life this long, with an attitude like hers. From her colleague Alex's disdainful sneer, I figured he was wondering the same thing.

"My resources are at your disposal," White decided.

"Sir!"

"However," White said, ignoring her, "one of my people will be with you at all times."

"I'll do it, Mr. W," Alex piped in.

"If I find you are using me, gentlemen," White continued, "your life expectancy will be even shorter than mine. Alex, you stay here. Madeleine will see to their needs."

"*What?*" she demanded.

"Go with them," White commanded. "Cooperate with them. Watch them."

"Frankie isn't worth the effort. I don't want this job." Her fists were balled, her voice simmered.

Guy White raised an eyebrow. "You don't have any choice, my dear. After all, he *was* your brother."

CHAPTER 7

"SO YOU TOLD HER NOTHING," ETCH SAID.

The old medical examiner, Jaime Santos, leaned against his porch railing.

Down below, winter mist filled the Olmos Basin. The pewter line of the dam cut through marshes and soccer fields, marching toward the hills where chimney smoke trailed up from the roofs of mansions.

"Nothing," Santos agreed. "I mean . . . what would be the point?"

Santos met his eyes, then looked away.

He's lying, Etch thought.

Doctors were not cops. They couldn't pull off a lie.

Santos had aged since retirement. His eyes had turned soft

and desperate. His chest caved inward. His hair had worn down to gray patches like a bad coat of primer.

"Miss Lee seems smart." Santos tried to sound casual about it. "She asked about the blood under Frankie White's fingernails."

Etch sipped his *atole*.

It had been years since he had the stuff. The cinnamon and chocolate sent him back to Christmas at his *abuela's*—stockings, presents, family dinners.

It had been a long time since he'd thought of Christmas as anything but sweep season for homicides.

"We got a DNA match," he told Santos. "Ana's husband—Ralph Arguello. Ana didn't want to accept that. She claimed the test was tampered with."

"One could fake something like that. You'd have to have access to the evidence room. You'd have to know what you were doing. But it's possible. Look at that big scandal in Houston. They had to shut down their entire DNA lab."

"What are you saying, Jaime?"

Santos shrugged. "Just that it wouldn't be hard."

Etch set his cup on the railing. There was a bullet hole dug into the rough-hewn oak. Etch put his finger on it. "Still the teenage snipers?"

"Damn kids," Santos agreed. "They get on that utility road down there with a .22. My windows are the only thing you can see on this side of the hill at night. They think I'm a damn bull's-eye. I keep calling the Alamo Heights cops . . ."

Etch nodded sympathetically. He took another sip of *atole*.

Christmas, nineteen years ago, Lucia and he had found Franklin White's third victim. A community college student, Julia Garcia had been raped and strangled off Mission Road, abandoned like a used tire. The spot had looked a lot like the marshland below Santos' deck.

Julia Garcia had been a few months shy of her twentieth birthday. She was the first in her family to go to college. Alive, she'd had a radiant smile. She volunteered with the barrio literacy program. She wanted to be a teacher. All that was cut short because she'd let a well-dressed young man pick her up at a bar.

Etch remembered standing in below-zero wind, watching the forensics team haul a draped gurney from the weed-choked gully.

Lucia said: *We'll get him, Etch. Don't worry.*

The father got away with it, he had told her. *Why not the son?*

Lucia's face darkened. She couldn't offer him any reassurance.

Guy White had never *killed* his women, but the distinction didn't matter. It was still the White family proving their power, taking the women of the old mission lands like the Anglo cattle barons had before them and the Spanish *alcaldes* before that. The lords of San Antonio never changed. They had to find the heart of the city, the deepest foundation, and violate it. Possess it. Make themselves legitimate by proving that the oldest inhabitants of the land, families that had been here for three centuries, were defenseless against them.

Like Lucia, Etch came from mission blood. He'd grown up within the sounds of the bells of San Juan and San José.

He'd also been a cop long enough to know how easily justice could be bought and sold. He'd seen how reticent the homicide detectives were to approach the White family, how swiftly White's lawyers counterattacked.

No one could bring Frankie White to justice. At least not in the conventional way.

No one would make him pay for snuffing out Julia Garcia's life.

Etch took another sip of Santos' *atole*. "You suggest anybody else for Miss Lee to talk to?"

The old ME wouldn't meet his eyes. "Why?"

"Just curious." He decided to risk a bit of the truth. "I have a guy tailing her."

"You think that's worth your time?"

"She's a fugitive's girlfriend. I have to assume eventually she'll hook up with Navarre. Be stupid not to have her tailed."

Santos' hands trembled. "I don't recall. We talked for just a few minutes."

Etch couldn't help feeling sorry for Santos. If he was Etch's suspect, if this had been a formal interrogation, the old doctor would've been dead meat. "You remember Larry Drapiewski, used to be with the Sheriff's Department? He told Navarre the hit man theory—Titus Roe."

"Yeah?"

"I wouldn't be surprised if there was some truth to that."

"I . . . guess it's possible."

"Jaime, I don't want the killer to be a cop. I wouldn't like it if people were sending that message."

"We take care of our own."

"Used to be that way," Etch agreed.

"So," Santos said, moistening his lips. "How's the sergeant in the hospital doing?"

Etch forced himself not to make a fist. He thought about Ana in that hospital bed, the uneven bleep of the heart monitor. He had stood at her window for an hour, hating himself, his hand in his pocket, fingering a small glass vial.

"Thanks for the *atole*," he told Santos. "Maybe we'll play a few holes some time?"

The old medical examiner nodded, his eyes cautious. "I'd like that, Lieutenant."

As Etch drove across the dam, he got one last glimpse of Jaime Santos standing on his back porch, two cups of *atole* steaming on the rail in the afternoon cold.

•   •   •

DECEMBER 1986, THE SAME CHRISTMAS FRANKIE White murdered his third victim, Etch's *abuela*, the ninety-two-year-old matron of the family, had died of a bad heart. What was left of the Hernandez clan came unraveled.

Etch's parents had died three years before—his father staring down the barrel of his old military service revolver, his mother shortly afterward from an overdose of sleeping pills. Etch's siblings drifted away to other states. His cousins stopped going to mass at San Juan. Even Etch moved out of the old neighborhood, to a nondescript little house on the near West Side where he could do his target practice in the surrounding fields.

His *abuela*'s funeral hit him harder than he expected. He finally realized he was alone. No family of his own. No wife or kids. Nothing but his job, and not many friends there.

Not that his colleagues disliked him. Everyone complimented Etch on his efficiency. Most of them trusted him to watch their backs. But nobody invited him for a beer. He did not radiate the kind of easygoing manner that made people want to hang out with him.

Except for Lucia. She went to the funeral with him. She held his hand during the lowering of the casket.

Afterward, they sat on her porch swing and drank tequila while inside the Spanish AM radio played old-fashioned *rancheras*.

"You should take the sergeant's test," Lucia told him. "I can see you as a supervisor. A lieutenant, even."

For a moment, Etch was too surprised to speak. "I'm a career patrolman, like you. You understand that."

She poured another shot of Cuervo.

She was wearing a charcoal dress, silver earrings, even lipstick. Her hair was freshly washed and curled. She smelled like jasmine.

"People make a wide arc around you," Lucia said. "They sense you're not one of the guys. That's okay. You're . . . detached. You're a born commander, Etch. You should stop worrying and play your strengths."

A Santiago Jiménez song played on the radio, the sounds of accordion and *basso* guitar pulsing through the screen door.

Lucia's daughter, Ana, was home from Lackland Air Force Base. It was her first weekend furlough after basic training. Etch could hear Ana inside, talking on the phone to a friend. A lot of twenty-one-year-old catch-up talk—*No way. Oh my God, you're kidding! He did what?*

Etch tried not to resent Ana's presence.

Lucia looked good tonight. It felt right to just sit next to her.

He'd thought, once Ana was grown and out of the house . . . maybe there'd be time to get closer to Lucia. He'd been trying for so long, building up his courage for the eleven years they'd worked together. They spent every day together.

In the field, they could read each other's body language perfectly, finish each other's sentences. Yet off duty, she still acted distant. Every time he edged toward telling her how he felt, she seemed to sense it and pull away.

"Lucia, I couldn't work a job where you weren't my partner," he said finally.

She smiled, but there was sadness behind it. "You should do more than this, Etch. You could run things better than the brass we got now, for sure. You're a good man."

"No, I'm not. Just lonely."

She said nothing.

"I know everybody in our beat," Etch said. "I know their kids and grandkids. And I've still got no one. I just can't—"

"Get close," she supplied, when he faltered. "It's like somebody stole that part of you—the part that lets you connect."

There was no need to answer. She described him as perfectly as the day she'd named him "Etch."

His heart pounded like a damn teenager's. He reached over and rested his hand on her knee. She didn't object. She laced her fingers on top of his.

Then Ana flew out the door, breathless. "Mom, can I borrow your car?"

Gently but firmly, Lucia brushed away Etch's hand.

Ana took a step back. "Oh—"

"It's all right, honey." Lucia forced a smile. "Etch, did I tell you Ana is applying for special police?"

"That's great." Etch tried to sound enthusiastic, though his heart felt like crushed paper. "You thinking about civilian law enforcement some day?"

Ana studied him warily, then nodded. "Four years in the service, then college. Then apply to SAPD."

She said it just like any twenty-one-year-old—as if life plans were carved in stone. It was hard for Etch to believe she was the same age as a monster like Frankie White.

"Uh . . . Mom?" Ana looked at the tequila bottle. "I thought you told me you'd stopped drinking."

Lucia rolled her eyes. She was only drinking to commiserate with an old friend, she said. Everything was fine.

Car keys were provided.

Ana promised not to be out too late.

Etch tried not to resent the look Lucia's daughter gave him—as if she thought he was *making* her mother drink. As if that was the only way Lucia would ever hold hands with him.

After Ana was gone, Lucia and he sat on the porch a while longer, but the moment for holding hands had passed.

A news break came on the radio, the Spanish DJ giving an update on Julia Garcia's murder. The witness who'd provided the description of a possible suspect had now turned up missing herself. Police would not say if they had other leads.

Music came back on, a ballad about love in the desert.

"Who was it?" Etch asked.

Lucia frowned. "Who was who?"

"The guy who broke your heart. What'd you say: 'stole a piece of your soul'?"

Lucia crossed her ankles. "That was a long time ago, Etch."

She drank her tequila.

The song played through.

He was so close to Lucia he could feel her warmth, but she wasn't with him anymore. Her thoughts were a million miles away.

For the first time, Etch felt the anger burning inside him.

He resented Lucia's past. He felt powerless, the way he'd felt watching the forensics team bring up the draped gurney with Julia Garcia's body.

"I could do something about Frankie White," Etch said.

Lucia set down her shot glass, leaned toward him. "Promise me you'll never say that again. Not even a hint."

"Lucia—"

"You become like them if you do that, Etch. It would eat you up. The only way to keep your soul from rotting when you deal with people like Frankie White is not to be like them. Don't hate them. Just do your job."

"Is that possible?"

Her eyes were intense, almost desperate. "It has to be."

They sat on the porch swing in their funeral clothes, listening to love music from the Mexican desert while the phone rang cheerfully inside—Ana's friends trying to reach her, optimistic young women all dying to chat about their wide-open futures.

●　　●　　●

ETCH WAS ON COMMERCE, THREE BLOCKS from the office, when he pulled over to take a call.

"Bad news," Kelsey said. "Ballistics can't match the bullets from Ana's leg with the gun we found at Navarre's house. Slugs are too badly mangled."

"Caliber?" Etch asked.

"Yeah. Right caliber: .357. But the blood on the shirt isn't Ana's. Could be Arguello's. They're still testing . . ."

His voice trailed off, wiry and nervous.

"What else?" Etch asked.

"A body turned up in a South Side dumpster this morning.

One of Zapata's cutters, shot point-blank in the gut. Our guys have been asking around. Seems there was a meeting that went bad at Jarrasco's last night. This guy and a friend met a heavyset Latino with a ponytail, about the same time that Ana was shot. The description kinda matches Ralph Arguello."

"You're saying Arguello has an alibi."

"A bad goddamn alibi. He was busy shooting a guy?"

"But that would mean he didn't shoot Ana."

"It's weak, sir. It's still gotta be him."

Etch heard the indecision in his voice.

Kelsey was the equivalent of an Abrams tank. As long as he had a clear target in the distance and wide straight road, he would roll over everything in his path. But as soon as he started doubting his aim or hit muddy terrain, he ground to a halt. He needed a good push to keep going.

"Kelsey," Etch said, "if you think you may have been too focused on Arguello, for whatever reason, if you think you've made a mistake, it's not too late . . ."

He could almost feel the steam on the other end of the line. Etch had dared to use the *M*-word.

"I didn't make a mistake, sir," Kelsey said tightly.

"All right."

"I'll keep you posted."

Kelsey hung up, hard.

Etch sat back and closed his eyes. He tried to convince himself everything could still work out.

With luck, Kelsey would now hound Arguello till Doomsday, and he would think it was his own idea. He would think Etch had tried to convince him not to.

Etch didn't hate many people, but Ralph Arguello deserved to go down. He'd gotten away with murder before. He was no better than the Whites. Worse. He'd married Ana, jeopardized the career Etch had helped her build.

Two years ago, watching them at the altar had been more than Etch could bear—Ana in her white dress, her face so much like her mother's, and a common criminal next to her, grinning like the devil.

Navarre and Maia Lee had been at the wedding. Then, as now, standing by Ralph Arguello, supporting somebody who didn't deserve it, watching him take Ana's hand.

Etch imagined Lucia sitting next to him, the way she had so many years on patrol.

Why did you do it, Etch? she asked.

It was an accident, he promised her. *It wasn't supposed to happen.*

She turned her face to the window. *It was no accident. You know better.*

The sound of his cell phone startled him out of his trance.

His surveillance man had a short report: Maia Lee had spent the last couple of hours inside the *Express-News* offices, probably going through the archives. Now she was at the Pig Stand, talking to the old guy behind the counter.

Etch hung up, hit the steering wheel with his palm.

"Miss Lee," he chided. "Miss Lee, Miss Lee."

He felt his anger building.

Jaime Santos had done more than a little talking. The old man was dangerous. And Maia Lee . . . she was too much like Ana. She was following Ana's trail too well.

If Kelsey didn't do his work right, if Arguello started looking bad as a suspect . . .

Etch searched for a fallback plan. Only one came to him—an idea that had been brewing since he debriefed the old deputy Drapiewski. It had a certain sense of justice to it.

He switched his phone to answering service. He radioed dispatch and put himself in the field. Then he put the car in drive.

He circled Travis Square and parked across the street from San Fernando Cathedral.

The man Etch wanted to see was doing business in front of the cathedral as usual. He was leaning over the portable cooler on his ice cream bicycle, offering a strawberry *paleta* to the girl who sold T-shirts at the souvenir stand.

At the end of the block, a beat cop was eating lunch on the hood of a pickup truck. A bored security guard lounged in front of the Catholic Family Center.

Hernandez didn't think they would recognize him. It didn't matter, anyway. This was his city, his territory. He could talk to an old collar if he wanted to.

He punched a request into his laptop, printed out some information. Then he got out of his car and walked across Mission.

"Titus," he called.

Titus Roe had been grinning at the T-shirt seller, but his smile evaporated when he saw the lieutenant.

Roe was grizzled and lanky, with a face like crocodile leather—all greasy bumps and hard lines. He wore a red flannel shirt rolled up at the sleeves to show his garden of flower tattoos—marigolds, roses, bluebonnets and cacti.

"Hi, uh . . . sir."

Roe's discomfort pleased Etch. He had warned the ex-con never to address him by name.

The T-shirt seller backed away. She was Latina, young and pretty, a little heavy on the mascara and hairspray. Just out of high school, probably, but Etch figured she could still sense the police aura. He was used to this effect on people—like he had some mildly frightening disfigurement that kept others from getting too close.

"I'm an old friend of Titus's," Hernandez told her. "Come on, Titus, pray with me."

He put an arm around Roe's shoulders and led him toward the cathedral.

Inside, San Fernando smelled of candles and newly hewn limestone. The recent renovations had taken the eighteenth-century mildew out of the air.

Hernandez wasn't used to the changes. The cathedral had been falling apart before, sure, but it had been familiar—the city's deepest taproot, an institution a year older than George Washington. Now the sanctuary felt raw, too open, too bright.

Up front, choir members were practicing a Christmas carol for tonight's Las Posadas celebration. A scattering of parishioners prayed in the pews. Hernandez and Roe slipped into the back row by the sacristy, where a bank of votives glowed.

"I almost had a date, man," Roe whined. "You know how long I've been working on her?"

"Work on her later," Etch told him.

Roe laced his hands together. "Who you looking for?"

Etch smiled.

Roe squirmed. "What? I've been cooperating, Lieutenant. Shit—you know I have."

True, Titus had given him some good leads over the years. Once upon a time, Titus Roe had been well connected, one of the busiest, if not best, assassins who worked locally.

He'd done two years in Floresville State for assault, but the only time Etch had a clear shot at busting him for capital murder, he'd let Titus go.

The hit had been a drug lord on the East Side—not exactly a loss to society. By sheer luck, Etch had found the murder weapon, tied it to Roe beyond a reasonable doubt, then set the evidence aside after explaining to Titus that it could come back anytime if he failed to cooperate. Since then, Titus had been a valuable informant.

"The Franklin White murder," Etch said.

"Aw, hell, Lieutenant. I didn't have shit to do with that. You think I'm crazy?"

Etch ignored the question. Of course, Roe was crazy. "You got any idea who did it?"

Roe's eyes drifted toward the front of the cathedral, where the choir was singing "Adeste Fidelis."

"Um . . . none," Roe said. "None."

"People are looking into it," Etch said. "Last week, Sergeant DeLeon. Now other people are stirring things up."

Roe's eyes narrowed. "And?"

"Maybe the person who did the crime should be nervous."

He offered Roe the slip of paper he'd printed out.

Roe read the information. He moistened his lips, stared at the crucifix above the altar. "Lieutenant . . . what exactly do you want?"

"Loose ends are difficult, Titus. That old gun of yours, for instance—if it should ever be found, come to the attention of the DA . . ."

Titus shivered. "I'm trying to go straight, Lieutenant. If this is some kind of test—"

"It's absolutely a test, Titus. I need a solution. I need to retire next month, understand? And when I do, your problems retire with me. You'll have nothing to worry about but selling *paletas* and dating the T-shirt girl."

"I—I can't."

"You can," Etch told him. "You've got no choice. Now memorize that paper and light a candle with it, you understand?"

Etch left him in the pew. When he looked back, Titus Roe was praying almost as if he meant it.

•   •   •

ETCH DROVE NORTH.

He passed Hildebrand, turned into Olmos Park, past Guy White's mansion on Contour. A mile further into the basin, he passed the wooded ridge above the dam where Lucia and he had once sat talking, the whole city spread below them, blood-red in the sunset.

Cops weren't supposed to fall in love on the job. They weren't supposed to break the law, or hate criminals, or kill, either.

Etch had tried to follow the rules.

He'd failed miserably.

After Lucia died, he'd thrown himself into the career track. He made lieutenant, just like she said he should.

The higher he rose in the department, the more he realized that professional ethics were like Kevlar vests. Cops wore them only because they were required to. They were supposed to be good for you, but what beat cop hadn't slipped off the damn vest once in a while, just to get rid of the scratchy hot confinement?

Etch vowed never to forget what had happened to Lucia.

He'd do whatever he had to. The truth could never come out.

He drove across the dam and parked downhill on the utility road.

Late afternoon, the sky was dark and cloudy. Cold seeped into the car the moment he cut the engine. Through the trees, he saw the deck of the house, the windows glowing large and yellow like the eyes of an enormous predator.

He got out of his car and opened the trunk.

•   •   •

IN AN ALLEY BEHIND SAN FERNANDO Cathedral, Titus Roe opened his ice cream cooler.

He moved aside boxes of banana *paletas* until his fingers hit cold metal—the Colt .45 he had promised himself never to use.

He unfolded the paper Lieutenant Hernandez had given him and read the information again. Two addresses. One in town, one in Austin. The car's make and color, with a license plate. A bad printout of a driver's license photo and the woman's name.

He folded the paper and put it back in his pocket.

He looked up at the rose window.

Retirement, he thought. *One month and the bastard will stop hounding me.*

He decided to start with the local address, go from there.

He muttered a silent apology to God and to the woman he didn't even know.

Maia Lee.

•   •   •

ETCH HERNANDEZ UNLATCHED THE LONG BLACK case and assembled the pieces.

He tried the scope, saw nothing for a moment but fuzzy leaves. Then he readjusted the lens and saw Jaime Santos standing on his porch, still drinking his *atole* and watching the clouds.

How could the old man stand the cold?

Go inside, Etch thought.

But the old man stood his ground.

Santos had sold out an officer. He would be dangerous in court. Whatever happened now was his own damn fault.

Etch murmured Lucia's name. He was hollow, nothing else inside him except her memory.

He lined the X-hairs on the old man's chest, and exhaled as he squeezed the trigger.

CHAPTER 8

"ARE YOU SURE THIS TIME?" I ASKED.

"Yeah," Ralph said from the front seat. "That's the bastard."

Nothing is more embarrassing than siccing the mob on the wrong person. Ralph's eyesight may have been laser-corrected, but thirty minutes ago at the Poco Mas Bar he'd mistakenly identified a burly Latino with a peroxide red buzz cut as one of the thugs who'd jumped him the night before.

We'd unleashed Madeleine White and watched the alleged thug get reduced to hamburger meat over the hood of the limo. The whole time, he swore up and down he didn't know anybody named Zapata. Finally Ralph realized we'd screwed up.

We left the poor dude sixty bucks for a new shirt, called an ambulance and scrammed.

Now, after three more conversations with my street friends and several twenty-dollar bribes, we were parked across Roosevelt Avenue from Mission San José, watching another burly redheaded Latino order a burrito at Taco Shack #3. The dilapidated look of the place made me wonder what had happened to Taco Shacks #1 and #2. I imagined they were turning into fossil fuel in the sedimentary layers below.

I squirmed in my new black suit.

A hot shower with scented soap and designer shampoo hadn't changed the feeling that I'd washed myself in grease, using a mobster's bathroom. My borrowed silk slacks were too tight in the crotch. The shirt collar was stiff with starch. Sitting in the back of the limo with Madeleine White, I felt like I was on my way to the mafia prom.

"Too many people around," Madeleine said, scoping out the scene. "I don't want more blood on the car."

"Sensitive type, aren't you?" I asked.

She glared at me like she was about to kick me in the face again.

Screw it.

Now that I realized who she was, I couldn't take her seriously.

I remembered her, all right. Frankie's little sister.

When I'd known her before, she'd been a ten-year-old kid with a dirty blond ponytail, a shrill voice and painter's pants decorated with Magic Markers. She always had bruises on her arms from getting into fights with her classmates. She used to sit in the bleachers during football practice and throw tennis balls at me. The coach never had the nerve to run her off because of her dad's reputation. Frankie called her the Brat.

Now, she must've been pushing thirty, but she looked closer to twenty. Proof positive she had Guy White's genes.

She didn't stick out her tongue anymore, but her *I-hate-you* expression hadn't changed.

"Listen," she told me, "*I* don't care if we draw attention. *I'm* not the one running from the police."

I wished I had a good comeback, or maybe just a better way of tracking down Johnny Shoes.

Unfortunately, Madeleine's plan was the best one we had. She'd said looking for Zapata's men would be easier than looking for the man himself, and she was right. When it came to moving around and avoiding detection, Zapata was slightly more paranoid than your average Third World dictator.

"What was that martial arts style you used on me earlier, anyway?" I asked her.

"Shen Chuan."

Ralph and I exchanged looks.

"Hell," I said.

As far as I knew, Shen Chuan was the only native Texas martial arts system. It was also a hard damn style to defend against. It was taught in the East Texas piney woods by one extremely good, extremely unconventional sensei.

"You study with Lansdale?" I asked.

"*Did*," Madeleine corrected. "He kicked me out of the dojo. Said I was over-the-top."

I tried to imagine what Joe Lansdale would consider over-the-top. Chain saws and atom bombs, maybe.

It seemed strange to me that a girl like Madeleine White would've taken up martial arts so intensely. Then I remembered something Ralph had told me. Mr. White had come to him for help when Frankie's problems got so bad they affected the family. I wondered what exactly that meant.

At the Taco Shack counter, the redheaded thug was getting his order.

"Come on," I said. "Let's interrupt this poor man's lunch."

"Hold up," Ralph said. "He's moving."

Sure enough, Mr. Thug had cradled his taco bag like an offensive lineman and was jogging across Roosevelt Avenue.

He didn't seem to have seen us, but he was moving at a good clip. He cut through the parking lot of San José and headed for the mission gates.

"Pull the car around," Madeleine ordered the driver.

"Why is he going to San José?" I wondered.

"Damn," Ralph said.

"What?"

"Zapata's mother."

"What are you talking about?"

The limo did a tight one-eighty.

I held the door handle to avoid slamming into Madeleine.

"Zapata's mom is a parishioner," Ralph said. "Ana told me once. I forgot. Zapata's family's been at the mission for, like, centuries."

Madeleine snorted. "You think Zapata is in there with his *mother?* What, praying?"

I tried to imagine Johnny Zapata as a good Catholic boy. Or even a good boy. Or even having a mother. I failed.

"I don't want this to go down in a church," Ralph muttered.

The limo stopped in front of the visitors' center.

Madeleine slipped a new clip into her nine. "Alex was right, Arguello. You are getting soft."

She kicked open the car door, looked at me expectantly. "Are we kicking someone's ass or not?"

•   •   •

AS A PI, I'VE LEARNED YOU get better help from people if you make an effort to like them. It's not about making them like you. You have to develop a genuine affection for disagreeable people. With the hard-luck cases I meet, often the best way to like them is to find something about them with which you can empathize.

With Madeleine White, that wasn't easy.

The ass-kicking woman who led us into the mission was as hard to love as the bratty little girl I'd known at Alamo Heights.

The only memory that made me feel any sympathy for her was so unpleasant I'd buried it for years.

My senior year at Heights, I attended my last Howdy Night celebration to kick off the new school term. It was a sultry September evening. Millions of grackles were screeching in the trees. The air was thick with mosquitoes and barbecue smoke and teenage hormones.

The football field had been converted into a carnival ground. Parents and younger siblings milled around everywhere. Teachers worked the standard game booths: the dunking chair, the sponge toss, the cakewalk.

I was supposed to be meeting my girlfriend Lillian, but she was running late, so I fell in with Ralph and Frankie White, who were trying the football toss and drinking Big Red sodas secretly laced with tequila.

Over by the fifty-yard line, Frankie's dad was talking to one of the city councilmen. Guy White wore jeans and loafers and an Izod button-down, like he was one of the common yuppies. His silver hair contrasted starkly with his deep summer tan. His smile radiated good humor. The field was crowded, but he had an open radius ten feet wide around him. Only little children who didn't know any better wandered close to him.

Frankie was getting angry because he couldn't get the football through the tire. He always griped that he should've made quarterback, but he couldn't throw to save his life. He kept giving carnival tickets to our bored English teacher, Mrs. Weems, and kept bouncing footballs off the rim of the tire, or throwing into the midst of screaming drill team girls by mistake.

Ralph was cracking up, which didn't help Frankie's mood.

After a few tosses his little sister, Madeleine, ran up to him. As usual, her clothes were decorated with Magic Marker designs—spirals, mazes, scary faces. She had a fistful of candy canes and her face was painted blue and gold. There was *cascarón* glitter and confetti in her hair.

"Share your tickets, Frankie," she demanded.

"Get lost, Brat," he growled.

Madeleine held her ground. "Dad said they were for both of us. He told you to share."

Frankie jumped toward her and faked throwing the football at her. She squealed and ducked her head.

Mrs. Weems, normally an innocuous soul, said, "Now, Franklin—"

"I told you to get lost," Frankie yelled at his sister.

"You can't touch me anymore!" Madeleine's chin was trembling. "Dad said—"

She never got to finish her sentence.

Frankie grabbed her by the scruff of the neck and marched her away.

"You want to play more games, Brat?" Frankie's face was bright red. "You want the apple dunk? Huh?"

She tried to fight him off, but he dragged her over to the tin washtub. Then he pushed her head underwater.

"Frankie," Ralph said. "Stop."

Frankie brought Madeleine up again, screaming and sputtering.

Mrs. Weems shouted, "Stop it!"

"You didn't get an apple, Brat?" Frankie said. "Gee, I'm sorry."

He shoved Madeleine under again. That's when Ralph and Mrs. Weems and I all got into the act.

Ralph pulled Madeleine away from Frankie while Mrs. Weems and I tried to restrain him, but Frankie had the weight advantage. He elbowed me in the gut, then pushed poor Mrs. Weems a little too hard. She stumbled backward.

"Stay off me!" he yelled.

"Franklin White!" Mrs. Weems got to her feet, furious, and slapped him hard across the face.

Frankie looked stunned. Then his face blanched. I was pretty sure he was about to kill our English teacher when a deep voice said, "Franklin."

Guy White stood behind us.

Frankie's shoulders hunched. He blinked hard, like a dog who expects a beating.

Madeleine was kneeling in the grass, crying and coughing up water, her face paint smeared. She got to her feet, but she didn't run to Daddy. Instead, she yanked her wrist free of Ralph's hand and took off into the crowd. Her father paid no attention.

His eyes bored into his son.

"Come with me," Mr. White told Frankie.

"I'm with my friends," Frankie mumbled. "I don't want to."

I couldn't tell which was stronger in Frankie's voice—hate or fear.

"Now," Mr. White said calmly.

"Hey, Frankie," Ralph said. "It's cool. We'll catch you later."

Mr. White glanced at Ralph, appraising him. Maybe he recognized that Ralph was letting Frankie save face. Maybe, in a cold way, he even appreciated that.

Frankie's fists clenched. He planted his feet, trying to ignore his father's order. But it was like watching a time-lapse movie—a granite hillside being slowly and mercilessly eroded by the sun and the wind. Finally Mr. White pointed toward the parking lot, and Frankie followed his father off the playing field. We didn't see them or Madeleine again that night. Soon, I was much more interested in my girlfriend and Ralph's tequila, and I stopped thinking about the incident with the Whites.

But looking back on it, I felt sorry for Madeleine.

I tried to imagine what it would be like living with two men like her father and brother, being kid sister to Frankie White, who could bring out the violent side in anyone, even a gentle middle-aged English teacher.

●   ●   ●

123

RALPH, MADELEINE AND I FOLLOWED THE redheaded thug into the grounds of Mission San José.

It was a cold Saturday evening, too late and overcast for much of a crowd. The *convento* was empty except for an elderly couple studying a tourist brochure. Ancient huisache trees lay flat against the ground and the foundations of ruined buildings made weird geometry in the grass. Along the fort walls, oak doors were fastened shut, as if the Indians who'd lived there two hundred years before were still inside, cooking dinner or stumbling through vespers prayers in their strange new Spanish language.

Mr. Thug toted his taco bag toward the *tiendita*—a tiny souvenir shop in one of the Indian apartments. The sign out front promised religious memorabilia and ice-cold bottled water. He went inside.

Ralph stopped. He stared at the shop door, his hand in the pocket of his new leather jacket where a borrowed .38 waited.

Guy White's manservant had taken one look at Ralph, then given him a tough-guy outfit—black jeans, leather jacket, boots. Me, I got a silk suit. Bloody typical.

"Zapata's mom," Ralph said. "I remember now. She runs the souvenir shop."

"Are we going in?" Madeleine asked.

"*Chiquita*, you ever meet Zapata?"

Madeleine's scowl reminded me of the angry little girl at Howdy Night—a ten-year-old foolishly determined to hold her ground.

"Call me *chiquita* again," she said, "and I'll cut out your tongue."

Ralph pulled out his .38, opened the door for Madeleine. "Ladies first."

Inside, the souvenir shop was crammed with postcard carousels, shelves bristling with plaster saint figurines, holographic Jesus portraits that smiled and suffered and ascended in 3-D.

Johnny Zapata stood at the jewelry counter with Mr. Thug, both of them getting yelled at by a gray-haired Latina cashier so hideously ugly she could only have been Zapata's mother.

She was waving a taco under Mr. Thug's nose and yelling, "*Tripas*, Ignacio! I wanted *tripas!*"

Mr. Thug/Ignacio raised his hands. "Mrs. Z—"

"Ma," Johnny Zapata cut in, "they don't sell *tripas* no more!"

"Bah!"

"I told you, Ma. It's illegal now."

The old woman made a barking sound. "Since when do you care about illegal? Huh?"

Had I been thinking more clearly, I would've backed out, let the three of them fight, and questioned the survivors later.

Unfortunately, they noticed us.

Zapata stood up straight when he recognized Ralph.

Ignacio started to reach for his coat pocket, but Madeleine stuck her gun in the side of his nose.

Ignacio raised his hands.

"Who are these people?" Mama Zapata yelled at her son. "More of your enemies?"

Zapata studied us.

He was just as huge as I remembered. His fashion sense hadn't improved. He sported a black and gray polyester shirt, white pants and white leather cleats. With his Mongolian features and his small evil eyes, he bore an uncanny resemblance to Genghis Khan out for a night of bowling.

125

"Old acquaintances," Zapata told his mother softly. He glanced at Madeleine. "You're Guy White's daughter. What you doing with these *babosas*?"

"We thought she'd get along with your mom," I offered.

"What?" Mama Zapata shrilled. "Did this little punk insult me?"

"Ignore him, Ma." There was nothing human about Zapata's voice. It was free of emotion, calm and ruthless, the way sharks would talk if they could. "This is Tres Navarre, the PI. He thinks he's funny."

"Eh, Johnny," Ralph said. "We're overdue for a chat. You sure you want your mother here for that?"

Zapata's eyes drifted from me to Madeleine to Ralph. He was trying to read the score. He didn't seem able to do it.

"Ignacio," he said, "this is the second time you failed me."

The henchman's face turned the same color as his peroxide crew cut. "Me?"

"You didn't do the job last night," Zapata said. "The wrong man died. Now you've led these people here."

"Wasn't my fault!"

"Take Ma outside," Zapata told him calmly. "When you come back, you choose what to lose."

Ignacio's face beaded with sweat. "Johnny, man, please . . ."

"You want me to let Miss White shoot you? That'd be quicker. Now take Ma and go."

Ignacio swallowed. He tried to take the old woman's arm, but she pulled away.

"I ain't going," she grumbled. "Who's gonna watch the store?"

"I'll watch the store, Ma."

"They gonna steal St. Peter."

"No, Ma. They ain't gonna steal St. Peter. Go on."

Before Ignacio could leave, Madeleine dug her free hand into his coat pocket and pulled out a Smith & Wesson. She said, "I'll hold this for you."

Reluctantly, the nervous thug escorted Mama Zapata out of the shop, the old woman still eyeing me like she expected me to filch her plaster apostles.

• • •

ZAPATA PEELED THE FOIL OFF A beef taco. "Well?"

The situation didn't need any more guns, but before I could try the diplomatic approach, Ralph pointed his .38 at Zapata's head.

"You set me up," Ralph told him.

"So?"

"Frankie White's sister is standing here. She wants to know whether you've really got a lead on Frankie's murder or if you were bullshitting. How about I count to five?"

Zapata smiled. "That would've been a scary threat, Ralph, back in the old days." He took a bite of flour tortilla, glanced at Madeleine. "You understand who you're working with, right? Ralph Arguello? He's old news. Gone soft."

"Five," Ralph said.

"Hey, Shoes," Madeleine said, "if I were you, I'd talk."

Zapata wiped his mouth. "You sure you want me to, miss? I hear a lot of things about your family. I got too much respect for Mr. White to go spreading rumors."

"Four," Ralph said.

"Respect," Madeleine said tightly. "You've tried to kill my father a dozen times. You've murdered his men."

"Just business." Zapata took another bite of his taco. "But

127

here's the thing, Miss White. I was bullshitting Arguello. I don't know nothing about your brother's death. If I did, I'd tell you. Bad misunderstanding between your father and me, years ago. Cost me plenty. I don't want all that stirred up again."

"Three."

Zapata kept his eyes on Madeleine. "Arguello called *me*. I knew he had to be desperate to do that. I've been wanting to take over his properties for years. So I told him what he wanted to hear. I set Arguello up so I could kill him."

He spread his hands, as if his intentions were completely reasonable.

"Two."

"Go on, Arguello." Zapata tapped his chest. "You're a fucking disgrace."

"One."

"You know why you can't? You married a goddamn cop. You got the perfect network set up for fronting drugs, guns, money laundering, you name it. And what do you do with it? Nada. You try to go straight. I offer you a fair price over and over and you don't take it. You're standing in the way of profit, Arguello. You need to be removed."

I put my hand on Ralph's wrist just as he shot. A plaster Jesus exploded on the shelf behind Zapata.

Zapata shook his head. "Pathetic."

I kept my grip on Ralph's wrist. His arm was like a steel cable.

"Zapata," I said, "you said yourself you want Ralph's pawnshops. Ralph started those businesses with Frankie White. Maybe Frankie was standing in your way, too."

He studied me, probably deciding whether or not it would be advantageous to insult me. "I'm not that stupid, PI."

"Not stupid enough to do it yourself," I agreed. "You could've hired Titus Roe."

His face reddened. "Titus Roe? Who the fuck would hire *him*? Who'd pay *anybody* to whack a loser like Frankie? I mean, Jesus, unless you were a woman—"

Zapata stopped.

"You were saying?" Madeleine's eyes had a dangerous gleam.

Zapata moistened his lips. "All I meant, Miss White: I had nada to gain. Think about it. Your brother getting killed was damn bad for my business."

Outside, Zapata's mother was arguing with Ignacio. She said she was sure she'd heard a shot, which meant her son had finished killing whoever he needed to kill. It was closing time and she had to get back to her shop.

I felt like I was standing in a meth lab, between vats of chemicals that could blow the neighborhood to rubble. I wanted to get out before that old lady came back in.

"Come on," I told Ralph. "Shoes doesn't know anything."

"Listen to the man," Zapata said. "And, Miss White—" He flicked his finger between Madeleine and Ralph. "Is your family leaning on this loser now? I mean, I knew Mr. White was sick and all, but—"

"Mr. White is not sick," Madeleine said. "He leans on no one."

"So if I was to see Arguello out on the street, without you—"

"I have no interest in whom you kill or who kills you,"

Madeleine said. "Just remember your place, Zapata—down there by the floorboards with the other insects."

Zapata's eyes glinted, like light off the edge of a scalpel. I doubted a woman had ever talked to him like that before.

He turned to Ralph, crumpled up his taco wrapper. "See you around, Arguello. Having your wife shot—that kind of thing should make a man reexamine his priorities. You still got a baby daughter to think about, don't you?"

I was glad I had Madeleine with me. It took both of us to get Ralph out the door without firing his gun again.

•　•　•

IN THE COURTYARD, MAMA ZAPATA WAS still arguing with Ignacio, whose face was pale and clammy. He looked at us like we'd come to deliver his last meal.

"Done," I told him. "Sorry."

I tried to steer clear of Mama Zapata, but the old woman stepped in front of Madeleine. "I know you. I remember your father."

"Excuse us," Madeleine said.

The old woman grabbed Madeleine's arm. "My son won't tell you, but I don't give a damn. Your brother got what he deserved. Punishment for your father's sins. *Entiendes*?"

"Get off me," Madeleine said.

The old woman spat in the dust at Madeleine's feet, then allowed a very ill-looking Ignacio to escort her back into her souvenir shop.

•　•　•

THE LIMO DROVE NORTH.

The chauffeur asked us where to. Nobody answered.

Along Roosevelt Avenue, run-down businesses were decorated with frayed Christmas garlands, weather-bleached Santas, grimy lights that had started to glow in the evening. This being South Texas, the Christmas lights stayed up year-round, but even a broken holiday is right once a year.

In the front seat, Ralph cradled his borrowed .38 in his lap. At Ralph's insistence, the chauffeur had anonymously called Ana's hospital and tried to get an update on her condition. They wouldn't tell him anything. Now Ralph was muttering something under his breath. The chauffeur was leaning as far away from him as possible.

I felt like I should say something to Ralph, but I was angry with him. My initial shock was wearing off, and I was starting to realize that he'd almost killed Zapata in front of my eyes. If I hadn't grabbed his arm, he wouldn't have missed.

A few uncomfortable facts were also starting to swirl together in my head: Frankie's reputation with women, Ralph's experience with his stepfathers, what Ralph's sister had said on the phone: *You know why he had to help Frankie, don't you?*

Ralph has always had a soft spot for abused women. Over the years, he'd gotten several prostitutes away from their pimps. He'd killed at least one wife-beater that I knew of. In fact, the more I thought about Ralph's violent reputation, the more I realized that when he picked the fight, he almost always lashed out at men who abused women. And he did so with no concern for his own safety.

I thought about Ralph's tone the night Frankie had roughed up little Madeleine. He'd had no tolerance for it—so why had he tried to save Frankie when his dad came down on him?

Ralph might have wanted to change Frankie, turn him

into something better. But I wondered what Ralph would've done if he realized Frankie was beyond redemption, if he started seeing how many women Frankie had hurt. Ralph would not have been intimidated by Frankie's mob father. For the first time, I wonder if the DNA test on the blood under Frankie's fingernails really had been faked.

Next to me, Madeleine cracked her knuckles.

I figured we'd better find her somebody to beat up soon or she'd start cannibalizing people in the limo.

"What did Mrs. Zapata mean?" I asked her. "What'd your father do?"

Madeleine picked a speck of dust off her slacks. "He's a mobster. Not much he *hasn't* done."

"I mean to women."

"You must not have been listening. She didn't say anything like that."

At the corner of Santa Rosa, a police car cut across our path on full code three, siren wailing, lights running. I resisted the urge to slink down in my seat.

"I remember you from Heights," I told Madeleine. "You used to draw on your clothes."

Her ears turned pink. "I'm an artist."

"An artist?"

"I got a BFA. That's what I did in college. You got a problem with that?"

I envisioned Madeleine doing tornado kicks in a painting studio, ripping canvases, karate-chopping brushes.

"I remember you, too," she said after another block. "You didn't like Frankie."

"How old were you when he died?" I asked. "Thirteen?"

She nodded.

"You remember the night of the murder?"

"I heard about it later . . . in a phone call. I wasn't around."

"What do you mean?"

"Don't act like you don't know. Everybody knows."

I didn't, but from her tone of voice, I got the feeling it would be dangerous to ask.

"My father's dying," she said to the window. "All that talk about optimistic doctors? That's bullshit. He's got two months, no more."

I wasn't sure what to say. *I'm sorry* wouldn't have been exactly sincere.

Before I could decide, my cell phone rang.

Madeleine scowled. "My father shouldn't have given that back to you."

"I forgot about it."

"Don't answer."

I checked the display. The number belonged to my housekeeper, Mrs. Loomis. She was calling from the cell phone I'd bought her for emergencies. She never used it. She hated phones.

I swore silently, then answered the call.

A man's voice said: "Who is this?"

My heartbeat syncopated until I realized who I was talking to.

"Sam," I said. "It's Tres."

"I know that, damn it."

"Why are you calling me, Sam? Where's Mrs. Loomis?"

"They can probably trace this. I told her it was a bad idea."

"Sam, I'm on the run here. Are you okay?"

"I told her not to worry. Irritating woman. The gunshot isn't that bad."

I sat up straight. "What gunshot?"

"Mine, damn it. I've had worse. I don't want you to come—"

Eight seconds later, over Madeleine's and Ralph's stereophonic protests, I was ordering the chauffeur to turn the car around, giving him directions to my office in Southtown.

FEBRUARY 2, 1968

DELIA MONTOYA KNEW SHE WASN'T HIS FIRST VICTIM, but she was determined to be the last.

Delia pulled into the police station parking lot right on time. She struggled to fix her makeup—hard to apply lipstick with three stitches in the corner of her mouth. She told herself she wouldn't cry. She would face the monster; she would give her statement.

Outside, the winter clouds were an unnatural mix of gray and sulfur. Even the city skyline looked wrong. To the east, a new tower was rising for the world's fair. The round top house was being hoisted up the five-hundred-foot column of concrete. It was about halfway today—like a ring awkwardly being lifted off a giant's finger.

Delia stopped at the doors of the police station. She took a shaky breath. She'd been here too many times over the last month, trying to get someone to listen.

Ever since her first visit, White's men had been shadowing her. They appeared while she was shopping, or baby-sitting her little cousin, or taking flowers to her mother in the nursing home.

They never threatened her, never spoke. But she knew who they were.

We are as close as your jugular vein, they seemed to say. *Don't ever forget that.*

Two weeks, three days, eleven hours since the attack.

135

She'd been shattered like a vase, glued back together imperfectly. She could still feel his fingers tightening around her wrists, his whiskers scraping against her throat. She could still taste the blood—first from biting his arm, then from his fist against her mouth.

She couldn't let him get away with it.

She'd spent two years fighting for other people's rights in California. She'd marched with César Chávez, blistered her feet on the dusty roads of the Central Valley, helped translate the stories of migrant workers for the media.

At New Year's, full of optimism and hope for the future, she'd come home to Texas to fight for *La Causa*. In that rush of confidence, she'd visited a South Side bar and felt comfortable rising to the challenge of a gringo who found her attractive. Why the hell not?

• • •

AN OFFICER ESCORTED HER INTO A green-tiled room with harsh fluorescents. At one end of the table sat a grim-faced detective, smoke curling from the cigarette in his hand. At the other end of the table, *he* was there, looking the same as the night he'd picked her up—clean, elegant, commanding. To his right sat another well-dressed man, the lawyer who'd visited her a week ago to explain how much she had to lose.

Mr. White has a wife and little boy, he'd told her. *Do you want to embarrass a man with a family?*

Since then, the losses had been piling up. First, her new job. Her boss at *La Prensa* let her go, mumbling something about budget problems, but she'd seen the fear in his eyes. Then she'd lost her lease. She was given one month to move out, no explanation. Most of all, she'd lost her privacy. White's men were everywhere she went.

She shouldn't have agreed to this meeting. They couldn't force her to make a statement with her attacker present. But even the police seemed to be playing by Guy White's rules.

"Miss Montoya." The detective was a grizzled man with a military haircut. The razor stubble on his cheeks was like frost. "We've made Mr. White aware of your accusations. We need to know now if you still want to press charges."

His voice sounded weary, like he'd done all this before.

White's eyes were a horrible blue.

If he'd shown any anxiety, she might've found her own strength. But there was nothing in his eyes but calm anticipation, as if he were patiently curious about what form of destruction she would choose.

She'd heard rumors about the previous victims. She knew she was only the latest in a long line of amusements. He had knocked her down the way a boy knocks down sand castles on the beach—just because he could.

She remembered his fingers around her throat, the taste of blood in her mouth.

Yesterday Delia had taken her seven-year-old niece to the playground. There'd been a man on the park bench, smiling at them. His eyes were dull with cruelty. Delia was certain the lump in his jacket pocket was a gun.

She remembered the lines White's lawyer had suggested. *All you have to say . . .*

She couldn't let him get away with it.

"It didn't happen," she muttered.

Silence. Cigarette smoke curled into the ugly lights.

"Excuse me?" the detective asked.

"I made it up to get attention," Delia said. "He never touched me."

She was conscious of the detective studying her—her stitched-up lip, the blue bruises under her eyes.

Please, she thought. *See that I'm lying.*

The detective looked down. He gently closed the file in front of him, rested his hand on it like a Bible.

"Well," Guy White said breezily. "That is that."

•   •   •

LATE THAT NIGHT, DELIA SAT IN her bathtub, warm water lapping against the porcelain, a candle burning on the sink. She watched the watery reflections of flame dance off her shower curtain and felt herself floating away.

She had betrayed herself.

No amount of washing could cleanse her. There was no way to stop the poison White had planted in her. Nothing to do but cut it out.

She used a razor—a momentary sting, then no pain in the warm water. She closed her eyes and willed herself not to cry, the water spiraling red around her naked body like firecracker smoke.

CHAPTER 9

MAIA WAITED BY THE CONCRETE PIG.

It was one of the more ridiculous places she'd been asked to rendezvous—a fifteen-foot-high grimy pink goliath of pork at the edge of the diner parking lot.

She glanced at the brown Acura parked across the street and prayed her police tail wouldn't decide to take her picture. Her only consolation was that the cop inside the car was probably as cold and bored as she was.

After eleven minutes, the old fry cook Mike Flume emerged from the diner. He wiped his hands on his apron and trudged toward her.

"Sorry, I got busy," he said. "Here."

He tossed her a house key rubber-banded to a slip of paper and started walking away.

139

Maia caught his arm. "Whoa, wait a minute."

"I got less than a minute, miss. There's nobody watching the oil."

"How'd you get the key?"

The old man glanced toward his diner.

He reminded Maia of a geriatric leprechaun—small, wrinkled and nervous, thinning orange hair, ears and eyebrows and nose all a bit too pointy.

"I rent the property from Ana. I put the stuff in the back. Figured she would come get it eventually, you know? She never did."

"What stuff?"

"Look, miss—Detective Kelsey's already gonna kill me for talking to you. He came by, you know, after Ana . . ." He shook his head. "Damn. I can't believe she got herself shot."

"If you want to help her," Maia said, "tell me what was wrong with the timing on the Franklin White murder."

The old man winced. "Hell, I only told Ana because it was her mom, for Christ's sake. It's probably nothing."

"You don't believe that."

"My waitress can't cook. I got meat on the grill."

"Mr. Flume—"

"All right, damn it. Etch and Lucia used to stop here before their shift. Every night, like clockwork. Etch parked his own car in the lot. Few minutes later, Lucia would bring the patrol unit around. Nine-thirty, every night, I'd give 'em both dinner on the house. Two cheeseburgers with rings. Lucia liked Big Red. Etch took a vanilla malt. They went on duty at ten."

Maia fingered the paper-wrapped key.

She stared at the signs painted on the diner windows—

FISH PLATTER, CLASSIC CAR FRIDAY. She imagined two uniformed officers sitting inside at the counter.

She had spent the last few hours at the *San Antonio Express-News,* buried in the news morgue, reading about the White family, Mission Road and any case involving Hernandez and DeLeon. What she'd learned had depressed the hell out of her, but it hadn't made things any clearer.

"The 911 call about Franklin White's body came in at just after ten," she recalled. "The ME's report placed the time of death at not very long before that."

"That's why Etch and Lucia asked me to talk to homicide for them. You look at their regular routine, they couldn't have killed Frankie White. They would've been here eating dinner."

"They were suspects? News reports said nothing about that."

Flume shuffled from foot to foot. "Look . . . Etch and Lucia were frustrated about Frankie White, okay? This was their beat. Kid kept coming down here, picking up women at the bars. Later, those women turned up dead. How would you feel? Longer the detectives went without arresting him, the more Etch talked about intimidating Frankie. He knew Frankie's car. He knew the bars Frankie liked. Sometimes Etch would follow Frankie around, to discourage him. Etch even told me . . . well, he said what he'd do if he ever caught Frankie on a dark street somewhere."

"And when Frankie turned up dead," Maia said, "Etch and Lucia were first at the scene."

"They couldn't have killed him," Flume insisted. "Etch might've talked about it, but Lucia never would've let him. She was the most even-keeled person I ever met."

"She killed a man once," Maia recalled. "Right in your diner, wasn't it?"

"That was different. Lives were at stake. She did what she had to—one clean shot. Calm and cool. But hitting Frankie White the way he was hit? I mean, no. No way. I told the homicide detectives Etch and Lucia were totally in the clear. I explained their routine."

"But?"

Flume tugged at his apron. "I didn't exactly swear *that* particular night was routine. They came in a little late."

"Both of them?"

He nodded.

"Together?"

"Separate. Lucia beat Etch for once. She rushed in about nine-fifty, couldn't believe Etch wasn't here. When he did come in, Lucia looked at him real angry, asked him where he'd been. He just stared at me and said, 'Mike, I got here the same time as usual tonight, right?' "

Maia cursed. "When did Hernandez come in exactly?"

"Ten o'clock. Maybe one, two minutes after."

Maia stared across Presa Street, at the brown Acura waiting in the dark.

The fry cook followed her gaze. "Aw, hell. You got a police tail? You didn't tell me that."

Maia pulled the rubber band off the old man's key, unfolded the piece of paper. "What am I going to unlock here, Mr. Flume?"

He shook his head. "Sorry, miss. My onion rings are burning." Fear was building in his eyes.

The old cook hobbled back toward the diner, leaving Maia alone with the key and a two-line message:

342 West King's Highway
Used to be Lucia's.

．　　　．　　　．

MAIA DROVE SLOWLY, SETTING HER PACE to the Dvořák on the classical station.

She knew the best way to lose her tail wasn't a high-speed chase. It was to bore him into a stupor.

She thought about Franklin White and the patrol nightstick that had killed him.

It was conceivable Franklin would've agreed to meet someone he knew well on the side of a rural road at night. Someone like Ralph Arguello. But it was also conceivable that he would pull over for a cop.

Kelsey had been on medical leave. Etch Hernandez and Lucia DeLeon had weak alibis for the murder time. But motive? The idea that Kelsey, even Kelsey, would kill because Frankie White had hurt his hands and endangered his job just didn't sit right with Maia. Neither did the idea that either Etch or Lucia would kill because Frankie White was murdering women on their beat.

Mike Flume was right. It took intense, personal rage to hit someone seven times in the head, to destroy their face. Whoever killed Frankie White had seen something in him that they hated deeply. They didn't just want to stop him killing. They had wanted to obliterate his image completely.

Maia meandered through Southtown, circled the blocks, braked to look at street numbers even though she knew the neighborhood.

She studied traffic patterns, counted the timing on lights, checked out side streets until she found what she wanted.

Her third time through the South Presa–Alamo intersection, where the traffic backed up, she put a delivery truck between herself and the Acura. Then she swerved into an alley between two cafés and shot through the back parking lot.

A moment later she was three blocks away in the residential neighborhood of King William. No sign of the tail.

"Amateur," she murmured.

She supposed there was no reason to have shaken the police. She wasn't about to lead them to Tres. Still, the idea of having a baby-sitter pissed her off.

The Dvořák piece ended.

Maia was about to change the channel to rock 'n' roll when a news break came on. An Alamo Heights resident had been found shot to death on his porch overlooking the Olmos Basin.

The sedate voice of the classical DJ sounded totally wrong to deliver such news: The victim, a retired Bexar County medical examiner, had been killed from a distance by a single rifle bullet. Police would not speculate whether the shooting was accidental or the work of a sniper, but stressed there was no reason to believe the general public was in danger. The name of the victim was being withheld until—

Maia turned off the radio.

The .357 in her shoulder holster suddenly felt heavy.

She thought about Jaime Santos' gnarled hands on his golf club, the sad smile he had given her.

Maybe the news was about someone else. How many retired MEs could there be?

She remembered Mike Flume's look of fear when he realized a cop was watching. *Detective Kelsey's already gonna kill me for talking to you.*

144

Don't think that way, Maia told herself. *Just drive.*

She turned on Guenther Street. In her rearview mirror, an old gray Volvo sedan pulled out from the curb.

Had she seen the same car at the Pig Stand? She'd been so focused on the obvious tail . . .

No. She was being paranoid. The police wouldn't have the time or manpower to pull something as devious as tag team surveillance.

She took a detour anyway—a sharp left out of King William, onto a nice straight stretch of South Presa, lined with stucco nightclubs and *taquerías.* She drove south until the buildings fell away and the landscape changed to country. She kept watch behind her, but the Volvo had disappeared.

She was about to reverse course when she noticed the street sign at the intersection ahead. The name hit her like a blast of cold air.

Mission Road.

Before she could give herself time to waver, she took the turn.

Half a mile south along a stretch of crumbling blacktop, she recognized the twisted live oak from the crime scene photos. The barbed wire fence had fallen down, the shrubs were a little thicker, but otherwise the place hadn't changed.

She pulled over, stepped out of the car.

It was getting dark. The wind was cold and sprinkled with rain. The smell of wild licorice drifted up from the nearby creek bed.

Or not a creek bed, Tres would've corrected her. An *acequia.*

He'd taken her on a picnic somewhere near here. The waterways in this part of town were man-made, two-hundred-

and-fifty-year-old aqueducts that had once irrigated mission fields.

Maia shivered.

She remembered Tres' words on that picnic, three months ago, right before she'd made her huge mistake.

Or *had* it been a mistake? The changes in her body were mixing her up so badly she could hardly remember. At the time, Tres' comment had seemed so insignificant. Just another one of his quips. Nothing worth changing their lives over.

She forced her thoughts back to the problem at hand. Franklin White. Frankie had died here—right where she was standing.

How far from the Pig Stand? Five minutes, max.

Witnesses?

She turned three-sixty.

Nothing but trees, fields and the road. The only light was a single streetlamp maybe half a mile north. Eighteen years ago, the place would've been even more remote, if that was possible.

She made a mental note to find out where Etch Hernandez lived back then. She wondered if this road was a route from his residence to the Pig Stand.

The wind picked up. Maia shivered again. Too many tragedies, too many lives ended here on Mission Road.

Somewhere along this stretch of blacktop, in the Sixties, Guy White had allegedly raped a twenty-two-year-old named Delia Montoya. The old newspaper article had been discreetly vague about the facts, but Maia got the idea. Delia and Guy had met at a bar. They left together. Delia was a fiery woman, a civil rights activist. She considered herself liberated. She could date anyone she damn well pleased, but she hadn't planned on being beaten up and raped by Piedras Creek. She filed a report with the police, but two weeks later, she abruptly withdrew the charges. She appeared at the police station, shaken and wild-eyed, and gave a new statement. She claimed she'd made up the whole rape story to get attention. Guy White was off the hook.

A similar story, five months later—a Latina secretary at a local law firm accused White of raping her at Mission Park. White produced an alibi for the night in question. He hired a private investigator to prove that the young woman had a sordid past with men. She was mentally unstable. Charges went nowhere. One month later, the young woman lost her job.

Twenty years later, in the 1980s, all of Franklin White's victims had been found within a square mile of this spot. Six young women, just as Jaime Santos had said—all six sweet and pretty, just entering college with bright futures. All of them strangled to death and abandoned in the woods.

Like father like son? Maia was tempted to think so, but Frankie's victims were so different from his father's, as were the ways the two men had destroyed those women . . .

Maia looked down the dark stretch of road. She imagined roadside memorials that might've decorated this barbed wire fence over the years—crosses made of flowers, bleached memorials moldering in the darkness.

A glint of metal drew her attention. To the north, at the very edge of the streetlight's glow, a car made a U-turn and headed away.

Maia tried to convince herself that the mist and gloom were playing tricks on her eyes.

It looked like a gray Volvo had pulled out from the shoulder of the road, as if the driver had been parked there, watching her.

•   •   •

TITUS ROE FOCUSED HIS BINOCULARS.

The Lee woman had nice legs.

Concentrating on that helped keep his mind off the pain in his hand—his first stupid mistake of the night.

Damn meat cleaver.

He'd assumed Lee would be at the San Antonio address. If she was making trouble for Hernandez, he figured, she was probably in town. Besides, the house was right down the street. Titus had started his search there.

For his trouble, he'd gotten squirted in the eyes and hacked.

He never even got a shot at the gray-haired woman, but he hoped the old Latino was dead. Titus was pretty sure he'd nailed that bastard.

Good trick, though, he had to admit—the old guy yelling *FBI!* and pulling a water gun.

Probably been pretending for years, rehearsing in front of the mirror. Old man sounded so convincing he threw Titus off balance.

The water smacked Titus right between the eyes and the old lady jumped at him with the meat cleaver, chopping his left hand as he tried to defend himself. Nursing Home of the Living Dead.

Titus had felt lucky to get off one shot and get the hell out of there.

Now, he watched the Lee woman standing in the middle of

Mission Road. She turned a slow circle, hesitating as she looked in his direction. No way could she see him, but her eyes seemed to stare straight into the binocular lenses.

She was clever. He'd already decided that.

He'd been heading out of Southtown, feeling sick from blood loss, when he spotted Lee's BMW cruising slowly down Presa Street like she was looking for an address. At first he didn't understand what she was doing. Then he spotted the policeman in the Acura.

Titus couldn't help but smile. If Lee hadn't been wandering around the neighborhood, trying to lose her tail, Titus never would've caught her.

He'd watched with admiration as she pulled the parking lot trick and disappeared. The cop was history, but Titus had killed half a dozen people here in the King William neighborhood, back in his glory days. He picked up Lee on South Guenther and gave her plenty of room.

Now that she'd stopped, he could shoot her. Mission Road was nice and deserted. Drive up, do her, drive away. But so much open ground made him nervous. She'd see him coming. He hated giving his victims time to think.

If he had a rifle . . . but he hated rifles, too. Rifles were for cowards who sat in deer blinds with six-packs of beer and pretended to be real hunters. A handgun was the only respectable tool for killing a human being.

He raised his good hand, tried to hold it steady. Damn arthritis. God had thrown him some cruel punches in his life, but the arthritis was the ultimate—payback for a guy who'd made his living with a steady hand, pulling the trigger on other people's enemies. Now he could barely aim. He had to keep his hands in an ice cream freezer all day to deaden the

pain. He figured it was safer not to mention that small problem to Hernandez.

Damn Hernandez. Fucking cop had had Titus' balls in a
vise grip for years.

The irony was, eighteen years ago Titus really had been approached about killing Frankie White. The parents of Julia
Garcia, one of Frankie's first victims, had come to see him, desperate for justice. They'd even offered him a grocery bag full of
twenty-dollar bills. Titus had looked into their hollow eyes and
felt truly sorry. He knew the hope of vengeance was the only
thing keeping them alive. If the target had been anyone other
than Guy White's son, Titus would've taken the job immediately. As it was, he asked for a few days to think about it.

Before he could give the Garcias an answer, someone else
had taken care of Frankie White.

Titus took one last look at Maia Lee, standing in the middle of the dark road.

He put the Volvo into drive, swung a U-turn and headed
back toward Presa. Lee would have to come back that way.
The other direction, Mission, led nowhere but a dead-end
cluster of trailer parks.

Titus pulled in behind the Loco Mart. He pointed the nose
of his Volvo toward the street and waited.

Three minutes later, Lee's black BMW drove by.

Titus followed, back toward King William.

Lee crossed the Arsenal Street Bridge and stopped on
Titus' favorite block—a row of bungalows hugging the limestone cliffs above the San Antonio River.

Upstream were Victorian mansions, warehouse art gal-
leries, architectural offices. The river was smooth and placid,
neatly walled by concrete.

But below the bridge, the water broke into a noisy stream. It spilled over the rocks and rushed, foaming, beneath the tiny run-down houses, as if the water were angry for being constrained so long, made to dress up for tourists.

Titus parked on the bank opposite the houses, in the Pioneer Flour Mill visitors' lot, where the curve of the river gave him a good view of the street. He got out his binoculars.

Lee was climbing the steps of a denim blue cottage with peeling white trim. Whirlybird propellers decorated the dirt yard. Beer cans pocked with BB holes lined the porch railing.

She tried a key in the lock.

Titus liked her hair from behind, the way her ponytail snaked between her shoulder blades. He wondered how the T-shirt seller girl would look in an expensive wool dress like that. He decided she didn't have the right figure for it.

Lee's key didn't seem to be working.

Titus wondered what she was up to.

Then he remembered it didn't matter. He was supposed to be doing a job, and this was his chance. He would drive by with his window rolled down, his Colt ready. He'd call her name, wait for her to turn—

But before he could start his car, Lee stepped away from the door. She shook her head, muttering something as if cursing herself for being stupid. Then she marched down the steps and around the side of the house.

Titus refocused his binoculars. The gravel drive led back to a tiny garage.

"Not in there," Titus murmured to her. "Come on back, honey."

Lee's key slid into the lock on the garage door. She rolled it open and stepped inside.

Crap.

Now Titus would have to get out of his car and walk up the drive.

At least he could shoot her out of sight from the street.

He wrapped the bloody rags a little tighter around his left hand. It hurt like hell, but it wasn't his shooting hand. Even with the arthritis, he could grip the .45 just fine with his right.

He pulled his Volvo out of the Pioneer Mill parking lot and headed across Soledad Bridge.

No mistakes, this time.

The pretty lady would never feel a thing.

•   •   •

MAIA STEPPED OVER A PILE OF shattered beer bottles and worked her way toward the back of the garage.

Stuff was piled everywhere—dusty baskets of women's clothing, plastic Seventies furniture, makeup kits and ammunition boxes.

In front of a grimy window overlooking the river, a worktable was spread with photo albums and scrapbooks—the only things not covered in dust.

Maia picked up a yellow legal pad scrawled with notes. She recognized the handwriting, the same shaky script as on the note Mike Flume had given her.

For some reason, in the not-too-distant past, the old fry cook had been making a timeline of Lucia DeLeon's life. He'd arranged Lucia's scrapbooks in chronological order, even marked certain pages with Pig Stand receipts.

First stop: A South San High School yearbook from 1964. Senior "Most Likely to Succeed" Lucia DeLeon looked uncomfortable in her bouffant hairdo, black dress and pearl necklace. Despite the requisite Sixties uniform, something decidedly rebellious flickered in her eyes—a challenge. Maia imagined the men back then would've picked her out of the crowd. They would've felt intrigued or threatened. Probably both.

The next album, Ana's baby book, started only two years later. Mike Flume had noted this, too, on his legal pad: *Ana born—1966.*

He'd bookmarked a photo of Lucia in her hospital bed. The new mother looked exhausted, sweaty, blue around the eyes as if she'd just been pummeled in the delivery room. An elderly couple, probably Lucia's parents, were holding the infant.

Standard childhood pictures followed: Ana with pureed yams on her face, Ana using Barbie dolls as drumsticks on her high chair tray. Ana with her first birthday cake. A family barbecue. The elderly couple again, looking frailer, holding toddler Ana up to a Christmas tree.

No pictures of Ana's father.

Maia could figure out that missing piece easily enough.

Unexpected pregnancy. The boyfriend cuts and runs. Catholic family. Abortion not an option.

Lucia's parents would've helped raise the child while Lucia completed her education, pursuing her dream of becoming a cop.

Maia looked out the filthy window at a clouded moonrise over the Pioneer Flour Mill.

What right did *she* have to turn coward?

She was older than Lucia DeLeon had been. Maia had money and a good career. She lived in a time when there was virtually no stigma for single mothers. Even if Tres took the news in the worst possible way, even if she told him her secret fear . . .

The memory rose up unbidden—the pale crippled body of a ten-year-old boy laid on a makeshift funeral bier, draped in the family's only white sheet. In his dead hands, a rare photograph of Maia's mother, dead since Maia's birth eight years ago. As Maia's father wept, her uncle—her only other living relative—pulled her aside. He smelled like incense and fish from the market stalls.

You'll live with me now, girl, he told her. *Your father will come for you soon.*

Maia never saw her father again. A month after the funeral, he refused an order from the Red Guard and was taken away for reeducation. It took her decades to realize her father had done this on purpose, as a form of suicide.

She pushed those images away, opened another album from Lucia DeLeon's life.

In this one, the time intervals between photos were longer.

There was a picture of Ana DeLeon as a young Air Force cadet, giving her mom an enthusiastic hug. Another picture at a policemen's picnic—off-duty officers clowning around for the camera, Lucia holding a pork rib like a gun to Etch Hernandez's head.

The last few pages were a montage of clippings from Lucia's police career. She'd saved both the good and the bad.

1968: A patronizing editorial about Lucia's graduating class at the academy—the first to include women trained alongside the men. The headline: *Cops in Pantyhose?* A photo showed Lucia and five fellow female grads, all wearing skirted matron's uniforms, looking like grim airline stewardesses.

Seven years later, a news article described Lucia's award for the medal of bravery. She'd confronted a coked-up ex-bouncer who had clobbered two officers unconscious at the Pig Stand and was holding a third officer hostage at gunpoint. Lucia drew the bouncer's attention, got him to aim his gun at her, then shot him. Her use of deadly force had been cleared by the review board. She became an instant celebrity.

1987: A brief mention of Hernandez and DeLeon as the officers who found Franklin White's corpse.

Two years later, a strange article for the scrapbook—a retraction of an earlier news piece. The *Express-News* had erroneously reported that an off-duty officer, Lucia DeLeon, had been pulled over for drunk driving. Now, a police spokeswoman said that Officer DeLeon had simply been taking cold medication and hadn't realized how impaired she was. DeLeon was a highly decorated patrol cop. Impeccable record. She'd voluntarily pulled over and accepted assistance from a fellow officer, Etch Hernandez, who happened to be passing by.

Maia read the article twice.

Happened to be passing by.

A month later, the police captain wrote Lucia a letter of commendation, asking her to head a new training program for the department. A scholarship for young women cadets was being created in Lucia's name, and the captain wanted Lucia to teach a course at the academy. The new assignment was quite an honor.

And one that would keep her off the streets.

Maia wondered what Lucia had thought about that.

She flipped back to the picture of Ana as an Air Force cadet, hugging her mother with so much pride. Ana had followed her mother's footsteps. She'd joined the police. She kept her mother's photograph behind her desk in the homicide division. Yet she'd rented Lucia's house to Mike Flume. She'd left her mother's belongings in this garage, gathering dust for decades.

On Mike Flume's yellow legal pad of notes, one final event was starred and underlined:

Lucia dies 1994—alcohol.

Maia wondered why Flume had felt the need to reconstruct Lucia's life, and why he'd rented her house for so many years.

He'd written *Lucia* with an upward slant.

He'd spoken her name with regret, maybe a trace of wistfulness. He still remembered what she ordered for dinner. He knew to the minute when she had shown up each night.

Maia's heart felt heavy. She didn't want to delve into the old man's longings, or know what he might've secretly felt for a lady cop whom he'd served dinner every night for years.

But it now made sense to her why Mike Flume might've lied to the police, if he thought he was protecting Lucia and her partner.

She was considering whether or not to take the photo albums when broken glass crunched behind her.

A cold prickle of danger went down her neck. Instinct took over. She dropped behind a pile of suitcases as the garage window exploded where her head had just been.

Maia drew her .357.

A shadow flickered across the ceiling—someone coming toward her.

She rose up, squeezed off a blast, and took out an impressive chunk of the wooden frame of the garage door.

Nobody there.

Her ears were ringing.

She heard feet on gravel—someone running away.

She cursed and charged out of the garage.

When she reached the driveway, a gray Volvo was peeling out in front of the house.

She could've let it go, but she was mad.

She dropped to one knee in the front lawn and opened fire—engine block, wheel, wheel, passenger's side window. The .357 did its work. The Volvo spun sideways, plowed down a brick mailbox and shuddered to a halt in the front yard of the neighbor's house. The windshield was shattered. Steam billowed from the hood.

The driver's side window rolled down. A Colt pistol was thrown out. A tattooed arm appeared, feebly waving a bloody white rag.

Maia advanced, weapon trained on the driver. The neighbors were coming outside to see the excitement. One called, "Officer? You all right?"

It took Maia a moment to realize he meant her.

She looked at the man in the Volvo.

He was a middle-aged Anglo, an ex-con judging from his tattoos. His forehead was lacerated, his left hand a bloody bandaged mess. Maia had never seen a more miserable-looking assassin in her life.

"He didn't tell me you carried a damn bazooka," the man complained.

"Who didn't tell you?"

He gave her hound dog eyes. "This is where it gets ugly, I guess."

"You got that right, Tattoo," she told him. "Get out of the car."

CHAPTER 10

I DIDN'T CARE IF THE COPS STAKED OUT MY HOUSE, but I wished they'd be consistent about it.

Apparently they hadn't been watching when some madman invaded and attacked Sam. But now that Sam was stuck inside, wounded and waiting for my help, Detective Kelsey and a uniformed officer had decided to camp out on South Alamo. They sat on the hood of a patrol unit, sipping coffee and having a nice little chat.

Fortunately we'd planned for this contingency.

I watched from the end of the block as Guy White's henchman Alex drove a delivery van in front of my house. He slowed down next to Kelsey. Ralph rolled down the shotgun window, whistled, and the van took off.

The effect was absolutely brilliant. Kelsey managed to spill

158

his coffee, tangle his gun in his holster and trip over his own shoelaces. By the time both cops were in their car and in pursuit, Ralph, Alex and the van were long gone.

"Pull around back," Madeleine ordered our chauffeur. "And keep the engine running."

"Alex *does* know how to evade police?" I ventured to ask.

Madeleine raised an eyebrow. "Alex's first job was driving for a drug cartel in Houston. Ten minutes from now, your friend and he will have changed cars three times and the cops will pull over some little old lady in that delivery van. You watch."

Not having much choice, I took her word for it.

We walked up the back steps of my house and entered Chez Bloodbath.

· · ·

RED WAS SPRINKLED ALL OVER THE linoleum. It made an arc across one wall and speckled the countertops.

In the midst of the carnage, Sam and Mrs. Loomis and my cat, Robert Johnson, were having chamomile tea at the kitchen table.

I said, "Holy Jesus."

"It's not as bad as it looks," Sam informed me. "Lot of blood, is all."

"Your *ear.*"

"What?" Sam cupped his hand around the mass of bandages on the right side of his face.

"The bastard shot off your ear."

"Only the lobe," Mrs. Loomis corrected wearily. "I put iodine on it."

"What?" Sam yelled.

Mrs. Loomis told me the story while Madeleine inspected

the scene. Robert Johnson lapped spilt tea and milk from Sam's saucer. Sam must've been more shaken up than he let on. He didn't bother shooing away the cat.

When Mrs. Loomis was done, Madeleine held up a newly rinsed meat cleaver from the sink. "You stabbed the intruder with this?"

Mrs. Loomis shrugged. "I wanted him to leave."

"Impressive," Madeleine said.

"I don't pay you enough," I said.

Mrs. Loomis tried to give me a reproachful look, but she was blushing too hard.

She described the intruder as a wild-eyed Anglo, grizzled hair, leathery skin, grungy flannel shirt and heavily tattooed arms. Unfortunately, that sounded like half the people I knew and several of my relatives.

"He said something odd," Mrs. Loomis added. "He said: *'Where is she?'*"

"Where's who?" I looked at Madeleine for her opinion.

She shrugged. "Maybe wrong address. Maybe he was a random burglar."

"Yeah, right," I said. "Or maybe he was Frankie's killer."

Sam perked up. "Frankie White?"

I wasn't sure what surprised me more—that he'd heard me, or that he knew who we were talking about. "Sam, you remember Frankie White?"

"What?"

"Franklin White!" I yelled.

"Yeah. Kid who got clobbered to death, right? Good money. I was the fourth or fifth PI the dad hired. Crazy damn family."

Madeleine's eyes narrowed. She was still holding the meat cleaver. "Who *is* this old man?"

I wondered if I should risk asking Sam more questions.

I'd learned never to assume he remembers anything, but also never to underestimate him. At times, he could tell me every fact about a case from thirty years ago. Other times, his memory was a house of cards. Put too much weight on it, and the whole thing collapsed.

"Sam, do you remember what you found out?"

He scowled at me over the rim of his teacup. "About what?"

"About Frankie White."

"He died. It was the father's fault."

Silence.

Robert Johnson pushed the empty saucer around with his tongue.

I said, "Um, Sam—"

"The father was bad news. Other PIs were afraid to tell him the truth. I think he knew, deep down. I tried to tell him, but hell, he didn't want to listen. He'd already decided it was some business rival did the hit. Nobody likes to hear, 'It's all your fault. You screwed up your own kids.' "

"Okay," I said. "Thanks, Sam."

"Daughter and son." Sam shook his head. "Both mental cases. Adolescent girl was institutionalized—manslaughter, I think."

Madeleine stared at her leather pumps. She seemed to notice for the first time that she was standing in a puddle of blood.

"Madeleine," I said. "Put the cleaver down, okay?"

She kicked over one of the kitchen chairs. The cat vaporized from the table.

"*Madeleine,*" I said again.

She threw the cleaver. It twirled past my head and impaled itself with a THWOCK in the corkboard by the oven.

The edge of the blade sank into the wall maybe two inches. The handle shuddered.

"I'll be in the car," she said gruffly.

The back door slammed behind her.

My heart started beating again.

"New girlfriend, Fred?" Sam asked cheerfully. "I liked the Chinese lady better."

Mrs. Loomis studied me with concern.

"It's okay," I told her. "If I leave, will you two be all right?"

She glanced apprehensively at the meat cleaver in the corkboard. "Nothing I can't clean up, dear. Just you be careful."

She'd never called me "dear" before. I tried not to think of it as a bad sign—the sort of kindness you'd extend to the recently deceased.

I pointed a finger at Robert Johnson, who had reappeared on the table the instant the offending visitor departed. "You take better care of these people."

The cat gave me a smug look. Translation: *As long as the tea and milk keep coming, I'm good.*

When I was at the door, Sam called: "Hey, Fred, be careful with that White family, okay? I'm pretty sure they got mafia connections."

I promised I'd be careful. Then I went out to the backyard where the black limo was waiting.

•   •   •

"DON'T ASK," MADELEINE SNARLED.

"I didn't."

She slumped in the back seat.

I'd expected her to ride up front now that Ralph was gone, but she'd climbed in back with me again. I guess she enjoyed torturing herself.

"I had a classmate in middle school." She exhaled shakily. "She made some comments . . . a particular comment about my brother. I lost control."

We drove past Alamo Plaza.

Shivering tourists were gathering for the evening ghost tour. Homeless men huddled like grubby gifts at the base of the forty-foot Christmas tree. Behind them, the old mission's facade glowed white—a frozen chunk of 1836, melting and forlorn in the middle of downtown.

Madeleine turned toward me, her eyes hungry. "I wasn't *institutionalized*. My dad's lawyers had to pull strings to keep me out of juvenile detention. They got me into a residential therapy program. Stokes-McLean. Four years."

Garlanded lampposts went by on Houston Street.

I knew something about Stokes-McLean. The facility was a former state sanitarium, a massive brick haunted-house-looking place not far from Mission San José. I'd seen what they did with problem kids—intense behavior modification sessions, usually six to nine weeks. I'd never known anybody who'd been sentenced to the program for four years.

"This was just before Frankie's murder?" I asked.

She nodded.

"You were trying to defend him."

She was silent through the next stoplight. "My dad promised me Frankie wasn't doing anything wrong. Right up to the end . . . he told me to ignore anything I heard."

"He also promised Frankie would stop hitting you."

She looked down, scratched a fleck of blood off her

knuckle. "Shut the fuck up. You don't know what you're talking about."

"Those bruises you sported in middle school weren't from your classmates."

"I shouldn't have said anything to you. I shouldn't even have tried."

"What did Sam mean about your father being to blame?"

Before she could answer, or more likely hit me, the limo lurched to a stop.

In front of us, traffic had backed up behind a police barricade. Half a block ahead, Main Plaza was filled with people and the glow of *luminarias*.

Las Posadas.

I'd told Alex and Ralph to meet us in Main Plaza, figuring it would be deserted this time of night. I'd completely forgotten about the Christmas celebration.

Our driver apologized. He said this was as close as he could get us to our rendezvous point.

"Let us out here," Madeleine ordered. "Circle the block. We'll be back in five minutes."

"And if we get spotted by the police?" I asked.

She glared at me. "Good point." Then to the driver: "If we get spotted by the police, Mr. Navarre will be dead and *I'll* be back in five minutes."

·   ·   ·

THE SCENE IN THE PARK WAS surreal enough to curl Salvador Dali's mustache.

Tourists mixed with candle-bearing pilgrims and carolers dressed like Hebrew shepherds. Children chased each other around the trees. Vendors worked the crowd with *fajitas, atole* and *cerveza.*

Through the middle of it all, Joseph and Mary led their donkey while mariachis sang at them in Spanish to go away; there was *no posada.* No room in the inn.

I couldn't help thinking: *This is San Antonio, man. We have three million hotel rooms.*

At the edges of the park, a dozen cops stood on duty. None of them paid us any attention. A public Christmas celebration probably wasn't the first place they expected dangerous fugitives.

Ralph and Alex were sitting on a park bench, watching the mariachis serenade the Blessed Couple.

Alex wore a navy blue suit and aviator's shades that must've left him completely blind in the dark.

My skin crawled when I saw him. He looked so damn much like Frankie. Or maybe my skin crawled because I realized he was about my size, and the accountant's clothes I was wearing might very well belong to him.

"You're late," he said.

"Any trouble?" Madeleine asked.

"With the getaway, no. With *you* supposed to be at your father's party half an hour ago, yes."

"He knows where I am."

Alex snorted.

"What?" she demanded.

"Nothing. Let's get out of here." Under his breath, he muttered something that rhymed with *itch.*

Madeleine grabbed his lapels, hauled him to his feet. "Navarre and Arguello, will you excuse us a minute?"

She dragged Alex away through the crowd.

Ralph didn't pay any attention. He was holding his wallet open like a tiny hymnal, staring at a photo of Ana and the baby.

I'm not sure why, but a wave of irritation washed over me. I told myself that wasn't fair. Ralph had every right to miss his family, to feel shock and grief. Maybe he even had the right to shoot at Johnny Zapata. It had been my choice to follow him out the window . . .

I stopped a vendor, bought a couple of beers.

I sat next to Ralph and handed him one of the cups. *"Salud."*

It took him a minute to focus on me. "Sam okay?"

I told him the story. I apologized that he'd risked getting captured just so I could check out a shot-off earlobe.

"S'okay," he said. "Friends help each other."

"Is that what we're doing?"

Ralph stared at me. I hadn't meant to sound so angry.

"Something you want to tell me?" he asked.

I should've shut my mouth, but I'd been saving up hurt I hadn't even known about. Now it was boiling over. Too many hours on adrenaline. Too many frayed nerves.

"Been a pretty shitty reunion. Longest we've spent to-gether since you got married. Look what we're doing."

"You saying it's my fault we haven't been hanging out?"

"You got a family," I said. "I understand that."

"I wonder if you do."

"Christ, Ralph, you pushed me away when you got mar-ried. You amputated your whole goddamn past. Watching you today with Zapata—I don't know. Maybe you weren't meant for a regular family life."

Ralph blinked. "I wasn't meant . . . *Vato*, if you were anybody else telling me this shit—"

"You'd what?" I demanded. "Prove my point? Shoot me?"

"You don't want to be here, *vato*, that's cool. I didn't ask you. But don't start jacking with me about who cut off who."

"Aw, come on—"

"We invited you over a dozen times, man. Whenever Ana saw you she'd ask you. I left messages on your machine. Don't tell me you didn't get them."

Ralph finished his beer, crumpled the cup. "Anybody's afraid, *vato*, it's you. I think it scares the hell out of you that I got a wife and kid."

"Bullshit."

"You hate it that you're the last person you know who hasn't settled down."

I wanted to yell at him how wrong he was, but my anger balloon had burst. I felt empty inside.

Mary and Joseph kept moving through the park. Their donkey must've made a deposit somewhere along the path. I caught a scent on the night air that was definitely not *fajitas*.

"We brought Lucia Jr. here last year," Ralph told me. "She was a newborn."

The Blessed Couple moved toward the cathedral doors across the street.

Ralph studied his wallet photo, then slipped it back into his pocket. "I got a bad feeling, *vato*."

"You're going to see them again soon," I managed.

"You'd watch out for Ana—"

"Stop it, Ralph. Besides, Ana doesn't need watching. She'd kick my ass if I tried."

"But you would, right?"

I sighed. "Yeah."

"Promise?"

"*Yes,* already."

I drank my beer, tried not to feel uneasy. Ralph was just scared for his family. He was entitled to sound a little despondent. We would get through this together. We'd been in scrapes this bad before. Almost.

The crowd shifted. I caught a glimpse of Madeleine giving Alex a deadly serious lecture. He was smirking at her. I wondered if his insolence was bravado, or if he actually had enough pull in the organization to stand up to Guy White's own daughter. I wondered what his plans were once the old man passed away.

"We could leave right now," Ralph said. "Forget the White family."

"We could."

"But the answer's back at the White house . . . isn't it?"

I felt as reluctant as Ralph sounded, but I had the same gut feeling.

I kept coming back to what Sam had said. Even if Guy White didn't want to admit it, the old gangster knew the truth about his son's death.

I wondered again about the intruder who'd broken into my house. I wanted to think it was the same person who'd shot Ana DeLeon, but I had a hard time believing it.

A guy who could set up a meeting with a homicide detective, calmly pull the trigger and walk away didn't fit the image of the man who'd broken into my place. Ana's shooter wouldn't have been vanquished by a meat cleaver and a water gun.

I poured out my beer, crumpled the cup in aggravation.

A tattooed man had broken into my house looking for a woman. He assumed she would be there. A woman other than Mrs. Loomis. A woman he wanted to silence.

A cold, slimy feeling poured over me.

I dug my cell phone out of my pocket.

"I thought you ditched that thing," Ralph said. "Don't be risking calls."

I hit speed dial #1.

Maia picked up, and she was even more direct: "You're insane. Get off the line."

"I'll keep it under thirty seconds."

"Tres, I've got my hands full."

"You're in danger. There's a guy with tattoos—"

"On his arms," she supplied. "Flowers, right?"

My stomach did a half-pipe. "Are you okay?"

"I'm fine. I'm holding a gun to his head. He's driving. We have a nice arrangement."

"Maia—Jesus, *what?*"

"I'm taking a picture. Hang on." A few seconds later: "Check your phone."

The wonders of technology. Camera cell phones had quickly become a necessity for PIs, but I never thought my girlfriend would be sending me photos of the men she held at gunpoint.

The grainy digital shot showed a fiftyish Anglo with grizzled hair and a pitted face. He was sitting behind the wheel of Maia's car, looking as if he'd just received an electric shock.

I put the phone back to my ear. "Maia, how—"

"No time to explain. We're looking for a quiet place to talk."

"Tell me where. I'll come."

"Too dangerous. I'm hanging up."

"Wait." I struggled to think of a plan.

Madeleine and Alex had finished their argument. They were trudging in our direction. The *Las Posadas* carolers had started their final song, welcoming Joseph and Mary to the church.

"Where are you?" Maia asked. "What's that singing?"

"Some newlyweds and a donkey. They're looking for a motel room. Look, don't interrogate that guy alone. Please."

"The problem is where. You have five seconds to suggest a safe meeting place."

Madeleine was only a couple of steps away. No doubt she was going to grind my cell phone into rebar. She wasn't going to be receptive to me giving her chauffeur any more directions, either.

I made Maia the best offer I could think of. As usual, it also happened to be the most insane: "You like mafia Christmas parties?"

DECEMBER 19, 1986

THE LAST THING THAT MADE JULIA GARCIA smile was her murderer's joke.

They were riding along together, his new silver Mercedes as smooth and silent as a magic carpet. She told him what she wanted to do with her life, and he said, "You don't want to be a teacher."

"Why not?"

"Because you'd have students like me."

She smiled and pushed his arm, but immediately she knew she'd gone too far. He tensed at her touch. His expression reminded her of the eight-year-old boy she'd volunteered with that afternoon, who'd flung the Dr. Seuss book across the room because he couldn't pronounce the word *know.*

She began to wonder if her friends at the bar had been right about this man. *Julia,* hija, *you gonna talk to* him?

They'd dared her twenty bucks. She'd taken the bet, conscious that the blond Anglo had been looking at her across the room, interested, intrigued.

She felt flush with success: Her first semester over, her grades excellent, her last exam put behind her that morning. By the end of the spring, her professors assured her, she could transfer to a full university if she wanted.

Shoot high, they'd told her. *Look at Yale. Look at Columbia.*

The names rolled over her like incantations—magical phrases from another universe. No one she'd ever known had gone this far. No member of her family had ever completed high school.

Earlier in the week, she'd dumped her senior year boyfriend. Life was too full of possibilities for her to marry him. She'd broken her last chain. Why not celebrate? Why not show off a little?

The guy at the bar was obviously from that other world she wanted—rich, powerful, groomed for success. It was as if he were put in front of her now, a symbol of what she could have. Did she have the nerve to take it?

They left together, and she turned to wink at her friends, knowing that tomorrow they'd owe her twenty bucks.

He pulled the Mercedes over on the side of a dark road. Mission, she thought, but she wasn't sure. A crumbling streak of asphalt marched off into the night, scrubby trees and barbed wire on either side like scar tissue.

Her companion's name was Frankie. That's all she knew. The name made him seem younger, though he had to be at least a few years older than she.

He put the car in park and looked up at the stars. The Big Dipper, Orion, a bunch of other constellations she couldn't name.

"Pretty," she said.

He didn't respond.

"So . . . you bring many girls out here?" She meant it to sound teasing, but when he looked over, the darkness in his eyes scared her.

"A couple," he admitted.

She shifted away from him, just slightly. Already planning exit strategies. She would tell him she still had an early exam tomorrow. No . . . she'd already told him she was done for the semester. What else would work? That her friends were expecting a call, maybe.

"My father used to come here," he murmured.

"Your father?"

"He used to bring women here. It killed my mother."

This was getting creepy now. Whatever Julia had been reaching for, this was not it.

"I'm . . . sorry." Julia tried to put herself into mentor mode. It was the only kind of training she could fall back on. Get him to talk. Put him at ease. A lot of kids . . . people . . . came from really bad homes.

"I got a sister," he continued. "Thirteen. Looks just like my mom. Doesn't even remember her, though. Not even a fucking memory."

"I'm sure your sister . . . really loves you, Frankie."

He stared at his hands, corpse-pale in the moonlight. Julia could see the anger draining out of his shoulders. She thought the dangerous moment had passed.

"She hates me," Frankie muttered. "Get me arrested if she could. Sometimes I wish I could bring *her* here. Show her . . ."

His voice trailed off.

Julia didn't know what he was talking about. She just wanted out.

"Look . . ." She tried to sound upbeat, not at all afraid. "I told my friends I'd call them, you know? Would you mind—"

"You told them you'd call."

"Yeah. Kind of silly, but, ah . . . we had a bet."

He stared at her as if there were an insect crawling over her face, something poisonous. "A bet. About me?"

She tried to keep her mind on good things—next semester, the children she tutored, getting her own apartment and a part-time job, moving to the East Coast. All that was waiting for her, just a few miles back down the road.

"It was just a joke," she managed.

"You bet your friends I wouldn't be able to perform?"

"No! Nothing like that."

He slapped her. It surprised her more than it hurt, but she saw a flash of yellow. Her mouth stung.

"Stop it!" She used the same tone she'd used on her boyfriend whenever he got out of hand. "Take me back—right now."

"You don't give orders," he said. "You don't even *look* at me."

He grabbed her by her hair and opened his car door.

The next thing she knew, she was being dragged outside, the grass scratching her legs. She kicked helplessly at the gravel. Her scream sounded thin in the night air—no one around to hear it. He threw her down, straddled her. His hands closed around her throat.

"Shut up," he warned.

She couldn't breathe. He was a black shadow above her, moonlight glinting on blond hair. Her throat turned to cement, a fire building up inside her chest.

If I just don't fight, she decided. *He will let me go.*

He kept one hand around her throat as he ripped open her blouse, then began tugging at her skirt.

He will let me go.

She prayed those words, over and over, but her hands still clawed weakly at his face. The gravel and barbed wire dug into her back.

His hand tightened on her throat, and she wanted to tell

him she would behave herself. She needed to breathe. If she could just get his attention, he would surely remember that.

She felt herself catching fire, as if her whole being were made of tissue paper. Her eyesight turned red, and the world faded into one small ember, slowly being smothered under Frankie's hand.

CHAPTER 11

ETCH ARRIVED AT THE CRIME SCENE HOPING TO FIND MAIA Lee dead.

Dispatch hadn't told him much over the radio. A shoot-out in King William between a man and a woman. Lucia's old address. Etch prayed Titus Roe had done his work.

Inside the yellow perimeter tape, the tow crew was loading a shot-to-hell Volvo sedan onto a flatbed trailer. The media vultures had cameras rolling. Neighbors wrapped in blankets shivered on their front lawns.

No ambulance or ME van.

Maybe the body was en route to the morgue.

Kelsey waited at the curb, his slacks splattered with what looked like coffee. He was holding his jacket over his crotch, as if that would hide the problem.

Etch gritted his teeth. Kelsey had been enough of an embarrassment for one day. Cops all over the city were already talking about his debacle of a car chase.

"So," Etch said. "The old lady you pulled over must've looked pretty dangerous."

Kelsey's ears turned purple. "We were baited. It was Arguello."

"You sure?"

"The old lady described the guys who switched cars with her. Arguello and a white guy."

"Navarre?"

"Maybe." Kelsey didn't sound convinced. "Whoever he was, he gave the old lady a hundred bucks and told her to keep the van. No VIN. Engine block numbers erased. Completely untraceable."

"Christ."

"And then we got this." Kelsey waved toward the shot-up Volvo.

Etch scanned the scene, trying to read what had happened. The Volvo had been hit at least four times by a large-caliber gun. No sign of Lee's black BMW.

The shooting had started in the driveway of Lucia's old house. Forensics had circled a spent casing on the concrete. Skid marks in front of the house indicated where the Volvo had peeled out.

Perhaps Lee had parked the BMW somewhere else—around the block so it'd be out of sight. She commandeered the Volvo, and Titus Roe had taken her down as she attempted to flee.

Etch tried to like that scenario.

He forced himself to look at Lucia's house.

The old fry cook who rented the place had trashed the

front porch with beer cans and lawn furniture. He'd desecrated the yard with his goddamn whirly bird decorations.

The idea of Mike Flume living here, sleeping in Lucia's bedroom, always made Etch's blood steam. Flume must've invited Maia Lee here to poke around for scraps of the past. God knew what else he'd told her. Etch should've taken care of him years ago, along with Jaime Santos. And as for Maia Lee . . .

"Hell of a shooter." Kelsey pulled his trench coat tighter. "Lee sure knew how to stop a Volvo."

Etch blinked. *"Lee* shot up the car?"

"Sorry, sir, I thought you knew. Witnesses up and down the block. Nice-looking Asian lady in a black BMW."

"You mean—"

"The guy in the Volvo tried to kill her and she turned the tables. Chased after him, blew his car to hell."

"She killed the guy?"

"No, sir. Took him out of the Volvo at gunpoint." Kelsey shook his head in disgust. "They drove off together in her car. Neighbors thought she was a cop, taking the guy into custody."

Etch's mouth felt like sand.

Maia Lee, goddamn her, had taken Titus alive. And with a screwup like Titus—it wouldn't be long before he gave up Etch's name. What the hell had Etch been thinking, going to Roe?

"Lieutenant?" Kelsey asked.

"I'm all right," he managed. "Been a long day."

Kelsey's eyes were as impersonal as microscope lenses. "You just come from the Santos case?"

Etch willed his hands not to clench.

The bastard was fishing, looking for a reaction.

"Yeah," Etch said. "Alamo Heights PD is cooperating. Ballistics is still working the scene."

"Tied to Ana's shooting?"

"Doubtful. Couple of weeks ago, Santos reported some kids down in the basin—"

"I heard." Kelsey's tone made it clear he didn't think much of the teenage sniper theory.

There was a loud, dull clunk. The tow crew lowered the Volvo onto their trailer.

"I got to sign for that." Kelsey studied Etch, as if the lieutenant was a much more interesting wreck-in-progress. "If you'll excuse me, sir."

•   •   •

ETCH STEADIED HIMSELF AGAINST THE SIDE of his car.

His knees felt weak.

He stared up the sidewalk at Lucia's porch.

The night of Frankie White's murder, Lucia and he had sat on that porch after their shift, as they'd done so many times before. Three in the morning. Out of uniform. Etch insisted on making margaritas. They sat together on the porch swing and drank in silence like mourners at a wake.

"We need to talk about it," Lucia said.

"No," he told her. "We don't."

"Etch, I don't want a lie between us."

She wore nothing special—jeans, her Houston Rockets T-shirt. Her feet were bare. Her short curly hair retained the faint impression of her patrol hat. She looked more beautiful than ever—the way people look when they're slipping away from you.

Etch set down his margarita. He slid off the porch swing

and knelt in front of her, his arms circling her chest, his head resting between her breasts. She ran her fingers through his hair. He could hear her heartbeat. Her skin smelled of clove.

"It was an accident," he told her.

"It was murder. The nightstick—"

"Lucia, don't. Please."

He couldn't make himself say what he'd planned. He couldn't explain why he'd been late to the Pig Stand that evening. All he had wanted to do was help her, save her. He had planned everything so perfectly, gotten up his nerve for weeks, and now his best intentions were shredded.

She allowed him to kiss her.

Later they went inside, shed their clothes. Their lovemaking was clumsy and desperate.

She told him she loved him, but the hollowness had begun.

A hole had been bored in Lucia's soul. The more Etch strove to patch it, the bigger it became, the further she slipped from his grasp.

In the years that followed, she kept up the facade of model officer. She pushed herself to confront the most dangerous situations. She got repeated commendations for bravery, but Etch began to see these incidents for what they were—suicide attempts, like the alcohol. Displays of contempt for her own life. He began to wonder if the shoot-out at the Pig Stand, years before, had really been about saving him, or if it had merely been her first flirtation with self-destruction.

He covered for her more reckless moments on the job, her drunk driving episodes. Her reputation on the force remained untarnished. They named a scholarship after her at the academy—a program for female recruits.

Seven years after Frankie died, Etch was at her bedside. He wouldn't allow himself to believe she was dying. She refused to let him call the doctors.

I'll be fine, she murmured. *Just need some rest.*

She convinced him to go home for the night, let her sleep off the alcohol.

Her last words, muttered half asleep as he closed her bedroom door: *Ana, is that you?*

Ana, the daughter who hadn't visited her in over a year.

•   •   •

"LIEUTENANT?"

Etch forced himself back to the present.

Kelsey was folding up his cell phone, slipping it into his pocket. "Another report on Navarre and Arguello. Assault and battery, four-twenty this afternoon. Arguello, Navarre, some woman—they approached this guy at the Poco Mas, got him outside and beat the shit out of him. Seems they were looking for Johnny Shoes."

Etch pondered that. "Who was the woman?"

"Anglo. Blonde."

"Not Lee, then. Who?"

Kelsey shook his head. "We're working on it."

"Work harder. They've already made fools of us enough this weekend."

Etch said *us.* He knew Kelsey heard it as *you.*

The detective rubbed the knife scars on his fingers. Etch could tell Kelsey wanted to say something, some half-formed doubt fluttering in his throat.

Etch decided to beat him to the punch. "Santos' death will

raise questions. Also, you know about the autopsy report, the rumors about the murder weapon being a nightstick."

Kelsey nodded.

"Ana would've investigated that," Etch said. "She wouldn't have been afraid to bust a cop, even if nobody in the department ever trusted her again. She would've done whatever she could to save Arguello."

Etch let the words slip under Kelsey's mind like a crowbar.

Even if nobody in the department ever trusted her again.

Etch's career was ending. He had nothing to lose. Kelsey was a different story.

"I came on in '87," Kelsey said. "I had a nightstick like that. A lot of times . . . things happened. People looked the other way. It wasn't like now."

"No," Etch agreed.

"But no cop would shoot one of our own. Somebody tried to kill Ana. Arguello is the one who ran. He and Navarre are out of control."

"Miss Lee will not see it that way. If she follows Ana's line of inquiry . . . it may be very easy for her to pin blame on the department."

"Can't let her. We need to bring in Navarre and Arguello, one way or the other."

Etch put on his best aggrieved face—the even-keeled lieutenant, trying to restrain the hot-tempered subordinate. He'd had a lot of practice playing that role opposite Kelsey. "We agreed to a forty-eight-hour delay before we publicize the DNA match."

"Navarre won't turn in his friend."

"Even so," Etch said, "if we make the DNA public, and the White family finds out . . ."

Kelsey had to believe this was his idea. He had to believe Etch hated it.

"I want to do the press conference tomorrow morning," Kelsey said. "We can't afford another day like today."

Etch gazed at the curb. "Twenty-four hours early. I don't know, Kelsey. I can't sign off on that."

"Are you going to stop me?"

Etch said nothing.

"First thing in the morning, then," Kelsey said.

Etch watched as his predictable tank stormed off toward the Arsenal Street Bridge.

•   •   •

AFTER THE CRIME SCENE CLEARED, ETCH drove north into Olmos Park. He parked at the ridge above the dam and stared at the lights of San Antonio.

He needed to go home. He needed sleep.

But there was so much to decide.

Stabilized.

He had called the hospital, a confidential talk with the doctor: Ana was expected to pull through. By tomorrow evening, it was possible she'd be conscious, and able to tell who shot her.

Etch exacted grave promises from the doctor that the information not be shared, for Ana's own safety. The doctor promised, clearly moved by Etch's concern. Etch hung up. Then he cursed Ana for inheriting her mother's toughness.

He couldn't do anything about her tonight. He was too tired. The men on guard duty would find it odd if he simply showed up. But tomorrow . . . Etch had already volunteered to take the morning shift by himself.

Everyone knew Ana was his favorite, his protégée. They imagined him by her bedside, holding her hand, waiting anxiously for her eyelids to flutter open.

He would wait anxiously, all right. He would see for himself how Ana looked. Then he could decide.

He rested his hand on the empty seat next to him. He remembered the night he and Lucia had made love here, at this very spot, for the first time.

They had shared their secrets. She had cried, weeping out years of frustration. *Finally,* Etch remembered thinking. *Finally, she will open up.*

And it seemed like she had, at first. She made love with a hunger that left him breathless . . .

You shot my daughter, Lucia said, somewhere in the back of his mind.

Etch tried to insist: He hadn't meant to.

He had rotated Ana to cold case because it was standard routine, given her a stack of old homicides, never dreaming that she'd come across Lucia's handwritten report, and see, behind the words, some truth about why her mother had fallen apart.

Ana had sensed the connection immediately, though she hadn't understood it.

Etch discouraged her, but she kept asking questions. He ran out of excuses for postponing the DNA test. She started pulling away from him, looking at him differently.

And inside, the old anger started to build. After all he had done for Ana, after all her mother had sacrificed . . . Ana had nearly ruined her career by marrying a criminal. She had repaid Etch's trust by digging into the one case he absolutely could not let her solve.

Finally, he had fixed the evidence. He had thrown some convenient facts her way about her husband's dealings with Frankie White. Then, and only then, he let her do the DNA test.

And why not? If he could save Ana from her marriage, remove Ralph Arguello, and protect his own secrets all in one act, why the hell not?

Only she hadn't believed it. She had refused to accept hard evidence.

And so Etch had gone to her house that night to push and provoke. To prove Ralph was a killer. He had learned that lesson from Lucia. Make them aim at you, then shoot them down. He hadn't meant to find Ana alone. He certainly never dreamed she would corner him like that.

If he could take it back . . .

You're lying to yourself, Lucia said. *If you wanted to hurt Ralph Arguello, you could have done so years ago. Same with the Whites. If you wanted to hurt them, you've had chances. It's not them you're mad at. You meant to do exactly what you did. That's why you took a .357, the same make as Arguello's gun.*

"Not true," he said aloud. "I never meant to hurt her. She's your daughter. She's the only thing left of you."

Exactly, Lucia said. *Exactly.*

He closed his eyes, tried to change Lucia's voice. He wanted to remember the night they'd made love, the night he'd decided they might actually have a chance together. For a few weeks, before Frankie's murder, it had seemed possible.

Everything I've done, I did to protect you, Etch said.

Even that is not true, Etch, Lucia said. *Even that.*

He opened his glove compartment. The small glass vial

was still there, the one he'd brought with him on his first visit to Ana's bedside.

Tomorrow, he told himself. Tomorrow, he would know what to do.

He drove toward home, the ghost of his partner riding beside him, silent and disapproving.

CHAPTER 12

"WELL DONE," MR. WHITE TOLD US.

Ralph, Maia and I stood in a semicircle around our prize.

The sauna room was tiled in milky white. Every drop of water or creak of the pipes echoed. Even White's anemic voice resonated. The air was thick and warm. I was getting nostalgic for the tamale truck.

In the middle of the floor, the hit man knelt, his hands tied behind his back. His face had had a close encounter with a steering wheel. His left eye was swollen shut. I wasn't inclined to feel sorry for a guy who'd tried to murder my girlfriend, but he was doing a pretty good job looking pathetic.

"Titus Roe," Ralph said. "Washed-up assassin."

"I know who he is." Guy White leaned forward on his cane.

He looked like he'd been made up for the party by a skilled mortician. His wasted face glowed with an unnatural mix of rouge and cream. His silver hair was freshly trimmed. His collar was starched, his tuxedo perfectly pressed, the shoulders padded. No doubt this was supposed to give the impression that Guy White was still healthy and powerful. Instead, he reminded me of some frail, soft-bodied creature slipped into a shell much too large for him.

Alex Cole stood at his side. His tuxedo matched Mr. White's down to the cuff links.

Madeleine was not present. As soon as we pulled into the gates, she'd been summoned for some "words with her father," and we hadn't seen her since.

"Roe was a suspect in Frankie's case," Ralph said. "The cop Drapiewski told us that. Now he's tried to kill Maia."

"And he refuses to speak," White observed. "How surprising."

Roe said nothing. He was doomed, and he knew it. His slumped posture told me he was conserving his energy for the last thing that would matter—withstanding pain.

"He's a pawn," Maia said.

A faint scowl played on White's lips. "I respect your opinion, Miss Lee. But a pawn for whom? That's what we need to know."

White held out his palm. Alex placed a nine-millimeter pistol in it.

White checked the magazine of the gun. "Twelve shots. They can be measured out judiciously, I think."

He offered the gun butt-first to Maia.

"No," she told him. "I'm not going to be party to torture."

"This man tried to kill you."

"He's an incompetent. Someone forced him to do it. He's a diversion."

White studied Maia, as if noticing small, unfortunate flaws in an otherwise valuable vase. "So . . ."

He turned to Ralph. "Titus Roe may be the man who shot your wife. At the very least, he is our best lead to find the one who did."

"Yeah." Ralph's voice was ragged.

"Mr. Arguello—Ralph—I understand you want to separate yourself from your past life, now that you have a family." White's face took on a look of sympathy that seemed as unnatural as the makeup. "Trust me, my boy, you can't. Neither of us can."

He offered Ralph the gun.

All I could think: This was my fault. I had brought Titus Roe here.

I hadn't looked any further than my gut reaction—to protect Maia by bringing her closer to me, to confront the man who'd dared to shoot at her. I hadn't thought through the obvious: what would happen to the shooter once he was in Guy White's grasp.

Water pipes shuddered. Somewhere above, someone was running a faucet, washing hands or scrubbing a wine stain from party clothes.

Ralph took the gun.

"Ralph, no," I said. "Don't."

"I should return to my party," White said. "Miss Lee, Mr. Navarre, accompany me."

"Ralph," I said, "wait—"

"Go on, *vato*." He looked at the nine-millimeter pistol in his hand as if it were a new part of him, a prosthetic limb he'd have to learn to live with. "You don't want to see what I'm cut out for."

"You heard him, Navarre." Alex smiled at me. He brushed his tuxedo jacket so I could see the other gun tucked in his cummerbund. No shortage of persuasion tools in the White household. "You need to enjoy the party."

I left my best friend alone with the hit man, Ralph's voice echoing richly against the tiles as he told Titus Roe he had five seconds to begin talking.

• • •

MAIA PUSHED PAST MR. WHITE BEFORE he could speak.

She stormed out the double glass doors, down the veranda steps into a throng of guests. Some of the tuxedoed men I recognized as business magnates, some politicians, some criminals. Mariachis strolled across the back lawn playing "Feliz Navidad." *Luminarias* glowed along the walkways. The pavilion tent was lit up white. The woods glittered with Christmas lights.

"Fine woman you have," White remarked.

I said nothing.

Alex hovered behind his boss. He kept a respectful distance, but near enough to hear every word.

White accepted a glass of champagne from a waiter. He held it up, studying the bubbles as if trying to remember the taste, but he didn't drink. "What did your lady friend expect, Mr. Navarre, bringing Titus Roe to me? Did she believe I would turn him in to the police?"

"My fault," I said. "I have trouble sometimes, thinking like you."

"You lost someone close to you once, Navarre." White's eyes were as glacial blue as his daughter's. "As I recall, you took revenge."

He was right. White knew many things about my past that I'd prefer he didn't.

"That wasn't cold-blooded murder," I said. "And I didn't get someone else to pull the trigger."

White smiled. "I understand Ralph Arguello. If you believe I gave him the gun because I did not want to do the killing myself, then I think I understand him better than you."

"You're a bitter old man."

He gazed across the lawn. Madeleine was down there in a red evening gown, a crowd of young men trying to gain her attention. She was ignoring them, staring up at me with a baleful look.

"I understand people, Mr. Navarre," White told me. "We only have two choices ever. To act, or fail to act. We feel better when we act. I have confidence Ralph Arguello is a man who will feel very good tonight."

"And if Titus Roe isn't the man who killed your son?"

"Oh, he isn't," White said. "One look at him, and I was certain of that. But if there's anything to be learned from him, your friend will find it. After that, let him get some satisfaction from vengeance. Titus Roe is worth nothing."

"The women Frankie murdered," I said. "Were they worth nothing, too?"

No change in White's eyes. No remorse. My comment wasn't even worthy of anger.

"My son didn't mean to kill anyone. He had trouble controlling his passions. I was much like him when I was young."

"A monster, you mean?"

"Think what you like, Navarre. It doesn't change the fact that some people are expendable. It's always been so. My son's life was worth more than any of the women he took."

Took. In the back of my mind, behind the cloud of anger, I found it an interesting choice of verbs.

"Frankie *wasn't* like you," I said. "He was broken inside. You knew exactly what he was doing to those women, and why."

"One thing about a terminal disease, Mr. Navarre. It makes you quite conscious of wasting time. If you'll excuse me—"

"What about your daughter?" I asked.

Down below, Madeleine was hard to miss in her swirl of red velvet, her blond hair and her angry expression. At the moment, she appeared ready to punch a young man who was trying to tell her a joke.

"Is she worth as much as your dead son?" I asked.

White set his champagne on the marble railing. His fingers trembled with rage. "I've done more to protect her than you can possibly know."

"Protect her from whom? Her own family?"

"Fortunately for you, Mr. Navarre, tonight is about keeping up appearances. Now if you'll excuse me, I have guests to greet. But be assured. When I find the one responsible for my son's death, I will not be handing over the gun to someone else."

He gestured at Alex to follow, then made his way carefully down the steps, where a city councilman was waiting to greet him.

Before Alex could leave, I took his arm.

"Where's the Secret Service?" I asked. "They weren't outside when we pulled up."

He smiled. "I made a few calls. I explained about Mr. White's party. Some of Mr. White's friends applied pressure. It was agreed surveillance on the night of Mr. White's party would be pointless. They could spare us for twenty-four hours so as not to embarrass a man of Mr. White's stature while he entertains his guests."

"You think of everything."

"I try."

I watched Mr. White hobble down the stairs, leaning on his silver cane. "This party was your idea, too, huh?"

Alex shrugged, trying to look modest, which immediately ruined his resemblance to Frankie. "As you heard, it's important for people to see that Mr. White is still in charge."

"No," I said. "I think it's important for you that they see firsthand how weak and old he is. And they see you walking behind him, directing him, calling the shots."

"I help as much as I can."

"And when the old man dies, there's Madeleine. Marry her off to the right man, and the dynasty could be on a solid footing again."

"Stranger things have happened."

"Unless she doesn't want to."

"Choices," Alex said regretfully. "We never really get to control our own choices, do we?"

"I hope they find your corpse floating in the river someday."

Alex clapped me on the shoulder as if we were old friends. "If you'll excuse me, Navarre. As Mr. White said, tonight is about appearances."

•   •   •

I MET MAIA AT THE BOTTOM of the landing.

She was watching the party guests circulate across the lawn, chatting and drinking and pretending they weren't freezing their asses off.

"Why do I keep listening to you?" she asked.

"My intoxicating charm," I guessed.

She was as beautiful as ever in a blue wool dress, her hair loosed from its ponytail, falling in a silky sheet down her back. She had a bandaged cut on her face from her gunfight with Roe. She'd arrived at the mansion not realizing she had a two-inch splinter sticking out of her cheek, just below her eye. The bandage made her look a bit like a refugee, a noblewoman fleeing a war, battling to maintain her composure

"Ralph is down there killing a man I delivered," she said. "If he doesn't finish the job, one of White's men will. Tres, you have to get out of here *now*. With me."

"I can't leave Ralph."

"Ralph's a criminal. He belongs here."

"Where would we go, the police?"

She looked like she was contemplating socking me in the gut. Instead, she wrapped her arms around my waist and pulled me toward her.

She was shivering.

The familiar scent of her hair made me wish I could leave with her—head up to Austin and forget everything, especially my old friend in the sauna room with the borrowed gun.

I told her about my day—Madeleine, Zapata, Sam and Mrs. Loomis. She told me about the old scrapbooks she'd looked through in Lucia DeLeon's garage, the women Guy and Frankie White had casually destroyed, the murder of the medical examiner Jaime Santos, the fry cook Mike Flume who'd had a crush on Ana's dead mother.

I thought about it all, trying to put the pieces together. The pieces didn't cooperate.

I tried to stay focused on Frankie White's murder, to imagine the nightstick that had clubbed him to death, but I kept coming back to what Ralph had told me earlier in the evening—that I had stayed away from Ralph, not the other way around.

I remembered his wedding reception. I'd stood next to Lieutenant Hernandez, watching the newlyweds cut the cake, and I'd heard him mumble, "This is a bad idea."

As Ralph's friend, I should've risen to his defense. One look at Ralph and Ana and you could tell they were in love. They shouldn't have belonged together. Their worlds should've exploded on contact. But you looked at the two of them, feeding each other cake, and you couldn't help having a sense of wonder, as if you were watching a juggling act with flaming torches—some impossible number of dangerous variables held aloft without a mishap.

I should have pointed that out to the lieutenant. Instead, I looked at his worried expression and a moment of agreement passed between us. *The marriage* was *a bad idea.*

It would never last. The pressure would be too much. Ralph would get restless. Ana would lose her job. Something would go wrong.

But really, those weren't my objections.

The marriage changed Ralph. It changed one of the constants in my universe, and it made me wonder if I would have to change, too.

Ralph was right. That had scared the hell out of me.

A bitter wind blew through Mr. White's party. Out on the lawn, guests moved toward the heated pavilion while mariachis belted out a *ranchera* version of "Silent Night."

"I have to tell you something," Maia said. "Something that might make a difference."

Her tone was like the edge of a thunderstorm. It made my senses crackle. I remembered our conversation in front of the Southtown office, what seemed like a lifetime ago—the desperate look Maia had given me.

"There *is* something wrong," I said.

"God, I wish I knew if it was wrong, Tres. Do you remember, a long time ago, I told you about my mother—"

She was interrupted by a woman's scream. Down on the lawn, the crowd parted. A bedraggled, bloody man had burst from the kitchen's service entrance and was loping across the property. He wore a torn flannel shirt and jeans, cut pieces of rope dangling from his wrists. Titus Roe.

Several of White's security men started to converge, but the crowd worked against them. The tuxedoed guests were surging away from the man and White's goons couldn't very well muscle their way through. Long before they could close the distance, Roe had reached the back of the lawn and disappeared into the woods.

"I couldn't do it," Ralph said.

I looked back and found him standing behind me, his face pale, slick with sweat. He wasn't holding a gun anymore.

"I know . . . he tried to hurt Maia," he stammered. "But I told him about the kitchen entrance. I told him to run."

I'm not sure who was more surprised—Ralph or me—when Maia threw her arms around him and kissed his cheek.

Ralph stared at her blankly. "He didn't shoot Ana. He convinced me of that. But I knew Mr. White . . . he would've had him killed anyway."

Mr. White, in fact, was standing by his buffet table down on the lawn, glaring up at us. Alex was whispering in his ear. I doubted he was advising hugs and kisses for Ralph.

I decided it was best not to wait for them to come to us.

"Stay with Ralph," I told Maia. I headed down the marble staircase.

I intercepted White and Alex at the bottom step.

"Inside," Mr. White ordered. "We need to discuss this."

"Titus isn't our guy. Ralph's convinced."

"Perhaps I did not make myself clear."

"You left the choice up to him," I said. "Isn't that right?"

White was having too much excitement for his condition. His complexion was turning gray despite the makeup. His breathing was shallow.

Alex put his hand on his boss's shoulder. "Let me deal with them, sir."

White trembled with anger. He kept his cold blue eyes on me. "Mr. Navarre, I seem to have been mistaken about your friend. I do not understand him any better than I do you."

"We'll leave then."

"I don't think so," the old man said. "We'll have you as our guests tonight. And in the morning . . . we'll talk."

He turned and walked back toward his crowd of guests, who were getting barraged with a new round of champagne and appetizers, security guards circulating amongst them, assuring everyone they could forget the rude interruption of the escaped prisoner.

I caught Madeleine's eye in the crowd. She appraised me

coldly, then turned back to the crowd of young men who wanted her attention a lot more than I did.

"Quite a show," Alex told me, amused. He raised one hand, and a heavyset security goon materialized at my right arm. "Virgil will show you to your room."

I had a feeling Alex would've said *your coffin* with the same good humor.

I looked up at the balcony. A couple of other goons had already found Ralph and were marching him inside.

And Maia was gone.

CHAPTER 13

MAIA DIDN'T WANT TO HOLD THE BABY.

"Just ten minutes?" Ralph's sister pleaded. She looked like a woman who'd just crawled through a wind tunnel full of baby food. "So I can take a shower? You're a lifesaver."

She handed over Lucia Jr., a bundle of grunting, kicking unhappiness, then disappeared down the hallway.

If Maia were in her place, she would've headed out the back door and driven away.

"Hey, sweetheart," Maia told the baby.

"Ah-ba!" Lucia Jr. complained.

Maia wondered if her head needed supporting. No, that was with younger babies. Lucia was almost a year old. She could sit up, use a cup, all of that.

Maia had been reading so many damn baby development

books, hiding them in the dirty laundry hamper whenever Tres visited, but she couldn't remember anything. Law school had been a snap compared to studying babies. Babies made no intuitive sense.

Lucia Jr. kept kicking and squirming.

Maia propped her over one shoulder, holding her by her terry-cloth-covered bottom. She got out her key chain. Babies loved keys. She put Lucia on the sofa and sat next to her and offered the keys.

"Ah!" Lucia went straight for the pepper spray canister.

"No," Maia said. "Not that."

She detached the pepper spray and put it in her pocket and Lucia started crying.

"Aw, come on, honey. Look, keys."

Lucia was having none of it. She wanted dangerous stuff or nothing. She was, apparently, her parents' child.

Down the hall, plumbing shuddered. Water began to run.

Hurry, Maia thought.

She bought a few seconds showing Lucia the handcuffs she kept in her purse. Lucia seemed to think they tasted pretty interesting.

Maia cursed herself for promising Ralph she'd stop by. The sister was clearly doing fine with the baby. But Maia hadn't been able to resist. Maybe it was her exhaustion, her frazzled state of mind, but earlier that evening, for the first time, she'd actually come close to liking Ralph Arguello.

•   •   •

THEY'D BEEN STANDING TOGETHER ON THE back veranda of Guy White's mansion. Without the glasses, Ralph looked older, weathered, like a Native American in a nineteenth-century photograph, staring across a landscape that was no longer his.

"I screwed up," he said, "cutting Titus loose."

Maia felt so relieved she couldn't speak. Never mind that Titus Roe had tried to kill her. Ever since she pulled him out of his Volvo, she'd known he was as much of an unwilling victim as she. She'd been foolish to bring him to White's house—a sure death sentence. Ralph had spared him. He'd lifted a huge weight from her conscience, and she was completely unprepared to feel so indebted to a man she so disliked.

On the lawn below, Tres was arguing with Guy White, trying to keep the old man and his henchmen from Ralph.

Maia knew Tres would stand in front of a tank if it meant saving Ralph or her.

"Hell of a way for me to repay him," Ralph said, following her eyes. "Tres kept me going, the last twenty-four hours. I haven't done shit but cause him trouble since high school, and he still risks his neck."

"I don't think Tres would see it that way."

"Stupid bastard," Ralph agreed. "Doesn't matter what I do wrong, he still backs me up. Covered my ass a million times. He makes me nervous."

Under different circumstances, Maia might've found that funny. Ralph Arguello, nervous of Tres.

"Did Roe tell you anything?" she asked.

"He wasn't going to. Said to go ahead and kill him, knew he was dead either way. Two years, three years ago, I would have shot him." Ralph leaned against the marble railing, rubbed his face with his hands. "Having a family, Maia . . . I don't know. First day I held Lucia Jr., it was like part of me went into her. Like she tapped me out. I can't kill people any-more. Even with Johnny Zapata, I hesitated. I kept seeing my baby. Does that make any sense?"

Maia reached over and squeezed his hand.

At the base of the steps, Guy White was not getting any happier. His men were closing ranks around Tres, like they were about to put him under house arrest.

"You need to go," Ralph told her. "Tres and I will manage. You gotta get out before White decides you're his guest, too."

"I can't leave you two."

"Keep searching. Check on the baby for me." Ralph looked over, and Maia was surprised by the sadness in his eyes. "I'd do anything for Tres. Used to figure he would be the one with the normal life—marriage, kids. I figured he'd have those things and I could kind of enjoy them through him."

Ralph reached into his shirt pocket, unfolded a thin piece of printed paper, like an oversized receipt. He handed it to Maia.

One glance and she understood what it was, but she was mystified how Ralph got it.

"In Titus Roe's pocket," he said. "Gave it to me after I cut his ropes. He wouldn't tell me who he got it from, but he said I'd figure it out. Said he owed me that much."

Men were coming around the edges of the veranda now, working their way toward Ralph.

"Take it," Ralph said. "Figure out who's left that we can trust."

Who's left we can trust.

For the first time, when he used the word *we*, Maia real-ized that Ralph trusted *her*. He approved of her. And when he talked about Tres having a normal life, having a family, he was including Maia as a given.

She didn't want to leave, but she knew Ralph was right. She had no choice.

She pecked him on the cheek, promised to see his child, and slipped into the mansion as Guy White's men came to secure their disobliging guest.

· · ·

THE BABY HAD THOROUGHLY SLIMED UP the handcuffs and was now checking out Maia's knee, tiny fingers grabbing at the fabric. Her wispy hair was braided and tied with plastic clips. The front of her jumper was stitched with a seal balancing a ball on its nose.

Maia could see the DeLeon family resemblance in Lucia Jr. She looked like her namesake—dark eyebrows knit with determination, as if everything was a challenge, and by God she would beat it.

Part of me went into her.

"You like my dress, huh?" Maia asked.

The baby looked up. Her mouth was open, drooling from intense concentration. Maia traced her finger over the baby's ear.

Ana had looked like this, in her baby pictures. Maia wondered if Lucia Sr. had sat on a couch with her, offering police paraphernalia to keep the serious little drooler quiet.

"I'm going to have one like you," Maia told the baby. "I'm in serious trouble, huh?"

The baby watched her lips move, but offered no advice.

Lucia Jr.'s eyes reminded Maia of someone. Not Lucia or Ana or even Ralph. She tried to figure out who.

Maia thought about her picnic with Tres in Espada Park. They had watched a mother and her toddler son walking by the old waterway. The little boy stumbled along, chasing a duck with a piece of tortilla.

"Cute kid," Maia had said.

Tres nodded, smiling at the boy's attempt to feed the duck by throwing wads of corn tortilla at its retreating butt. The mother chased after, herding the boy away from the water whenever he strayed too close.

"Count your blessings," Tres said. "That could be you."

Maia wasn't sure why he said that. Maybe because the woman was about Maia's age, a little old for having children.

Tres and she never discussed marriage, much less having children. But last summer, during a particularly dangerous case, Tres had brought Maia a friend's child for safekeeping. He had told his friend that she was perfect for the job. Maia had wondered, ever since then, if he'd been trying to tell her something.

Count your blessings. He sounded almost regretful.

Or maybe she was projecting.

"Hard to imagine," she told him.

The mother and child moved on downriver. The moment passed.

But the next week, Maia forgot to get her birth control prescription refilled. She kept putting it off. She told herself it was just because she was busy.

Two weeks after, she spent the night with Tres. She told herself she wasn't taking a risk.

She had sworn never to have children. She had sworn when she was nine years old, watching her father weep by a makeshift funeral bier.

Pregnancy itself was far from her worst fear.

And yet . . . here she was.

The faucet in the bathroom squeaked shut.

Maia tried to imagine what Lucia Sr. had felt like, in her position. An unwed mother. She thought about Ana on the day she married Ralph, how happy she'd looked despite the naysayers, the disapproving looks from her police friends.

Maia understood, for the first time, why Ana had fallen in love with Ralph. Whatever else one might say about him, Ralph was *present*. He was like Tres in his fierce commitment to people. Ralph had been the man in his family since he was an early teen. Maia knew that. It was impossible to imagine him being an absentee father, being an absentee *anything*.

She stroked Lucia Jr.'s cheek.

Something about the baby's face still bothered her . . . some resemblance, but before she could give it more thought, Ralph's sister came out of the bathroom, toweling her hair dry, bringing with her a cloud of jasmine-scented steam.

"Thanks a million," she said. "I forgot how good that feels."

Maia nodded. She picked up the baby in spite of her squirming protests and gave her a hug. She kissed her forehead.

"Cute, isn't she?" Ralph's sister said. "But *hijo*, tons of work. You got kids?"

"No," Maia said. "No kids."

"Still time."

Maia said her goodbyes. She had another stop to make.

The paper Ralph had given her was still folded into her pocket—a police printout with her name, her address, Tres' address. Everything one would need to give instructions to an assassin.

It was high time she paid the police another visit.

•　　•　　•

THE SAPD EVIDENCE ROOM, LIKE MOST that Maia had been in, was a cold basement, perpetually lit by corpse-colored fluorescents. A chain link wall separated the outside from rows of metal shelving, cardboard boxes, trunks and refrigerators.

A bored-looking supervisor sat behind a Dutch door, filling out paperwork. On the counter next to him was a logbook for signing in and out.

Maia had freshened up in the car while she was putting together her cover story. She couldn't do much about the bandage on her cheek, but she'd fixed her makeup otherwise. She'd made sure she was wearing enough perfume.

She leaned against the Dutch door, a little closer to the supervisor than was necessary, and smiled. "Long night?"

She got the desired effect.

In his haste to stand up, the supervisor dropped his clipboard. "Oh, um, no."

He was about thirty. Pale. Dark hair and chewed cuticles. Like most cops who gravitate to lonely jobs in the bowels of the department, he looked like a classroom pet that was used to being alternately ignored and terrorized.

Maia offered her hand. "My name's Lee, from Austin. They tell you I was coming down?"

"Um, no, ma'am . . . I mean, I would've remembered if they mentioned somebody like you."

His hand was cold and damp, but Maia gave it a nice firm shake—friendly, uninhibited. "It's about the Orosco case. I hate to bother you, but I wanted to see the evidence. It is here, right?"

She handed him a slip of paper with a case number written on it. Finding a believable cold case to investigate, and the accompanying file information, had taken her all of five minutes—one phone call to an acquaintance in Austin.

The supervisor looked at the number. "Oh . . . oh, yeah. Been here for years. Yuck."

"Would it be okay if I—" She gestured to his side of the door, gave him a smile that was just a bit playful. She was overdoing it. No female cop would flirt like this. But she was betting the supervisor wouldn't object.

He didn't.

"Just let me—um, here, sign in . . ."

He opened the gate while Maia scanned the logbook, saw the entries she wanted to see, then signed herself in as *Minnie Mouse* and put the incorrect date and time. The supervisor didn't notice.

Once inside, he was more than happy—thrilled, he insisted—to walk her back to cold storage.

"Thanks, these places are such mazes," Maia gushed gratefully. "I don't know how you keep it all straight."

"Oh, well, yeah . . ."

Maia figured it was time to make her point. She asked the supervisor if she could make a quick cell call.

"Oh, sure," he said. "Don't know if you'll get a good signal in here."

She got a signal. She was just calling upstairs.

"This is Maia Lee," she said into the phone.

Momentary silence, then the man on the other end said: "We need to talk to you in person. *Now.*"

"I know," Maia said. "I'm in the basement."

"What do you mean you're in the basement?"

"See you soon."

She hung up, gave the evidence supervisor a conspiratorial smile. "Bosses. Such a pain. Please, lead on."

The piece of evidence she pretended to want was a human pelvis from a stabbing murder back in 1998. The victim and the prime suspect had both been from Austin, so SAPD and APD had cooperated on the case. The weapon had never been found. The pelvis, with penetration wound, had been kept in cold storage—just in case they ever found a blade to match it against.

It boggled Maia's mind that anyone would keep such a thing, rather than just making a cast of the wound, but her contact had assured her it wasn't the strangest thing in the evidence room's freezers.

"Here you go," the supervisor said proudly.

"Wow." Thankfully, Maia's nausea was never bad at night, but it still took all her willpower not to gag. She promised herself she would never stand in front of a refrigerator wondering what to eat again as long as she lived.

"That's a pelvis, all right," she managed. "You sure it's okay . . ."

"Oh, hell, nobody cares about this stuff. Help yourself. It's a cold case. Literally, right?"

He sounded proud of his little joke. Maia tried to smile.

She took a closer look at the entrance wound, acting like she knew what she was doing. Finally she sighed. "No . . . damn. I was looking for a secondary laceration, but . . . well, I guess it's back to the drawing board."

"Aw, really? I'm sorry."

She closed the refrigerator. Her host didn't notice the blood kit in the small evidence bag which she'd slipped into her pocket.

They walked together toward the front of the evidence room.

"So," she said, "hypothetically speaking, if somebody wanted to switch a DNA sample in the evidence room, how easy would that be?"

"Impossible."

"Why?"

He shrugged. "I witness everything in and out. No chance."

"What if the person were a cop?"

He laughed uneasily. "You're kidding, right?"

Maia smiled, though she felt depressed as hell. She'd found out what she wanted. Sure—the supervisor on duty would keep out ninety-nine percent of the people. Nobody off the street could waltz in. But with somebody who was determined, who knew how departments worked—no evidence was safe. Like beat cops who regularly left their patrol cars unlocked, most deterrence inside a police station was cop aura. Cops had a hard time believing that anyone would be crazy enough to mess with police property.

And the names on the log-in book . . . Maia was trying to figure what to do with that information when her supervisor friend stopped dead in his tracks.

Detective Kelsey had understood her phone call. He was standing red-faced at the Dutch door, swinging the supervisor's clipboard by its broken pen chain.

•   •   •

KELSEY SLAMMED THE INTERROGATION ROOM DOOR. "You have any idea how many charges I could level?"

Maia nodded. "I also have a fair idea how much embarrassment I could cause the department."

"Worth it, to get you disbarred."

Maia took the evidence bag out of her pocket, put it on the table. She did not feel particularly calm, but she was determined to act it.

"Detective, I didn't lie. I didn't coerce. I just batted my eyes and walked out with some poor fool's DNA sample. *Help yourself,* your supervisor told me. Your security is a joke. The blood match on Arguello is a joke. Somebody tampered with the evidence."

Kelsey looked at the evidence bag like it was poison. A vein throbbed under his left eye.

"Check the logbook," Maia said. "You won't find my name. How many other holes do you think there could be?"

"You will not drag this department into the mud."

"Kelsey, the DNA testing for the White murder was sent to the lab about ten days ago. Your name is on the logbook several times for that week. Lieutenant Hernandez's, too."

"Every detective in homicide—"

"Yes," she agreed. "Makes it easy to prove access, doesn't it?"

Kelsey leaned across the table. "Miss Lee, tomorrow morning we're issuing a warrant for Arguello for Franklin White's murder. We're pressing charges against Navarre for aiding and abetting. When that happens, your carping is going to look exactly like what it is: typical defense attorney crap."

"You gave us a window. Forty-eight hours."

"That window just closed."

She forced herself to breathe normally. Not to think that she'd just signed Tres' death warrant.

"Detective." She tried to moderate her tone. "We have a mutual problem."

She opened her purse and unfolded the police printout. She pushed it across the table.

Kelsey read it, at first blankly. Then she could see comprehension spread across his face like hardening cement. "Where did you get this?"

"Titus Roe, a two-bit assassin. We had a little misunderstanding earlier. He, ah, got away from me before I could ask him many questions, but he gave me that. He said I could figure out who gave it to him."

For the first time, Maia saw something human in Kelsey's eyes: fear. But fear for what, she wasn't sure.

"I have only your word for this," he said slowly.

"It's a police printout. Directions for an assassination."

"No."

"Titus Roe was an obvious choice. He was a suspect in the Franklin White murder eighteen years ago. He's a Judas goat. Just like Ralph."

"Ralph Arguello is a murderer." The words didn't need to be loud. Kelsey's voice was saturated with loathing.

"Kelsey," Maia said, "tell me you didn't try to have me killed."

"You've got the nerve—"

"You were off duty the night of Franklin's murder. You had reason to hate the Whites. A cop nightstick was the murder weapon. Someone is desperate, Kelsey. Someone tried to frame Ralph, then Titus Roe. How long before they try to frame you?"

His face was pale and yellow, like something belonging in the light of the evidence basement. "That's enough, Miss Lee."

"Show me you're on the right side," Maia said. "Give that

printout to Internal Affairs. Postpone the arrest warrant against Ralph."

Kelsey picked up the paper. He crumpled it into a ball, kept it tight in his fist. "Listen to the news tomorrow morning, Miss Lee. And if you have any influence with your boyfriend, get him in here tonight."

"You really want the media involved? You want them to hear about my visit to the evidence room?"

"What visit, Miss Lee? You said yourself—you're not on the logbook. As far as I'm concerned, you were never here."

He opened the interrogation room door.

He didn't bother escorting her out.

If you have any influence with your boyfriend . . .

Before she was even out of the building, Maia had her phone in hand and was punching the number.

CHAPTER 14

AS CAGES GO, MY BEDROOM IN THE WHITE MANSION WAS a nice one.

Spanish Colonial bed. Oak bookcases. Fireplace. Saltillo tile floor with a Guatemalan rug. Disregard the surveillance camera mounted on the wall, the armed guard outside the door, the iron bars on the window, and it might've been a room at the Palacio del Rio.

I had to look hard to find evidence that the room once belonged to Frankie. In the back of the closet was a box of football trophies, pictures and an Alamo Heights *Olmos* yearbook from 1985. There was Frankie's Mules jersey, his football helmet, baseball bat, water polo ball. His senior letter jacket looked very much like the one I had torched in a fit of angst during my college years.

Frankie's collection of stuff creeped me out. I could've

been looking through my own mementos. The same shots of friends, the same parties—there were even a few group pictures with me in them. If I had died at age twenty-one, my closet might've been preserved like this. His legacy and mine would've been hard to distinguish.

The only thing different in Frankie's stuff was a nine-by-twelve framed sketch—a portrait of Madeleine White, twelve years old, her face done completely in shades of blue pastel. The likeness was unmistakable, yet the blue tint made her look different from the little girl I remembered. She stared out with a lost expression, like a shadow that had gotten separated from its owner. The inscription at the bottom, in childish letters that didn't go with the expertly drawn portrait: *To Frankie, From Maddy. Xmas, 1986.*

I put the portrait back at the bottom of the box.

I searched for clothes that would fit me, but there were none in the closet. Madeleine's goons had repossessed my suit, taken my phone, left me nothing but silk pajamas and no shoes, just to be sure I wouldn't try running anywhere. The only footwear options in Frankie's closet were a too-small pair of cleats and some enormous teddy bear-shaped slippers—a joke birthday gift, maybe.

I wasn't that desperate.

I paced across the cold Saltillo tile floor.

Sleep was out of the question.

I tried the bars on the windows, just out of principle. They were fast.

The guard Virgil outside my door was still there all three times I opened it. He said he would not be willing to get me a glass of water. The third time, he locked the door from the outside.

I threw Frankie's letter jacket over the surveillance camera, just to be petulant, and crashed on what used to be his bed.

I looked up at the exposed oak beams on the ceiling.

Outside, party music was still going, though the sound of voices was getting softer. The bedside clock glared 11:52.

I wondered if Zorro felt like this, trapped in the *alcalde's* hacienda. I wished I had a black mask and a sword.

Mostly, I wished I had Maia Lee. If I pretended hard, I could imagine her lying next to me, warming the right side of the bed. I listened for her breathing—that deep sigh she makes sometimes in the middle of a dream.

I thought about her expression at the party. *I have to tell you something.*

I thought about that a lot.

She had mentioned her mother, who died having Maia. Maia had told me the story only once, and I'd gotten the message that she was not willing to share details. I knew Maia's uncle had raised her after her father got sent away to a Communist reeducation camp. Her parents, Maia assured me, were not an emotional issue for her. She had never known her mom, never been close to her dad.

Which did not explain why she was thinking about her mother now.

I closed my eyes.

One of the photographs from Frankie's closet bothered me. It was a fuzzy snapshot of Ralph and Frankie on graduation night, still in their electric blue AHHS graduation robes, drinking tequila in the Skyride at Brackenridge Park. I knew the location because I'd taken the picture. It was the last time I'd seen Frankie White alive.

For reasons that would only make sense to drunken teen-agers, we'd bribed the Skyride operator a hundred dollars of Frankie's money to let us take an after-hours trip above the park.

The Skyride was in its last years of operation. The cables were loose. The motorized winch smelled of burning oil. The Skycar itself, a canary yellow box just big enough for three people and a tequila bottle, had a rusted floor and creaky seats and a door that didn't quite close. The operator stopped the ride for us at the top, a hundred feet in the air, so we could sway in the night wind and savor the possibility of plunging to our deaths on graduation night. When you're eighteen, such things sound like great fun.

We talked about the future.

I was going to Texas A&M to major in English.

Ralph and Frankie had a good laugh over that.

Ralph was disdainful of college. He was going to go into business and make millions. In truth, he'd already been in business for years, "finding merchandise" for Alamo Heights students. If we wanted a new Walkman, or a watch, or a James Avery charm bracelet, we knew to talk to Ralph first. His locker had better prices than the mall.

"What about you, Frankie?" Ralph asked. "Dad get you into Harvard?"

Immediately, Frankie's mood turned sour.

I doubt Ralph paid any attention to GPAs or college ad-missions, but I'd heard the rumors. I knew that despite Guy White's sizable bank account and lofty expectations for his son, Frankie had gotten in nowhere. With his grades and his terrible discipline record, he'd graduated only by the slimmest of margins.

"SAC," Frankie grumbled.

We both stared at him. San Antonio College, derisively known as San Pedro High, had an unfair reputation as the bottom rung on the local education ladder. It was, in our teenage minds, only one step up from a career at McDonald's.

Ralph burst out laughing. "SAC? What the hell for? You don't need to work."

Frankie took another swig of tequila. He shifted his weight and the Skycar bobbed back and forth precariously. "Punishment."

His face was scary in the dark—pale and brutal, his hair deathly white.

"Man," Ralph sympathized, "if I had your dad—"

"You'd dump him in a trash can," Frankie growled. "Yeah, that'd be nice. And you'd still have your mom, too."

Ralph didn't say anything.

The night wind smelled of fish spawn and lantana from the Sunken Gardens somewhere below us in the dark. Headlights glowed on McAllister Freeway. A line of traffic was still snaking its way down Hildebrand from Trinity University, where we'd had our graduation ceremony—all the good students who'd stayed for the reception with their families, unlike us.

Guy White had been at that party, no doubt, giving the other parents strained smiles, looking around for his errant son, probably contemplating what punishment he would have to inflict on Frankie when he came home.

"I want to kill him," Frankie mumbled. "I wish to hell—"

"Hey, man." Ralph punched him in the shoulder. "Don't worry about it. Tres and me will always be around for you, right?"

Ralph looked at me. He knew damn well I was out of the picture. I couldn't wait to leave town. Even if I'd been staying, Frankie White was the last person I'd want to help.

But the way Ralph talked, you could almost buy into his optimism. He made everything sound so reasonable. He described his business plans, said Frankie could help him out.

Ralph would open some pawnshops. He loved talking to people. He loved hearing their problems and pricing their most precious possessions. How much for a wedding ring? How much for the guitar that was supposed to take a kid to L.A.?

"Pawning is life, *vatos*," he said with a grin. "You want to understand somebody, look at what he's willing to give up."

Sometimes he would even save his customers' lives. Front them a little cash, keep the loan sharks away. Even if it was only for a few days, Ralph could do some good while he made a profit. What could be better than that?

I'm pretty sure Frankie heard very little of what Ralph said, but the tone of Ralph's voice seemed to calm him down. We sat drinking in our rusty Skycar, Ralph and I contemplating the future, Frankie contemplating murder, until the cable lurched and the Skyride started moving again, carrying us down through a hundred feet of darkness toward the end of the ride.

·   ·   ·

THE CLOCK ON FRANKIE'S BED STAND blinked midnight.

From the wall behind my head, I heard tapping. I wasn't sure at first, but then recognized the beat. "La Bamba."

Ralph.

I got out of bed. The knocking was coming from behind a Guatemalan tapestry. I draped it over the bedpost to get it out of my way, then ran my hand over the wall. Plaster and sheetrock. I tapped until I found a spot without a stud.

I went back to Frankie's closet and got his baseball bat.

What the hell.

I gave the wall a good battering-ram strike, dented it pretty nicely.

The guard didn't open the door. Maybe he was used to prisoners throwing tantrums. Maybe he was just scared I'd ask him for water again.

The second hit, the aluminum head of the bat went into the wall and ripped through insulation.

The third whack, I felt something give on the other side.

I put my face down at the hole.

From the other side, Ralph's voice said, "Al Capone's vault. May I help you?"

I couldn't see him very well—just a shadow against more shadows. Still, it was reassuring to hear his voice.

"Maia get away all right?" I asked.

"Yeah. I'm pretty sure."

"So what do you think?"

"Besides the fact that we're totally screwed?"

"We still got tomorrow," I said. "Let White get some sleep. I bet the old bastard will be chipper at breakfast."

Silence. The hole smelled of chalk and dust and mildew.

"I'm sorry, *vato*," Ralph said. "What I said earlier, about you being afraid of me and Ana . . . that was out of line."

"Forget it," I told him. I didn't add that he'd probably been right. The comments he'd made were still stinging a little too much.

I knelt next to the hole, waiting for Ralph to speak again.

Then I heard voices outside my bedroom door—the guard and someone else.

I slid the baseball bat under the bed and threw the wall hanging back over the hole. I swung around just as Madeleine White came in the room.

She'd been drinking. I could tell that because I'm a trained detective. Plus she had a half-empty bottle of champagne in her hand, her red dress was slipping off one shoulder and her eyes were half closed.

"You fucking idiot," she told me.

"Sure, come right in."

Behind her, my personal doorman protested, "Miss White—"

"Get lost, Virgil."

"But—"

She wheeled at him. "Get—the fuck—lost."

Virgil did the smart thing. He got lost.

Madeleine slammed the door. She stared in my direction as if I was in several different places at once. "What is your friend's problem, letting that fucker Roe escape?"

"Three *fucks* since you walked in," I said. "Even by my standards, that's impressive."

She scowled. "What?"

"If you want to know something about Ralph," I said, "you're in the wrong room."

"Don't wanna talk to him."

"Why not?"

" 'Cause I got the call for you, didn't I?"

She set her champagne bottle on the nightstand, fished around in her purse, brought out my cell phone.

I tried to take it.

She pulled it away. "You and Arguello—what are you really after?"

"What was the call, Madeleine?"

"First explain why he let Titus go. Then I'll decide whether to tell you or my father."

"Ralph didn't want to shoot an innocent man."

"Innocent? Bullshit."

"You saw Roe. You really think he killed your brother?"

She sat down hard on the bed.

The straps of her evening dress fell around her arms. Her newly curled hair was coming undone.

She reminded me of one of those elaborate trick knots—the kind that look seaworthy but come apart when a single end is pulled.

"I don't care whether Roe did it or not," she said. "I just don't want my father pissed."

There was fear in her voice—the terror of somebody facing down an old phobia, staring into the dark closet that scared her as a child.

"If you mean he'll take it out on you," I said, "then I'm sorry."

"I didn't say that."

She was still holding my phone. I resisted the urge to grab it.

"Madeleine . . . why did Frankie kill those women?"

She made a fist in the quilt, pulled it over her lap. "You know why. My dad did the same thing when he was young. He liked having power over them. With Frankie . . . it just went too far."

"No," I said. "That's your father's excuse, but it wasn't

about power for Frankie. Frankie strangled his victims. It was about hatred."

Madeleine said nothing. She rubbed her arms, as if she could still feel the bruises that used to be there when she was ten years old.

"Frankie hated your father," I said. "Your father drove your mom to an early grave. Frankie couldn't take out his anger on his dad, so he took it out on everyone else. Teachers and police. You. Finally, the women along Mission Road, the same area where your father once preyed. Frankie couldn't hold your father accountable. He didn't have the courage or strength for that. So he killed those women instead. It was the best he could do."

Madeleine stared at the letter jacket on the security camera. "I hate this room."

"Your father put you in that treatment facility partly for your own protection," I guessed. "He was worried what Frankie might do to you."

She didn't answer.

"Don't try to please your dad," I told her. "Don't try to follow in his footsteps."

"Who says I am?"

"Walk away. Move. Go out of state. Wouldn't he let you?"

Madeleine smoothed the quilt over her lap. "You moved to California for a while, right?"

"Yes."

"Did that work for you—just leaving?"

Direct hit.

"Alex is jockeying to take over the operation," I said. "Once your dad dies, he'll either force you to marry him or kill you. He'll have to."

"He wouldn't dare."

"He as much as admitted it," I said.

Madeleine stood, steadied herself on the bedpost. "Your friend's wife, the cop lady—she's getting better."

I had to make an effort not to look at the hole in the wall. "Is that what the call was about?"

"The call? No. Her condition is a secret. My dad has strings he can pull. Even with doctors. Well . . . especially with doctors, these days. They're keeping her sedated to keep an eye on her heart rate, but they'll probably try to bring her around late tomorrow, maybe Monday."

"And she'll tell who shot her."

Madeleine nodded. "And maybe who shot Frankie."

"Who else knows this?"

"Just the cops, I guess."

That didn't make me feel better, after all the things Maia had told me.

"The lady who was here earlier," Madeleine said.

"Maia Lee."

"You two . . . serious?"

I nodded.

Madeleine said, "Oh."

She picked up her champagne, staggered toward the door.

"That's who called," she threw over her shoulder. "She wanted to talk to you. I said you were busy."

"She must have loved that."

"She sounded pretty desperate. Guess that's why she trusted me with the message."

"What message?"

" 'The news is coming early.' "

"That's it?"

"I thought she meant the news about the police lady in the hospital getting better. But now . . . I'm not sure. She said you needed to meet her as soon as possible. I got the feeling she wanted you out of here—fast."

I tried to look puzzled instead of scared for my life. I'm not sure I pulled it off. I glanced at the bedroom door behind Madeleine, and wondered, briefly, if she were drunk enough for me to overpower her and make a break for it. Probably she wasn't.

"Why would your girlfriend want you out of here?" she asked.

"Jealousy," I speculated. "Because I'm having too much fun."

Madeleine studied me. "You're weird."

"You wouldn't consider letting Ralph and me out?"

"Another two prisoners running across the lawn in the middle of my dad's party? I don't think he'd like that. I delivered the message. That's my risk for the evening. G'night."

"Thanks, Madeleine."

"Hope it works out with you and Maia. Depending on this . . . news."

She closed the door behind her.

I waited for five seconds, then checked the deadbolt. Blessed be the inebriated. She'd forgotten to relock the door. I was thinking about how to jam it open when I heard Virgil's voice outside, talking to some other guy.

I stayed still, waited.

The guys were right outside the door. Virgil grumbled something about Madeleine. The other guy laughed.

Neither of them checked the lock.

I could bust out and surprise them, but two against one,

me with only a baseball bat and fashionable silk pajamas—I didn't like the odds. I could take down two men, maybe, but the house was still full of people. Armed people. I wouldn't get far.

I went back to Frankie's bed. Ralph was calling my name through the hole in the wall.

"You catch all that?" I asked.

"Most," he said. "Ana—she's—"

"Gonna make it, yeah. But the news coming out early—"

"The DNA." He hesitated. "*Vato,* I was about to tell you before . . . something I gave Maia, from Titus Roe."

He described the police printout with Maia's personal information and my address.

Once the news sunk in, I was tempted to put a few more holes in the wall. "Goddamn it."

"I'm telling you, *vato.* It's Kelsey."

I tried to wrap my mind around the idea. It still seemed wrong. But who else? Hernandez? I thought about the lieutenant in his Armani suit and his fatherly smile. It seemed even more unlikely.

Then again, I thought about the client I'd killed a couple of days ago, Allen Vale, the well-dressed physician with the friendly smile and the loaded shotgun.

What had Maia said? *Tres Navarre, impeccable judge of character.*

"We gotta get out of here," I said.

"*Claro.* You got any ideas?"

I told him about my door. "You want to try it?"

A long pause. "Yeah, but wait a few hours. Let the party die down."

His voice sounded heavy.

It made me realize how tired I was. The long day was catching up with me—too much adrenaline, too much worry. As dangerous as it was to wait, if I tried to pick a fight in my present condition, I'd be committing suicide.

"You're right," I said. "A few hours sleep."

I lay back on Franklin White's bed and stared at the ceiling.

I told my body to wake me up at 3:00 A.M. Then we would make our escape. With luck, Ana would be conscious tomorrow. She'd get us all off the hook.

I had a bad feeling in my stomach as I fell asleep. Maybe I knew, even then, how incredibly wrong things would go.

CHAPTER 15

ETCH WAS UP WHEN THE CHURCH BELLS STARTED RINGING.

After thirty years in the neighborhood, he could anticipate St. John's sunrise service. Every Sunday, he rose before the bells and dressed in coat and tie, though he hadn't been to mass since Lucia died.

It wasn't that Etch had stopped believing in God. He just figured the two of them had nothing more to say to each other.

Still, the bells comforted him, the way watching family picnics comforted him when he was riding in a police car. He liked knowing some people could have a normal life.

He chose a brown wool Italian suit, teal shirt, mauve tie, leather loafers. The temperature outside had dropped below freezing. He could tell from the knock in the water pipes, the color of the sky out his window. A Blue Norther had rolled in—a snap of Arctic air that had no business in Texas.

He turned and stared at his empty living room.

He was down to a coffee table and sofa. No television. No knickknacks. No photos.

Over the last year, anticipating retirement, he had slowly pared his possessions down to nothing. Every week, another box went down the street to the church's donation bin, until his entire life seemed to have dissolved.

Travel had been the idea, originally. Etch told his colleagues he was buying an RV, striking out to see the United States. Except for his college years, and a few business trips here and there to pick up fugitives, Etch had never left San Antonio. He deserved to travel.

The problem was Etch never bought the RV.

He kept just minimizing his possessions without making preparations for anything new. He felt like he was erasing himself, a little at a time, and something about it felt satisfying.

He loaded his nine-millimeter, attached the silencer.

Not many people in San Antonio owned silencers, but Etch had a collection. He enjoyed shooting in the early morning.

The parishioners didn't want their prayers interrupted. The neighbors didn't want their dreams punctuated by small arms fire. Etch tried to be sensitive to their wishes.

He loaded a fresh clip. He went out the back door.

Etch's house sat on a stretch of Basse Road that hadn't changed much in the last three decades. To the north, the city grew like a cancer, eating up more rural land every year, but here on the West Side, nobody much cared about progress, or strip malls, or adding a Starbucks to every block.

The boulevard was lined with weeds and cactus and scraggly live oaks. The houses on either side were shotgun shacks on huge lots. Etch's own was a two-bedroom clapboard, painted the color of provolone cheese. It wasn't really so small, but it looked that way surrounded by fields of spear grass.

In the spring, the back acre would be flooded with bluebonnets and Indian paintbrush, but now, in the winter, there was nothing but yellow grass.

Etch's target range was an old olive Frigidaire, sitting in the field between his house and the church. At least once a week, he opened the refrigerator and loaded it with cans, bottles, boxes, whatever he had left in the pantry. Etch still did grocery shopping, though somehow he never got around to eating much. He liked to shoot the contents of the refrigerator, then hose out the remains.

He worked his first clip. He took out three cans of sardines, blew up a two-liter soda bottle, plugged a few shots into the door and watched the recoil whap it back and forth on its hinges.

He knew he was putting off what he had to do this morning. Eight o'clock already. He had to get going before people started waking up and the hospital shift changed. He had arranged to take over starting at nine. That would give him a good hour before the doctors came in to check on Ana—plenty of time to make his decision.

He imagined Lucia, sitting just behind him. If he looked back, she would be there at the picnic table under the huisache tree. She'd be holding a cup of coffee, wearing her patrol uniform.

You can't murder my daughter, Etch.

"She betrayed you. She isn't yours."

She is, Lucia said. *You're not going to win, love.*

He feared she was right. He couldn't carve a victory out of this. He'd been buying time for eighteen years, but if it came down to keeping himself alive or keeping his secrets hidden, he wasn't sure which he would choose.

Etch checked his gun. One round still chambered.

He thought about Ana lying in her hospital bed, heart monitor bleeping steadily. The more he had tried to love her, help her, see her mother's qualities in her, the more he hated her.

He remembered a meeting he'd had with Ana, shortly before her mother died.

She'd invited him to coffee. He had gone, feeling a bit uneasy. And irritated.

Ana was twenty-six, just out of college after the Air Force, her first month into the SAPD police academy. By all accounts, she was excelling. There was no doubt she was worthy of her mother's legacy. There was also little doubt that *Ana DeLeon* wouldn't be spending her entire career on patrol.

It rankled Etch every time someone said that, as if the work Lucia and he had been doing since Ana was a little girl was meaningless. A job for the unmotivated.

They'd met at the Pig Stand, down the street from Lucia's. Etch wondered if Ana had picked the spot as some kind of message. Etch hadn't been there in almost three years. After Frankie's death, his old routines with Lucia had slowly unraveled. Everything seemed tainted by the night of the murder.

Ana insisted on buying his coffee, as if with the seventy-five cents, she was proving her adulthood, her independence. Etch never paid for anything at the Pig Stand anyway, but he let her put down the money.

She was only a few years younger than Lucia had been when Etch started patrolling with her. Ana had the same glossy black hair, chopped short in a utilitarian wedge. She had the same plum-colored lips, the same challenge in her eyes, though that look that had been draining from Lucia's eyes over the last few years.

"I'm worried about my mother," Ana said.

Etch counted to ten before answering, trying to keep his anger inside.

"Maybe you should go see her," he suggested. "How long has it been?"

In truth, he knew exactly how long. Six and a half months, since the huge fight when Ana had poured all her mother's liquor into the river behind her house.

Ana set her coffee cup on the counter. "She doesn't want to see me."

"You sure? Or do you not want to see her?"

"She's destroying herself. She won't talk to me about it. I thought maybe you could—"

"Ana, your mother's a strong woman."

"With a great reputation in the department. A real role model. Yeah, Etch. I know. Everybody is so goddamn busy protecting her reputation, they're not helping *her*. She's drinking herself to death."

Mike Flume, the fry cook, was putting orders on the pickup counter, getting a little too close to the conversation. Etch stared at him until the nervous bastard's freckled red face disappeared back into the kitchen.

Ana sat forward, took Etch's hands, which made him uncomfortable as hell. "Etch, you're her best friend. You've got to talk to her. Please. Find out what's wrong."

"She's a police officer. She has a lot of stress. You should understand—"

"This isn't stress. Something's eating her up from the inside. Something specific. For the last . . . I don't know . . . couple of years, it's been getting worse. She needs therapy, or—"

"Therapy?" Etch pulled his hands away. "You think she's crazy?"

"No. I don't mean that. But there has to be some reason—"

"I'll talk to her," Etch promised. "But Ana, seriously, you need to go see her yourself."

Ana nodded morosely. Etch knew she had no more intention of seeing her than he did of talking to Lucia about her drinking.

"Thanks for the coffee," he said.

He left her at the Pig Stand counter, cradling her cup and staring out the window, looking so much like Lucia that Etch began dreading the day Ana would wear an SAPD uniform. He hoped the academy trainers were right. He hoped Ana made some plainclothes division in record time. He did not want to see her in the same uniform her mother wore.

Ana had gotten every break Lucia never had. Lucia had sacrificed so much for her, and Ana had made a mockery of that by marrying Arguello.

Not only that—she was proud of it. She was happy. She balanced a family and a career.

Etch and Lucia never got that chance.

He raised his nine, took careful aim.

There would be no winning. But there might be justice, and justice was different than the law. Nobody understood that better than a cop.

Don't, Lucia said. *Walk away, Etch.*

He shot his last round into the freezer door, opening a hole in the olive green metal at the level of a human forehead.

• • •

"LIEUTENANT?"

Etch spun, his gun still raised.

Kelsey stood ten feet away, staring down the barrel of the nine. He raised his hands slowly.

Etch lowered the gun.

His face burned. He felt like a damn amateur, getting startled like that.

"Sorry," he mumbled.

Kelsey put his hands down. He pointed with his chin toward the target refrigerator. "Fucking major appliances, huh? I got a washing machine I should shoot."

"Yeah," Etch said. "It's therapeutic."

He was grateful to Kelsey, trying to defuse the situation, but he started to realize how wrong it was for Kelsey to be here.

Kelsey's eyes were bloodshot. He hadn't changed clothes since last night, which meant he'd never been to sleep. And he had never come to see Etch at home unannounced before, even for the most urgent cases.

Kelsey picked up a clip from the picnic table, turned it in his fingers. "You didn't answer the front door so I, uh, poked my head into the living room. You moving out, sir?"

"Travel," Etch said. "Life on the road."

"Must be nice." He didn't meet Etch's eyes.

Across the field, the sound of the church organ seeped through the stained glass. A recessional hymn. "Joy to the World."

"Are you going through with the DNA announcement?" Etch asked.

Kelsey exhaled steam. "Public relations signed off on it. The press is already champing at the bit."

"But?"

"I got some news."

Etch reloaded his pistol. "About Ana's condition?"

"About the woman Navarre and Arguello were with yesterday. I think I got an ID on her. She's Madeleine White."

For a moment, Etch was too stunned to speak. Then, despite himself, he felt a little impressed. "I'll be damned."

"Pretty ballsy," Kelsey agreed. "But you can appreciate, this changes things."

"How so?"

"If Navarre and Arguello are working with White, and we make an announcement while they're under his, uh, protection . . . They won't last a minute."

Etch aimed at the refrigerator. He thought about which soda bottle to shoot for. "You ever find Miss Lee?"

"Yeah. I found her."

Etch shot the Sprite bottle. It ruptured, exploding white foam out the front of the fridge. "And?"

"She let Roe go. She said he was part of a setup. She said the DNA was, too."

Etch studied him, trying to figure what Kelsey was holding back.

"You see where she's going," Etch said. "She's going to blame you."

Kelsey's ears turned red.

"You and Ana have a history," Etch continued. "So did you

and Frankie White. Lee will say you have a motive for the Franklin White murder. It's bullshit, but she'll use it."

Kelsey's fingers had whitened on the nine-millimeter magazine. "Ana's on the mend. She'll tell us the truth."

"I hope so. Maybe you should wait on the announcement. If Lee shook you up—"

"She didn't shake me up."

"All right."

"It's just, if Navarre and Arguello are with White—"

"They're trying to beat you to the punch. You gave them a deadline. Now they're trying to hand Guy White his son's killer early. And it sounds like they've settled on you as a patsy. But maybe you're right. God willing, Ana will come around and tell us the truth. Today. Or tomorrow."

Etch could tell Kelsey was turning now, aiming his anger back in the direction Etch wanted.

"Anything else Lee said?" Etch prodded, his tone full of concern—the fatherly lieutenant, protective of his people's welfare. "Anything that might put you in a bad light?"

Kelsey licked his lips. "No . . . no, sir."

"You want to go ahead with the announcement? It's your call, son."

The *son* did it.

Kelsey stood a little straighter. He set the clip back on the picnic table. "I'll go ahead with it. We don't owe Arguello and Navarre anything. Nothing else we can do."

•   •   •

ETCH STOOD AT HIS WINDOW, WATCHING the parishioners leave St. John's. The old married couple who always parked in front of his house were just getting into their car. Every year, they got a little more stooped. The old man's coat got a little more threadbare and his wife's hair got bluer. But they were still together. Must be pushing ninety.

Etch wished them well. He hoped they died together some warm summer night, holding hands in bed. Nobody should die in winter. It was too depressing. Too cold and impersonal.

He looked down at the windowsill where he'd placed a few of his last possessions—a tiny black velvet box and an evidence bag.

He opened the evidence bag, brought out the vial and syringe—the same glass vial he'd had in his pocket the first time he visited Ana.

Etch hadn't investigated homicides for fifteen years without picking up a few interesting methods of killing. The vial was a souvenir from a chemistry professor at Trinity University who used his postgraduate research to plan his wife's perfect murder. If he hadn't confided in his lab assistant, Etch never would've caught him.

Clear liquid. Damn near untraceable. Etch would need one minute to inject, no more. The effects would take maybe an hour to manifest. Coma. Organ failure. Everything you'd expect from a gunshot victim who suddenly took a turn for the worse.

He doubted the ME's office would run toxicology, but even if they did, this stuff wouldn't show up on a standard scan.

Etch's first visit to Ana's bedside, there'd been too many people. No opportunity. Then Maia Lee had shown up and rattled his nerves.

Etch turned the vial, watched a small air bubble float through the poison.

Maia Lee was becoming a major problem. She'd gotten to Titus Roe. She'd rattled Kelsey. She was putting together Ana's line of investigation much too well. Depending on how much she'd told Navarre and Arguello . . . Etch needed a way to tie up all the loose ends at once.

He slipped the poison into his pocket. Today, one way or another, he would finish things.

He remembered sitting with Lucia on her porch, a few hours after they cleared the Frankie White crime scene. He'd wanted to tell her why he was late to their shift that evening. He'd been rehearsing in front of his bathroom mirror, practicing what he would say to her, worrying about whether he was doing the right thing.

But Frankie White had ruined everything. As usual, the Whites got in the way.

Etch picked up the black velvet box from the windowsill.

He opened it and stared at the white gold engagement ring, the small stone that was all he could afford, eighteen years ago.

He hadn't had the courage to propose that night—not after the murder. And in the following weeks, Lucia started drifting away. He never found the right moment. He feared that she would say no.

Lucia never saw the ring.

Like so many of Etch's dreams, the velvet box got tucked away, a secret *what if* he never showed to anyone. It was all Frankie White's fault. The bastard had deserved every hit with the nightstick.

Lucia spoke to him: *It isn't the Whites you're mad at, Etch, any more than you're mad at Ralph Arguello.*

"You're wrong," Etch said.

You're mad at me. Because I couldn't be there for you, not one hundred percent.

"That wasn't your fault."

It's still true, love. You meant to kill Ana. As soon as she looked into the case, you stole that poison from the evidence room. You were already thinking about how to stop her.

"No."

Don't kill her, Etch.

"She betrayed you. She left you. She doesn't deserve anything from me."

Ana's words mixed with her mother's: *Everybody is so goddamn busy protecting her reputation, they're not helping* her.

Etch had no choice. He hadn't chosen any of this.

He made Lucia a silent deal: *If you want it stopped, you'll have to stop me. Otherwise . . .*

He slipped the syringe in his coat pocket.

He closed up his empty house. As he walked toward his car, he imagined that his steps were erasing themselves behind him, leaving no trace of the path he'd walked for the last eighteen years.

CHAPTER 16

SO MUCH FOR BIOLOGICAL CLOCKS.

When I woke up, it was already light outside. I was upside-down in Frankie White's much-too-comfortable bed. The clock read 9:02.

I cursed and ripped off the covers. My head felt like it had been used as a guacamole pestle. I was still wearing the silk pajamas.

I grabbed the baseball bat, started to go for the door, but the tiled floor was like ice. I tiptoed my way to the closet and searched for shoes.

Frankie's too-small football cleats? Wouldn't fit.

My only other choice: the teddy bear slippers. I swallowed my pride. At least they were warm, and I figured they'd be quieter than cleats.

I went to the door and tried it—still open. Virgil was still standing outside, bleary-eyed, reading a NASCAR magazine.

He turned, stared at me in surprise.

I gave him my most disarming smile. " 'Morning, Virgil."

Then I rammed the baseball bat in his gut. He doubled over, allowing me to clonk him on the head and roll him into the room. He curled into fetal position on the tiles and moaned. Not quite unconscious, but he wasn't going to be running relay races anytime soon.

I took his gun and his keys, apologized, and was about to leave when I thought, *Shoes.*

I checked him out. No good. Feet way too small. For the time being, I was stuck with the teddy bears.

I locked Virgil in Frankie's room and trotted next door to Ralph's. No guard outside. The hallway was clear in both directions.

I suppose I should've felt honored Virgil chose my door to stand outside. He'd obviously concluded that I was the more lethal threat, or maybe he simply didn't want to listen to Ralph snore. And Ralph *does* snore.

I rapped lightly on the door—*Para bailar La Bamba.*

A muffled grunt, then silence.

I rapped again. Ralph doesn't sleep much, but when he finally gets to deep REM, he tends to stay there.

Finally his voice: "You better have breakfast."

"A .38 or a baseball bat," I murmured. "Take your pick."

"Thirty-eights give me indigestion."

I found the right key and unlocked his door. He was wearing black sweatpants and a T-shirt. His hair was frizzy, tied in a haphazard ponytail like the Wicked Witch of the West.

He looked down at my animal slippers. "Nice."

"There's a story behind those."

"When the mother bear catches up with you, it's your problem." He grabbed the bat. "Which way?"

We headed for the main staircase.

I was hoping several things: First, that I could find my way back to the service entrance in the kitchen. I mean, why mess with a classic strategy? It had worked for Titus Roe. Second, I was hoping the White household was mostly asleep, this being the morning after the big party. Finally, I was hoping we could find a car and get off the property alive.

All those hopes pretty much fell apart when we ran into Madeleine.

·   ·   ·

WE WERE CROSSING THE BALCONY OF the main entry hall, heading for the final flight of stairs, when she emerged from a door right next to us.

I'm not sure who was more surprised, but her hangover must've still been slowing her wits. I had time to raise my gun.

Her jeans and oversized button-down were spattered with acrylic paint. She smelled of turpentine. She had three green freckles on her cheek and a slash of sky blue in her hair.

She stared at the .38 like it was a dead rat. "What are you doing?"

"Leaving," I said.

"The hell you are."

"Come on, Madeleine. Just . . . go take a shower or something. We'll be out of your way."

"You son-of-a-bitch. Where's Virgil?"

"Upstairs with a stomachache and a headache. Look, you never wanted us here. It didn't work out. We're going to keep looking on our own."

The scary thing was, I almost thought I'd convinced her.

She gazed down into the entry hall, as if thinking hard. Then I realized she was looking at the front door. Our favorite mafia boy Alex Cole had just come inside, carrying a Sunday paper, his car keys and a box of Krispy Kremes.

He was moving fast. Red-faced and scowling, he marched toward the stairs like he absolutely *had* to get his doughnuts somewhere important. He froze when he saw us.

"You bitch," he said to Madeleine. "What are *they* do-ing out?"

Madeleine blinked. "What did you just—"

"It was on the car radio." Alex pointed at Ralph. "It was *him*. The police have DNA. Arguello killed Frankie. That's why he shot his wife. She was about to bust him."

Madeleine looked like she'd taken an uppercut to the face. She turned toward me.

"It's a frame," I said. "Madeleine, we wouldn't be here—"

"Hey, wake up!" Alex shouted at the house. "Security! Wake the fuck up!"

Madeleine's fists clenched, but her eyes were brittle, the way they'd looked when she was ten, running under the high school bleachers to get away from her brother. "How. How could you—"

"It wasn't me, *chiquita*," Ralph told her. "I tried to help Frankie. You know that."

"Wake up, somebody!" Alex yelled. "Aw, the hell with it."

He dropped his keys and doughnuts on an end table and

started up the stairs toward us. Footsteps behind us—at least two guys, running from the upstairs hall.

"*Vato,*" Ralph yelled, "*vámanos!*"

We pushed past Madeleine, who didn't try to stop us. We ran toward the bottom of the stairs and Alex.

Two guards were coming behind us. Both were armed, but looked half asleep, baffled by what they saw.

"What are you waiting for?" Alex yelled. "Shoot them!"

One of the guards: "But—"

Alex started to say, "Shoot, godda—" when Ralph and I crashed into him. Not the most graceful takedown, but it worked. Alex crumpled backward in an unintended somersault.

Ralph and I burst through the kitchen doorway just as the guards opened fire.

•　　•　　•

RALPH RAN STRAIGHT FOR THE SERVICE exit. A bullet came through the window and shattered a bottle of brandy on the counter.

He hit the floor, put his back against the door.

"One more guy outside." He reached up, threw the deadbolt.

The interior door had no lock, but it was right next to the refrigerator. I dragged the fridge in front of it. With all the adrenaline coursing through my body, I probably could've stacked a stove and a couple of cars, too.

Alex was cursing in the living room. He told one of the guards to wake up Mr. White. Madeleine said something and he yelled at her to shut up. Somebody battered on the interior door. The beer bottles rattled in the fridge.

The wall phone was right next to me. I thought about calling the police, but I decided it wouldn't do any good. We already had enough people on the premises who wanted to kill us.

Maia was my only other option, but I hesitated. As much as we needed her, as much as I wanted to hear her voice, I didn't want to put her in danger. I had a bad feeling that if I called her, it might be our last conversation.

A guard's face appeared in the back window. I shot at the pane just above his head, then scrambled over to where Ralph was sitting.

"We need a third exit," Ralph said. "Maybe a distraction."

WHUMP.

The interior door shuddered. The fridge moved a couple of inches.

Brandy from the broken bottle was dripping off the counter. There were maybe a dozen more bottles left over from the party. Right by the gas stove—and the window above the sink.

An insane idea started to form in my head, but Ralph was way ahead of me.

"Check that drawer by the oven," he said. "Find me some matches."

As Ralph was lighting what might be our funeral pyre, I gave in to desperation. I picked up the phone.

CHAPTER 17

SUNDAY MORNING THE STREETS WERE DESERTED, which was not good for Maia's safety. When she was angry and nervous, she drove as fast as traffic would allow. This morning, that was very fast indeed.

As so often happened for her, the answers had woven together in her mind at 3:00 A.M. Unable to sleep, dreading the onset of morning sickness, she had followed Ana DeLeon's thought process through to the end. Maia knew who had shot Ana. An 8:00 A.M. call to the hospital front desk, a few questions about the police security detail had confirmed Maia's fears about what he would do next.

Etch Hernandez.

Two things had decided her. First, the look on Kelsey's face last night had not been the look of a guilty man. Stubborn, angry, defensive, yes. But guilty men don't look quite so lost. They tend to have a smug calmness somewhere inside—a certainty that they are right and will be vindicated. Kelsey didn't know what the hell was happening to him. He looked like a hopelessly outmatched boxer who'd decided to tuck in his chin, squeeze his eyes shut, and throw as many blind punches as possible before he got KO'd.

The second factor was the photograph of Hernandez and Lucia from Ana's bulletin board. Maia had studied it a hundred times. She kept trying to read the strange uneasiness, the tense body language between the two partners. The way they stood together, the way Etch seemed entirely conscious of Lucia . . . *Timing is wrong.*

Maia wondered if Ana realized how ironic her notation was.

She suspected she knew more than Ana did. She thought she now understood the motive behind Franklin White's murder, and that was the most disturbing puzzle piece of all.

She fishtailed into the hospital lot and took a reserved space.

She rummaged through the toolbox she always kept behind her driver's seat—a few simple items that opened most doors. One was a stethoscope.

She tucked it in the front pocket of her blazer and headed toward the lobby.

As she walked, she thought about Tres.

She'd slept in his bed last night. The pillows smelled like him. The cat curled between her feet, but the sheets weren't warm enough.

The longer Tres and she were together, the more she missed

his warmth when they slept apart. He was always hot—always just a degree shy of a fever.

She woke to winter sunlight through bare pecan branches, the creaking of pipes and the smell of melting butter and fresh-baked cinnamon rolls downstairs.

Despite her uneasy stomach and her sense of foreboding, she ate breakfast in the kitchen with Sam and Mrs. Loomis.

Even with a bandaged ear, Sam was in an excellent mood. He ate three cinnamon rolls with bacon and had two cups of coffee.

He thought Maia was one of his operatives. He kept asking her questions about clients. Maia did her best to fabricate good answers.

Mrs. Loomis talked about her children—two boys, both grown and moved out of state. Her husband the policeman had died when the boys were very young. She'd raised them on her own, hadn't seen either of them now for several years.

"That's a shame," Maia said.

Mrs. Loomis spooned scrambled eggs onto their plates. "Oh, it's not so bad. I miss them . . . but mostly I miss them being young. They drove me crazy so many years. I can't help getting nostalgic."

Maia must've looked perplexed, because Mrs. Loomis laughed. "You'll understand when you have a child, dear."

When. Not *if.*

A decade ago, Maia would've protested. She'd fended off many such comments, resented the assumption that because she was a woman, she would someday be a mother.

The last five or six years, those comments had become fewer and fewer.

Maia was almost grateful to hear someone make the assumption again. It sounded . . . optimistic.

Maia ate her eggs. She tried to push away the image of her father grieving, his years of anguish and worry finally breaking him, turning his bones brittle as surely as the disease that had taken his ten-year-old son, Xian, wrapped in funeral white.

Maia knew she had to get going, but she didn't want to leave the comfort of the kitchen. She felt safe here, part of the makeshift family of Tres' foundlings.

She thought about her own apartment in Austin, the view of Barton Creek out the kitchen window. She'd only been away from it twenty-four hours, but she had trouble picturing what it looked like. She had even more trouble thinking of it as home.

"Undercover work on the loading docks today," Sam told her. "Be careful nobody finds you out."

"I'll be careful," she promised.

She met Mrs. Loomis' eyes. The older woman smiled as if she'd just seen a photo from her own past—something simple and poignant, with faces of children who had long since grown.

• • •

"IS DR. GAGARIN IN ICU?" MAIA asked, using a random name from the hospital directory.

The hospital receptionist looked up. What she saw: an Asian woman in an expensive black pantsuit, a stethoscope in her pocket and a confident, impatient expression—a woman who was used to having her questions answered. "I don't know, Dr.—"

"Never mind," Maia said. "I'll go up myself."

"I can page—"

"No, thank you. No time."

Maia strode down the hallway to the elevator.

Nobody stopped her.

Maia wasn't surprised. She'd played doctor numerous times. Never once had she been challenged. She liked to think that was because of her great acting skill, but she feared it had more to do with hospital security. They weren't any better than police stations.

Maternity wards were the worst. Maia had already put that on her list of things to worry about, six months from now . . .

The elevator opened on the third floor.

As Maia feared, no police officers were stationed outside Ana DeLeon's room.

Sunday morning, off-duty cops could make big bucks directing traffic for the local churches. It wouldn't have taken much to convince the uniforms to take off this shift.

Maia walked toward Ana's room. Halfway, she froze. At the far end of the hall, by the nurse's station, Etch Hernandez was standing with his back turned, talking to an orderly.

If he'd already done something, if Maia was too late . . .

Morning sickness snaked its way through her stomach. She fought down the nausea and slipped into the room.

Ana's heart monitor showed a strong pulse. Her eyes were closed. She still looked wasted and pale, but the improvement over yesterday was striking.

Her face had some color to it. Her chest rose and fell with regular breathing.

Maia suddenly felt foolish.

Perhaps she'd been wrong about Hernandez. He'd been

here before her. He hadn't done anything. Would he be in the hallway, casually chatting with an orderly, if he was planning murder?

Maia went to the bedside and held Ana's hand. Ana's gold wedding band felt warm against her skin.

Maia prayed Tres had gotten her phone message. It had been a desperate, stupid thing to do—trusting White's daughter, but Maia had been shaken. She'd felt a compulsive need to explain Tres—to protect him. And she'd sensed something in the young woman's voice—a receptiveness. God, if she was wrong . . .

The DNA match would be announced anytime. It wouldn't be long before someone in White's household heard the news.

The pain in Maia's gut was getting worse. She wanted to lie down, curl into a ball, but she couldn't give in to it—especially not *this* morning.

Ana's eyes moved under her lids, as if she were dreaming.

"You'll be okay," Maia told her shakily. "You're a tough lady."

She heard footsteps coming down the hallway.

Maia slipped behind the bathroom door and aimed her cell phone camera through the space between the hinges.

Etch Hernandez came into the room.

He was well dressed as usual—a chocolaty wool suit, teal shirt, mauve silk tie. He regarded the woman on the bed with his usual sad expression, as if he'd simply come as a dear friend. Then he reached in his jacket and took out a syringe and a small vial.

Maia snapped a picture.

Hernandez moved toward Ana's bed. Maia pulled her gun and stepped out of the bathroom. "Lieutenant."

Hernandez turned, his eyes as glassy as a sleepwalker's. He was right next to Ana. The syringe was full.

"I got a nice picture of you about to poison your protégée," Maia said. "Try it and I'm going to blow a hole in your fucking Italian suit."

Hernandez regarded Ana. The needle was three inches from her forearm. "I should've killed you first, Miss Lee. That was a mistake."

"I think we can agree that your priorities are fucked up," Maia said. "Now step away from Ana."

Hernandez focused on a spot in the air, as if he were listening to some other voice. "Miss Lee, you don't understand. I'm not interested in saving my own skin."

"No," Maia said. "You're interested in saving Lucia's memory. And if you don't cap the syringe, I'll tell everyone the truth about Frankie's murder."

She wasn't sure she truly understood until that moment, when his eyes turned cold and bright. "You've shared your thoughts with Navarre and Arguello?"

"*You're* going to do that," she said. "We're going to go see them right now."

"And why should I agree?"

"Because you want the truth to come out. Deep down, you won't be satisfied with someone else taking the blame. Part of you wanted Ana to pick up that cold case. You wanted to hurt her. You wanted Ana to know, Etch."

She'd never addressed him by his first name before, and it seemed to unnerve him.

He lowered the needle. He wiped it with his handkerchief, capped it, put it back in his jacket pocket. "You plan to walk out of here holding a police lieutenant at gunpoint?"

"Not at gunpoint," Maia said. "I'm taking your sidearm and putting mine away. We leave together. If you try anything, I'll break your neck with my bare hands."

•　　•　　•

THEY LEFT THE HOSPITAL TOGETHER. HERNANDEZ was calm. Way too calm. He made no attempt to run or yell for help.

When they got to Maia's BMW, he took the wheel without complaint. Maia got in the passenger's seat and took out her gun. Second time in one weekend, she thought grimly, that she'd had a hostage chauffeur.

She doubted Hernandez would remain compliant once she told him they were going to the White mansion.

She was about to give him his driving directions when her phone rang.

The sound distracted her only for a second, but that was enough. Morning sickness dulled her reflexes. Before she knew what was happening, Hernandez had wrenched the gun out of her hand and was pressing the muzzle under her jaw.

The phone kept ringing.

Maia sat perfectly still, her heart pounding.

"Change of plans, Miss Lee," Hernandez said. "You'll be driving. This is going to end where it began."

Without taking his eyes off her, he managed to find her purse and fish out the phone. He answered it on the fifth ring.

"Mr. Navarre," he said. "What a surprise."

CHAPTER 18

AFTER THE CALL, I DIDN'T CARE MUCH ABOUT THE KITCHEN burning around me, or the men with guns outside. All I cared about was getting out, getting to Maia.

"Twenty minutes?" Ralph cursed Etch Hernandez with Spanish epithets even I had never heard. "That's impossible, *vato*."

"Bigger fire," I advised.

We splashed more brandy, piled on grocery bags and washrags and cardboard boxes, and in no time we had a nice blaze going along the back wall. Soon the curtains and the back door were in flames.

Ralph smashed out a window with his baseball bat. He threw a Molotov cocktail toward the driveway and was rewarded with a loud BA-ROOM and some surprised yelps from the men outside.

"The kitchen's on fire!" one of them yelled.

Full points for powers of observation.

They banged on the back door, found it too hot to touch.

"Around to the front!" somebody yelled.

Perfect.

The guys on the interior door hammered away with new-found zeal. The refrigerator rattled and rocked.

"Another few seconds," Ralph said.

"Smoke," I warned. "No time."

I could barely see. Forget breathing.

Ralph climbed onto the kitchen sink. He kicked open the only window that wasn't in flames and jumped. I was right behind him.

The diversion almost worked. At least, there was no one waiting to shoot us as we crashed through a pomegranate bush and tumbled onto the back lawn.

We wove between banquet tables, trying to avoid broken champagne glasses and soggy paper plates of leftover food.

We were just passing the pavilion tent, about halfway to the woods, when Alex Cole yelled, "Freeze!"

He had anticipated our plan well enough to position himself on the back veranda of the house. He'd exchanged his Krispy Kreme doughnuts for an automatic assault rifle. Even from halfway across the yard, I was pretty sure a full clip would turn us into Swiss cheese.

Ralph dropped his baseball bat. I lowered my gun. I couldn't bring myself to drop it. Not yet.

Alex smiled. He should've shot us immediately, but he was

too busy enjoying the moment, surveying us as if we were two more fixtures on the estate that would soon be his.

"Come on over," he called amiably. "Let's talk."

Smoke boiled from the kitchen windows, making a black twister that stretched into the winter sky.

Behind Alex, the glass doors opened. Two mobsters wheeled out a very annoyed-looking Guy White in a hospital chair. Madeleine stood behind him, still in her painting clothes, still looking stunned.

I called, "Good morning, Mr. White."

Alex turned involuntarily.

Mr. White snapped, "Watch *them,* you idiot!"

That moment of surprise was all we needed. Ralph and I dove through the doorway of the pavilion tent and hit the ground as the assault rifle opened fire, ripping through the cloth sides of the tent, shattering punch bowls and glasses.

The firing stopped.

My ears were ringing, but, miraculously, Ralph and I both seemed to be unharmed.

Mr. White was wheezing, "—thousand-dollar rental tent! Put that damn rifle away!"

Alex: "But—"

"Go get them, you idiot! Madeleine, you, too!"

Ralph and I were surrounded by broken glass ornaments and smashed finger sandwiches. Red punch made a waterfall off the edges of the tablecloth.

"Go out the back," Ralph told me. "I'll distract them."

"They'll kill you."

"*Vato,* you got to get to Maia—"

"No, Ralph. We leave together. Come on."

I didn't wait for an argument. I ran for the back exit, but before we could bust through, the tent flap opened. I found myself staring down the barrel of Madeleine White's pistol.

"Drop it," she said.

I couldn't think of anything better to do than comply. I set the .38 on a folding chair, in the middle of a platter of shrimp.

"Madeleine," I said. "Thirty feet, we hit the woods and we're gone. Maia is in trouble. Please."

She stared at me bitterly, as if I were offering her an impossible choice—a decision where all her options were fatal.

"Step aside," I pleaded. "Five-second head start. Anything."

"I have a better idea," said a voice behind us. Alex was standing at the front of the tent, his rifle aimed at my chest. "Why don't you two come with me, and we'll start the morning over again."

● ● ●

I DISLIKE EXECUTIONS. ESPECIALLY MY OWN.

Guy White sat in his portable wheelchair in the gazebo, before the giant Christmas tree. He listened in deadly silence as I told him about my phone conversation with Lieutenant Hernandez.

Alex stood at his boss's side, assault rifle ready. Two other guards, plus Madeleine. Our odds of survival were somewhere south of hopeless.

I noticed small details with perfect clarity. White had an oxygen tube strapped around his nose, but it wasn't plugged into anything. There was a toothpaste stain on his burgundy Turkish bathrobe. His white flannel pajamas were missing the middle button. In the morning light, his skin was translucent, every vein in his hands and face inked in perfect detail.

The air smelled of smoke. The column billowing up from the house could probably be seen for miles. Sirens wailed in the distance.

I'd lost the bear slippers somewhere between the kitchen and the gazebo. Under my feet, the frozen grass felt like ice shards.

"You expect me to believe this," Mr. White said at last. "You expect me to believe a police lieutenant—"

"He has my girlfriend." It took every ounce of my will not to run, to make a mad dash across the lawn. "He's going to kill her. We have to leave *now*."

"How foolish do you think I am?" White's voice trembled with rage. He looked at Ralph. "Why did you kill my son?"

Alex Cole cleared his throat. "Sir, the police'll be here any minute. If we're gonna take care of these—"

"I want to hear," White said. "I want to hear his reasons."

"Sir," Alex insisted, "the house—"

"Let it burn."

The house obeyed that order. Flames flickered in the second-story windows.

White stared at Ralph, waiting.

If Ralph was scared for his life, he didn't show it. His feet were flecked with grass, his sweatpants sooty, his T-shirt peppered with shrapnel holes and red punch stains. Bits of broken glass glinted in his hair. But he stood up straight, looked Mr. White in the eyes.

"I didn't kill Frankie, *patrón*," he said. "You did that."

The old man's tiny supply of blood collected in his cheeks. "How dare you."

"Maybe you didn't hold the murder weapon," Ralph said, "but that doesn't matter. Frankie died because he hated you.

He told me what was going to happen. I just didn't understand."

"I trusted you—"

"To save him. I know. Couldn't be done. Couple of nights before he was murdered, Frankie came into the pawnshop. He'd been drinking. He said he'd had an argument with you. Said you were trying to arrange a marriage for him."

White closed his eyes, his face like paper. "It was for his own good."

"Frankie confessed to me about killing those women. He said he couldn't control the anger. He wished you'd sent him away, like you did Madeleine. He said Madeleine was the lucky one to get away from you."

Madeleine stared at Ralph. White's guards all wore the same expression—as if they'd just stepped into a nest of rattlesnakes.

"Frankie wanted out," Ralph said. "He was going to keep killing until somebody killed him or you were forced to send him away. And you know what the worst is? I thought about doing it. About killing him. After he told me about the women . . . I was thinking to myself: I might have to do it. I even thought Mission Road would be the best place."

Ralph looked at Madeleine, his eyes full of sympathy, as if she were the one with the terminal disease. "I'm sorry, *chica*. Some people can't be saved. I've kept that in mind ever since Frankie died. Every time I had to hurt somebody, kill somebody—I pictured Frankie. And I pictured your father. I imagine you felt the same way."

The specks of paint on Madeleine's face, the streak in her hair, made me think of the portrait in Frankie's closet—a twelve-year-old girl, composed entirely from shades of blue.

The sirens got closer. We were losing too much time. Even if I left right now, I wasn't sure I could make it to Maia.

"I should kill you," Mr. White said. With his translucent skin and the air tube around his nose, he looked like some sort of ancient, disoriented catfish, brought to the surface for the first time in its long life.

"Not going to solve anything, *patrón*," Ralph said. "Let us go. Let us help Maia."

Alex raised his rifle. "Let me, sir."

White said nothing. His eyes were colorless in the morning light.

At that moment, I knew Alex would make the call for him. We would die. As soon as he shot Ralph and me, Alex Cole would come into his inheritance. He would become Guy White's willpower, his voice, his decision-maker.

I was bracing to charge—to risk pushing Alex down and making a break for it—when Madeleine said, "Alex, put down the gun."

Guy White had trouble focusing on his daughter. "Madeleine?" he said hazily. "Go to your room."

"My room is on fire, Daddy."

It was the first time I'd heard her call him anything but *sir*.

She took a set of car keys out of her pocket, threw them to Ralph. "Go on. Help your friend."

"*What?*" Alex protested.

"Madeleine." Mr. White's face was weary and pale. "You have no right—"

She wheeled on him so fast his voice faltered.

"I—have—every—right." She turned toward the guards. "My father isn't well. I'll watch after him. You two go to the front yard. Wait for the police."

One of them said, "But—"

"He isn't well," Madeleine repeated, "so you're going to listen to me. I am his daughter. I am responsible. Understand?"

"These men," Mr. White said, staring at Ralph and me. His tone sounded watery, petulant. "They burned my house, they killed my son . . ."

He seemed to be trying to summon up his anger, but he couldn't do it. His thoughts trailed off, lost in the smoke. He gazed at his mansion, now burning with an audible roar.

Madeleine raised an eyebrow at the guards. They got the message. They made a wide arc around Guy White's daughter and left the gazebo, heading toward the front yard.

"The keys are for the white Lexus," Madeleine told us. "Hurry."

"This is bullshit," Alex growled. "They move an inch—"

"Alex," Madeleine said, "you will stand down. Arguello, Navarre—go."

Emergency lights flashed against the trees, maybe a block away.

We had no more time.

We left the gazebo, jogged over the frozen grass. Every step, I expected to be shot between my shoulder blades. I knew the only thing keeping us alive was Madeleine's sheer force of will.

Somehow, her willpower held. We made it to the corner of the house. We found the white Lexus. By the time the police vehicles and the fire truck came screaming up Contour Drive, we were a block away, a column of smoke rising behind us from what used to be the White kingdom.

CHAPTER 19

HERNANDEZ AND MAIA WERE WAITING on the shoulder of Mission
Road.

Hernandez sat on the hood of Maia's car. He was immaculate as always in a chocolate-colored suit. No anger in his
eyes—just a chill, dangerous calm.

Maia stood two feet in front of him. She wore her black
wool pantsuit, a Band-Aid on the cut under her eye. Hernandez
and she might have been mistaken for a rich couple, broken
down on the side of the road on their way home from church.

I didn't see a gun on Hernandez, but that meant nothing.
Maia wouldn't be standing there if she saw any chance of
overpowering him.

"Plan?" Ralph asked me.

My throat felt raw. Neither of us was armed. Madeleine's charity had not extended as far as providing firearms.

We were dealing with a killer, in a place where he had killed before.

"It's you he wants," I told Ralph. "Stay in the car. Let me talk to him."

"He'll kill Maia."

A small hot wire threaded its way through my chest. I'd already decided I would have to take down Hernandez, one way or the other. If it came to Ralph or me getting hurt, there couldn't be any choice. Ralph had a family.

But Maia being here . . .

"We go talk to him," I said. "If it gets bad . . ."

We both knew there was no backup plan. We couldn't call the police. Sunday morning, a cold winter day on Mission Road—there would be no witnesses, no passersby, no help.

We got out of the car.

When we got within twenty feet of Hernandez, he held up his hand—*stop.*

"You're late," he said.

"Tres, go," Maia pleaded. "Get away."

She clutched her stomach. Her face was ashen. I realized why she wasn't trying to fight Hernandez: She was in pain, close to collapsing.

I wanted to run to her. I wanted to get her safely into the car. Most of all, I wanted to pulverize Hernandez—to do to him what he'd done to Frankie White.

"How'd it happen, Etch?" I asked. "Did Frankie say something to you when you pulled him over? Something so bad you had to destroy him?"

"Franklin White deserved to die, Navarre. Surely we can agree on that."

"Tres," Maia said, "you don't understand—"

Hernandez grabbed the back of her neck. From under his jacket he produced a .357 Magnum, identical to Ralph's. "No need to confuse him, Miss Lee. Arguello, come here."

I wanted to tell Ralph not to go, but my voice wouldn't work. All I could do was stare at the muzzle of the gun against Maia's throat.

Ralph stepped forward. "What've you done to my wife now?"

"Nothing yet," Hernandez admitted. "Miss Lee interrupted me. But there's time. Ana won't be conscious for several hours at best."

"Let Maia go," Ralph said.

"As soon as you join me," Hernandez said. "Right here by the car, please."

"Ralph, no," I said.

I thought about a story Maia had once told me, about a killer in San Francisco who'd controlled eight people with a Smith & Wesson .22. He'd directed his victims to tie each other up. Then one by one he shot each in the head. They could've overpowered him easily. Instead, they followed orders. They trusted the man's reasonable tone. Maia and I had promised each other we would never allow anyone to control us like that.

And yet there I stood, frozen, as Ralph walked toward the BMW. He stopped where Hernandez told him, next to the left headlight, just out of reach of Maia.

"Now, Miss Lee," Hernandez said, "go to your boyfriend . . . I'm sorry, your *client*."

He gave her a shove. She stumbled forward. When she got close, I pulled her to me, hugged her tight. Her skin was warm. Her hair smelled of cinnamon.

"Stay back when it starts," I murmured in her ear. "Please."

"Tres—"

"Please."

"What now, Hernandez?" Ralph spread his hands. "You shoot me like you shot Ana?"

Hernandez's expression turned almost apologetic. "I thought about it. I truly did. But you know what? It'll work better if I let you live."

He turned the gun on Maia and me. "Start practicing your story, Arguello. I killed Frankie White. I killed these two with the same gun I used to shoot your wife. I'll be amused to hear you try to convince Kelsey."

"Lieutenant." Maia's voice quavered. "This isn't what Lucia would want."

Hernandez's eyes were glassy with self-loathing. He looked the same way Dr. Allen Vale had, standing on his estranged wife's front lawn, just before he fired his shotgun. "Don't talk to me about Lucia, Miss Lee. She never got what she wanted. She never had a chance."

"Let them go," Ralph said. "You want me, let them go."

"I didn't want you next to me so I could kill you, Arguello," Hernandez assured him. "I brought you here to get the angle right. You'll shoot them from here, you see, because they were about to betray you. They were about to turn you over to me. This is a good spot for betrayals, Arguello. One of the best."

Wind rustled in the live oaks. Frozen leaves crackled like glass. I imagined Frankie White standing here in the final moments of his life. The last thing he would've seen: a stretch of barbed wire, a stand of cactus, a crumbling stretch of blacktop.

A car engine roared somewhere in the distance, the squeal of tires back toward South Alamo. I knew it couldn't have anything to do with us. There was no luck along this stretch of road. Too many lives had ended here.

"It'll be your word against mine," Hernandez told Ralph. "Try convincing Kelsey. Tell him I'm going back to the hospital later to kill your wife. I'll love to hear you plead."

I squeezed Maia's hand. I would shield her as best I could, put myself in front of her. Maybe I could charge Hernandez, close the fifteen feet between us, throw off his aim.

The car engine got louder behind us.

"You're going to jail, Arguello," Hernandez said. "Your daughter will grow up without you, knowing her father is a monster. You'll live without friends, without your wife. You'll have a taste of what my life has been like."

"Etch," Maia said. "You didn't kill Frankie."

I didn't know what she meant, but Hernandez's jaw tightened. "You think like Ana, Miss Lee. I'm afraid that's why you need to die first."

He raised the gun toward Maia's heart and I charged, knowing I would die.

Fifteen feet. No chance.

But Ralph was a lot closer.

He tackled Hernandez and both men slammed against the hood of the BMW. The .357 exploded—a thunderclap in the cold morning air.

I crashed into them, tearing Hernandez away from Ralph, shoving the lieutenant to the ground. I slammed my fist into his nose and the Magnum skittered across the asphalt.

"Tres!" I heard Maia scream.

I turned around. Ralph stumbled backward. He collapsed against the barbed wire fence, pulled his knees up to his chest. Maia screamed again.

A shriek of tires. A black sedan fishtailed to a stop behind us.

Kelsey and a young plainclothes officer got out.

The younger guy drew his piece, aimed it at me. "Step away from the lieutenant!"

I was too dazed to wonder what they were doing here. I was too dazed to move.

"Now!" The young guy's hands turned white on the handle of his gun.

Kelsey scanned the scene. He took in Ralph, Maia, the Magnum in the middle of the street.

"Stand down," he ordered his companion. "Call an ambulance."

"Sir?"

"Do it!" Kelsey barked. He marched toward us, grabbed the lieutenant and pulled him into a sitting position.

Hernandez's nose was broken. There was a lightning bolt of blood under his left nostril.

"Kelsey? How—"

"Madeleine White," Kelsey said tightly. "She called with an interesting story, suggested you might be here."

"You believed her. You came with no SWAT team."

"No, sir. I was hoping—"

"You could resolve things without force."

"Yes, sir."

"Full of surprises."

Kelsey looked back at his colleague. "Bring me some

handcuffs." He looked at me grimly. "You, take care of your friend."

"What?"

"*Now,* goddamn it," Kelsey growled. "The ambulance is coming."

Only then did I come out of my shock enough to realize what had happened.

Maia was kneeling next to Ralph. His face was coated with sweat. He was holding his gut. There was blood between the cracks of his fingers.

I rushed over to him, reached instinctively to move his hands, but Maia said, "Don't, Tres."

"*Vato*—"

"Damn it, Ralph," I said, my voice cracking. "Why did you do that?"

He raised his eyebrows. *"Qué más?"*

What else?

I imagined we were back at graduation night, sitting in the Brackenridge Park Skyride, Ralph trying to convince Frankie and me that anything was possible, trying to sell us on his crazy dreams as we balanced precariously a hundred feet in the air.

"*Vato,* tell Ana . . ."

"Don't talk," I said.

I heard a distant siren, or maybe it was just my desire to hear one. The ice on the road melted against my jeans, soaking into the denim.

"Remember what you promised," he croaked.

"You're going to get better," I told him. "And when you do, I'm going to kick your ass, you hear me?"

He gazed at the bare branches overhead. He seemed to be

looking for something. Behind us, I heard Kelsey snapping plastic cuffs on his superior officer, reading Hernandez his rights.

I put my hand on Ralph's forehead. His skin was cool and damp.

By the time I was sure I heard a siren in the distance, Ralph's eyes seemed to have found something to focus on—something small and bright and remarkable, far above us.

CHAPTER 20

A WEEK LATER, MAIA SAT IN ANA'S HOSPITAL ROOM, WATCHING Lucia Jr. sleep against her mother's breast. Tres sat next to her while Ralph's relatives buzzed around, trying to make Ana more comfortable. Ralph's niece fussed with the flower arrangements, which had been arriving by the crateful. Ralph's sister was sure Ana needed more pillows. Ralph's cousin tried to convince Ana she was ready for the tamales he'd brought.

"Thank you, José," Ana said weakly. "But it's a little soon for venison."

Every time her focus started to drift, the bustle of the relatives increased. Ana's attention was immediately needed. Which sympathy cards to keep? Which toys for the baby's stocking? Which outfit would Ana wear home?

Maia understood this approach to tragedy, so much like

269

her own family's. Grief was a crack to be filled, a stain to be scrubbed out. Don't think about it. Don't talk about it. Keep busy. Keep working.

Somehow the baby slept through the commotion, which Maia found reassuring. The baby would have enough to contend with. She'd have years of commotion and grief ahead. It was good that she was a sound sleeper.

Tres reached out and stroked the baby's hair.

His face was sallow. He'd lost too much weight in the last week. He looked like he was recovering from a bad case of pneumonia.

At least he hadn't distanced himself from Maia. He'd asked her to stay with him, not go back to Austin for a while. They spent every night together. Every afternoon, they came here to be with Ana, keep the relatives at bay, talk about Ralph, or just watch the long squares of winter light slide across the tile floor.

Ana touched Tres' hand. "Go on. Your appointment is waiting."

"It's only the police," he said. "They can wait."

"No. Go on. You can, um . . ."

She rolled her eyes toward Ralph's cousin, who was trying to pass out tamale samples to the nurses.

"Right," Tres sighed. Then he announced to the room, "Come on, everybody, Ana needs her rest."

There were protests, hugs and kisses, some last-minute arranging of flowers and cards.

Tres didn't look happy to leave either, though Maia knew his last round of meetings with the DA wouldn't be so bad.

Charges would be considered. Tres' PI license might still be revoked. But the true killer, Hernandez, was behind bars.

In the end, he had confessed to everything freely, including Franklin White's murder. He planned to plead guilty. Much to his lawyer's exasperation, Hernandez had not even bargained for a plea agreement that might spare his life.

Hernandez was unlikely to face retribution from the White family. According to Madeleine, her father had taken a turn for the worse over the last week. He was now confined to his bed twenty-four hours a day, allowed no visitors except nurses. Madeleine offered no comment to the press about Hernandez's arrest, but rumors were flying that she had other things on her mind. A purge was underway. Madeleine was swiftly consolidating control of her father's organization. A fresh slew of bodies had begun turning up in the San Antonio River or dumped in the fields off Mission Road. One of the victims was a mobster named Alex Cole. He'd been shot through the forehead at point-blank range.

With all that for SAPD to worry about, with all the bad press about the head of homicide being a killer himself, felony charges against Tres for aiding and abetting a fugitive would do no one any good, legally or politically. The city didn't want any more publicity to come out of this affair than it had already gotten. Nor did it want to face scrutiny for the false DNA match that had led to Ralph Arguello's murder. Eventually, Tres would go free.

Ralph's sister gently picked up baby Lucia, who fussed in her sleep but allowed herself to be resettled against her aunt's shoulder.

At the door, Tres looked back. "Maia, you coming?"

Maia met Ana's eyes. An understanding passed between them.

"You go ahead," Maia said. "We have some girl talk."

Tres hesitated.

"It's okay," Ana promised him. "I won't keep her long."

•   •   •

MAIA HELPED ANA DRINK SOME CHICKEN broth.

After a few spoonfuls, Ana sat back, her head cratered in the pillows.

As often happened in quiet moments, Maia felt a fissure expanding in her chest—the raw, painful absence of Ralph.

Before she could lose her nerve, she said, "I've got something for you."

From the bag at her side, she pulled the photo album she'd found in Lucia DeLeon's garage—Ana's baby book.

Ana took the album, ran her fingers over the cover. "You looked through my mother's things in the garage."

"Yes."

"What'd you decide?"

"The same thing you did, I imagine."

Ana studied her wistfully. "You're pregnant, aren't you?"

"You're changing the subject."

"Oh, boy." Ana sighed. "That's a yes."

She opened the baby book to the first page, traced her fingers over her mother's picture—Lucia Sr., looking battered and exhausted and terribly young in her hospital bed, her parents holding newborn Ana.

Maia remembered the look of Ralph's face. He had died with his head against her shoulder. She'd felt his last breath against her forearm.

It wasn't fair. A childish protest, but Maia couldn't help it.

He'd taken one bullet. He'd gotten attention faster than Ana had. He should have lived.

The doctors talked about tissue damage. They talked about point-blank range. The only thing Maia really understood was that he'd absorbed the shot meant for her, kept the damage inside himself, shielded her completely. And he'd left Ana to raise a child alone, just as Ana's mother had done.

Ana turned a page in the album—a picture of her first Christmas, her grandfather holding her up to catch an ornament.

"How old was your mother?" Maia asked.

"When she had me?" Ana murmured. "Just barely twenty. Nineteen when . . ."

"When she was raped," Maia finished.

"She never admitted it until I was in high school, but by then I'd figured it out. I didn't understand the whole story . . . the truth . . . until I started looking into Frankie White's death."

She stared at the yellowing pictures of herself as a baby, eating yams, opening presents, grabbing at her grandfather's spectacles.

"How did your mother meet Guy White?" Maia asked.

"They must've met at one of the clubs down on South Alamo." Ana looked almost relieved to be concentrating on it, as if it felt good to slip into her professional self, to hold her life at the distance of a case file. "I figure White would've been about thirty-two. My mom was nineteen. She was pretty. Willful. She wasn't afraid to talk to men. Perfect prey."

"She didn't tell anyone that White raped her."

"No. I'm not sure she even knew who White was at first, but she would've found out. He was on the rise. He was getting a reputation as a man you didn't cross. She would've had no choice except to stay quiet."

"She kept you."

"She kept me."

"White never knew?"

Ana gazed down at the photo of her grandparents. "My mother tried to avoid Guy White after she became a cop. The sad thing was—I don't think he even remembered her. I'm sure *I* never occurred to him."

"Your mother told Etch about the rape," Maia guessed, "once they got to be friends."

"They were more than friends," Ana corrected. "But, yes. She must have. Etch loved her. For him, I was always a reminder of what White had done to her."

"And when Frankie White started victimizing women just as his father had—"

"It brought back all my mother's worst memories. She was a wreck. Her drinking got worse. I didn't know why at the time. Now, it makes sense. When I started looking into the Franklin White murder, I thought I understood. Etch had killed Frankie, out of revenge for my mother. He loved her. He hated what Guy White had done to her. I figured my mother had committed suicide with alcohol because she knew what Etch had done, and that knowledge was killing her. It wasn't until Etch shot me . . . Something in his eyes told me I'd put the case together wrong."

"So you know."

Ana stared at the ceiling. Her heart monitor beeped steadily. "My mother killed Frankie White. She had the patrol car. The area Frankie cruised was on the way from her house to the Pig Stand. She must've pulled Frankie over. He must've said . . . something. I don't know. He grabbed her, enough to scratch her. It must've brought back the rape, years of anger and fear she couldn't share with anyone. She lost control."

"And Hernandez covered for her."

Ana closed the photo album. "For years. Too perfectly. He protected her reputation so well she never got help. But it was my fault, too. I was afraid. I couldn't stand what was happening to her. I stayed away, and she died without me there."

Maia took DeLeon's hand. It felt as warm and fragile as a bird. "Your mother wouldn't blame you."

"I don't know. I hope not. She raised me alone, and . . . she was good to me. But distant. Terrified of love. I was so determined not to repeat her mistakes, when I met Ralph . . ."

Maia felt the fissure opening inside her again. She could only imagine how bad it was for Ana—Ralph's absence a gaping canyon, every word, every thought a walk along the precipice.

"What will you do?" Maia asked.

"Medical leave. Six months. I'm taking it all to be with Lucia."

Maia had to do a momentary mental shift to remember which Lucia Ana was referring to. "You could retire with full pay, full benefits."

Ana shook her head. "I'm going back to the job. I have to. It's part of me."

"And Ralph's shops?"

"I'm keeping them," Ana said with no hesitation. "Some of Ralph's cousins have offered to help out. But I think . . . I think that's what Ralph would've wanted. He worked so hard for so many years. I don't think he ever wanted the shops to leave the family."

Maia felt dizzy thinking about the challenges Ana was facing. Guilt pressed against her ribs.

And yet Ana sounded strangely confident. She would have

enough money. She'd be surrounded by Ralph's relatives whether she liked it or not—all the cousins and nephews and siblings Ralph had quietly helped over the years, now taking Ana as one of their own, another orphan in need of a family.

More than that, Maia saw a resilience in Ana's eyes that was nothing like the old photographs of her mother. Maybe Ana would not be raising her daughter quite the same way.

"What about you?" Ana asked.

"Me?"

"The pregnancy. Are you close with your mom?"

"Male relatives," Maia managed. It seemed selfish, ridiculous to open up her own problems in the face of what Ana was going through. "An uncle raised me, mostly."

Ana seemed to sense there was more. She waited.

"My mother died in childbirth," Maia said. "Having me. The women in my family have a tendency to die in childbirth."

"And now you're pregnant."

"I'm scared shitless, Ana."

"Things are better now than they were in our mothers' generation. Medically. In a lot of ways."

"There's more."

It was the first time Maia had ever explained it to anyone. She had trouble finding the words, but something about Ana's grief, the fact that she was already hurting, somehow made it easier for Maia to talk.

When she was done, Ana didn't offer any consolations.

They sat together, Ana in her bed, Maia at her side. Steam curled off the chicken broth.

"That's a lot to consider," Ana admitted. "Are you going to have the baby?"

Maia said nothing.

"What about Tres?" Ana asked. "Would he help?"

"Yes. Maybe. I don't know."

"You'll have to tell him soon. I mean, what, you're about six weeks along?"

"Eight and a half."

"Wow." Ana folded her hands over the photo album, rested her head against her pillow. "Being a mother is the best thing I've ever done, in case you're wondering. I can't . . . I can't pretend I have your concerns. But Lucia is the best thing in my life."

"What about Guy White?" Maia asked. "Are you going to confront him?"

Ana's eyes shone clear and intense. "Maybe when I'm stronger. I can't do it now. The idea of having his blood inside me . . ."

Maia nodded. "I'll keep it our secret."

Ana turned up her palm, gave Maia's hand a squeeze.

"I'll need the rest," Ana said. "I'll need time just to be a mother for a while."

Maia thought back to her brief baby-sitting stint with Lucia Jr. "I wouldn't call that rest."

Ana put her hand in a square of winter sunlight that was sliding across her bedspread. "You got that right, sister. You got that right."

JULY 14, 1987

THE MERCEDES PULSED RED AND WHITE in Lucia's emergency lights.

Despite all her years on the force, her courage wavered when Frankie White got out of his car.

He looked so much like his father, especially in this place, on this isolated road.

She watched him trudge toward her patrol unit, his blond hair and white shirt ghostly in the dark.

He was almost at her car door, intolerably close, before she got out to meet him.

"Well?" he demanded.

"Who's in the car, Frankie?"

He glared at her as if she were a traffic signal—some annoying mechanism of society. He probably didn't remember or care that they'd met before, that she'd warned him to stay away from her beat. Why should he? He'd been dealing with cops for years. They all called him by his first name. He was like their goddamn foster child.

"Nobody's in the car," he said. "I'm alone."

Lucia glanced at the tinted windows of the Mercedes. She couldn't see anyone inside, but back on South Alamo, when she'd first spotted him, she thought she saw a silhouette in his passenger's seat—a young woman. When Frankie had turned on Mission Road, she'd had no choice but to follow.

"You don't mind if I check it out." She started forward.

He surprised her by grabbing her forearm. She yanked it away, felt his fingernails rip into her skin.

"*Back off.*" Her heart was pounding. "Kneel on the ground. *Now.*"

"Go away, lady," Frankie told her, not moving. "Get out of here while you still can."

"You threatening me? A police officer?"

His eyes were icy with rage. "The police are a fucking joke. You couldn't arrest my father. What makes you think you can touch me?"

He pushed her shoulders, hard enough to send her staggering backward a few steps.

She drew her nightstick.

"*Stop.*" Her voice sounded shrill, even to herself.

She knew she should follow procedure. She had a violent subject. She should call for backup. She should not be arguing with him.

But her training was dissolving—the heavy blue thread she'd used to stitch her life together was swiftly coming unraveled. She was nineteen again—a young girl being shown that her power was nothing but an illusion.

"Get on the ground," she ordered. She heard the wobble in her voice and hated it.

"Fuck you."

"Do it, Frankie."

"*You* get on the ground, bitch."

Lucia's arm was bleeding. He'd broken the skin.

So much like his father, yet the anger in his eyes was more volatile—more like what Lucia saw when she looked in the mirror, when she thought about Mission Road.

You couldn't arrest my father.

Frankie turned. He started back toward his car.

He would drive away, leave her standing there. She was meaningless to him. The years with the badge, the years building herself back up from a thousand shattered pieces, they meant nothing.

She was a girl again, abandoned in a cold ditch, her back snagged on a line of barbed wire, the orange moon glowing above her through the naked branches. Another man was walking away—a man in a beige suit who had just crushed her soul like a balsa wood toy.

Later, she would not remember raising the nightstick, but she felt the crack of wood against bone reverberate in her fingers. Franklin White crumpled.

Her rage left her. Years of police officer composure shed off her like winter clothes. She was alone, horrified.

Afterward, talking to Etch, she would realize how many mistakes she'd made. She would try to piece together what really happened and wonder if she was going crazy. Had she only hit him once? Hadn't she left the murder weapon with her fingerprints on the handle?

At the time, she had no thought but getting away, running from that place.

She dropped the bloodied nightstick and fled.

CHAPTER 21

THE STATE OF TEXAS LET ME KEEP MY PI LICENSE.

My less-than-heartening conclusion: They looked at how many times it had almost gotten me killed and decided that letting me keep my job was the best possible punishment.

As for Guy White, his only punishment was living his final months under his daughter's care. Madeleine got him a private nurse, allowed no visitors without her permission. The fire damage Ralph and I caused to the White house was not that extensive, but Madeleine announced that the mock-presidential mansion which had been the symbol of her family's power for a generation would be razed by New Year's. She would rebuild to better suit her tastes.

A new police lieutenant was shuffled into Etch Hernandez's homicide position, but Detective Kelsey became the true

281

power in the department. He moved into Ana's office. Word was he'd make sergeant by the end of the month. Given that the department had few options for positive publicity, they were using Kelsey as a hero—proof that the SAPD would not tolerate wrongdoing within its ranks, even if it meant busting a superior officer.

The real support of the rank and file went to Ana DeLeon. A cruiser was almost always parked in front of her house—some colleague, making sure she and the baby were okay. Gift baskets, home-cooked dinners, offers for baby-sitting poured in. The police fraternal organization set up a college scholarship fund for Lucia Jr.

Once, and only once, Johnny Zapata sent his lackey Ignacio around to talk to Ana, to see if she would sell off Ralph's pawnshops. Within forty-eight hours, the SAPD had found reasons to shut down all of Zapata's front businesses. Ignacio was tossed in jail on several outstanding warrants. Madeleine White personally visited Zapata's mother at Mission San José to let her know that her son was bothering a defenseless widow who happened to be a close friend of the White family.

Johnny Shoes got the message. Ana never heard from him again.

As for Ralph's legacy, nobody, even the cops, had a negative word to say about him. He'd given his life to stop the man who shot his wife. He was a hero. Who had ever doubted that Ana's marriage to him had been the right choice?

I kept waiting for the shock to wear off. I kept busy, took new clients, spent a lot of time with Maia. I knew the pain was somewhere inside, waiting to rip me apart, but my heart felt like it had been given a shot of morphine.

I drove past Ralph's old childhood home, now occupied by

another enormous family. I brought marigolds to San Fernando Cemetery, where Ralph's simple gray tombstone stood next to his mother's, near a spot where we'd once had lunch during *Día de los Muertos*. I visited Sunken Gardens, the Blanco Café, the stadium at Alamo Heights High School—all the places that had defined our friendship. I kept remembering Ralph's irreverent grin, his wisecracks, the way he treated the world as a dangerous toy.

And every day I talked to Ana DeLeon, until eventually I got up my nerve to ask her advice about a problem.

• • •

CHRISTMAS EVENING, I PUT TISH HINOJOSA'S "Arbolito" on the stereo.

The Southtown house smelled like homemade tamales—a gift from some of our neighbors. I hadn't had the heart to tell them I could no longer tolerate the smell of steamed venison and *masa* without thinking of Guy White.

Mrs. Loomis, miracle worker that she was, had decorated the house, bought a ten-foot Scotch pine for the living room, and cooked us all turkey dinner.

Sam still had a bandaged ear, but otherwise he seemed in a good mood. He and I had decorated the tree. We'd made *ojos de dios* out of string and Popsicle sticks to keep away evil spirits. I got a bunch of small frames and helped Sam make ornaments with pictures of his relatives. We made one for Ralph, which Sam seemed happy to add to his collection.

Santa Claus brought Robert Johnson a new scratching post, which he sniffed disdainfully. Then he jumped under the wrapping paper and got crazy eyes.

Sam got a bigger-caliber water gun. Mrs. Loomis got a raise and a new set of kitchen knives, since she couldn't stand to keep the cleaver she'd used on Titus Roe. She protested that I couldn't afford either luxury.

"Don't worry about it," I said, and tried to smile confidently.

I told Maia not to open her present yet.

She gave me a funny look, but set the poorly wrapped shoebox aside.

"After dinner," I said, and gestured with my eyes toward the front porch.

•   •   •

WE LEFT MRS. LOOMIS AND SAM in the living room, drinking spiked eggnog and getting sentimental about Nat King Cole.

Maia, the party pooper, was nursing a mug of herbal tea.

She leaned against the porch rail. "Thirty years in America, and I still don't get Christmas."

"You decorate a tree," I said. "Spend a month shopping for crap nobody wants. Pretend there's a fat guy in red velvet who flies around the world. What's to get?"

"Thanks for clearing it up."

Maia's unopened present sat next to me on the rail. I tried to get up my nerve to say what I needed to say. "Hey, uh, Maia . . ."

She looked at me hesitantly.

". . . I know you're pregnant."

Her eyes were amber, beautiful and immensely sad.

An electric current arced through my chest.

She folded her hands around her tea mug, looked out at South Alamo Street. In the window seat of the café across the street, an old couple was having dinner, dressed in their church best. They must've been eighty-something. They were holding hands.

"How'd you figure it out?" she asked.

"The night at the Whites' party, you mentioned your mom. I kept thinking about that. And the way you'd been acting. Besides, I'm a detective."

"I'm sorry." Her eyes were glistening. "I'm really messed up about it."

I felt like I'd been ripped out of my own life and placed in someone else's. I was used to solving family problems for other people. I was used to custody battles, adoptions gone wrong, unfit parents, delinquent kids—all the horrors of parenthood from the outside.

This . . . this was like reading through a mirror. Everything felt backward.

I wondered if Ralph had felt this way when he learned he was going to be a father. I realized I'd never be able to ask him.

Suddenly, the morphine wore off. My best friend was dead. I'd spent the last two years of his life trying to push him away.

You want to understand somebody, Ralph had once told me, *look at what he's willing to give up.*

I steadied myself against the porch rail.

"Tres?" Maia asked.

"I'm all right."

She studied my face, knowing damn well I wasn't all right.

Across the street, the older couple toasted each other with glasses of champagne. Nat King Cole kept singing from the living room.

"I want this baby," Maia told me. "But it's dangerous."

"Better health care," I managed. "The doctors are good."

"No. There's something else. My brother."

"You don't have any siblings."

"Present tense, that's true. But . . . I did. An older brother. He died at age ten. He never saw a doctor. We couldn't get good treatment because of who my family was—warlords, landowners, traitors. We didn't even know what was wrong with him. He was frail, clumsy. He broke bones a lot. Finally his body just . . . quit on him. Since then, since I came to America, I've figured out what he had."

I was silent for a verse of "We Three Kings." "Muscular dystrophy?"

"I've been talking to doctors," Maia said. "It passes through the mother's side, even if the mother doesn't have it. A boy child would have about a fifty percent chance of inheriting the disease."

"And . . . is it a boy?"

"I don't know yet, Tres. I kind of don't want to know."

Maia's present was still next to me on the porch rail. I stared at the green bow and said nothing.

"You didn't choose to be a dad, Tres. You're not obligated to help. Especially not . . ."

She didn't finish, but I understood: *Especially not after Ralph's death.*

I slid her the present. "Open it."

She looked at the battered shoebox. One of the many things I've never mastered is gift-wrapping. The box looked like it had been packaged by a clumsy, color-blind kinder-gartner.

Maia set her tea on the railing and opened the box. Inside,

wads of tissue paper and a smaller box. Inside that, a still smaller box. This one black velvet.

She opened the hinged lid.

"Corny, I know," I said. "Ana helped me. She guessed the right size."

Maia held up the ring like it was critical case evidence. "Tres—"

"I didn't know about diamonds. The guy said that one was good. I didn't figure you for a diamond person, but Ana thought it was the right thing. So—"

"Tres—"

"If you think it's a bad idea . . ." My face felt hot. "I mean, I know it's weird."

"You're proposing to me?"

"You could keep the Austin apartment for business. The house here is huge. I mean . . . I never figured myself for old-fashioned, but the kid needs a dad. I mean, he's got one, but he *needs* one full-time. So, yeah. I'm proposing. Marriage, I mean."

"Jesus."

"Is that a no?"

She threw her arms around me and kissed me hard. The tea hit the porch and went rolling, splattering all over the place. The diamond ring dug into my neck.

When she finally let go I felt dizzy, like I'd just been pulled back from the edge of a cliff.

"That's a yes, stupid," she told me. "A very big yes."

She kissed me again, and I tried to force myself back into my life, but I couldn't do it. Something had changed. Something huge.

Nat King Cole was playing inside. The air outside was getting colder.

Mrs. Loomis called to us from the front door. She had *atole* for us to try. She and Sam were waiting to play Old Maid. We'd promised them a game.

Maia ran her hands through my hair. "Tres, do you have any idea what you're getting yourself into?"

"None," I admitted. "Absolutely none."

"That makes two of us," she said. "Come on."

She took my hand and led me inside, where the rest of our makeshift family was waiting.

JULY 14, 1987

WHEN SHE WAS SURE THE POLICEWOMAN was gone, thirteen-year-old Madeleine White opened the passenger's door of the Mercedes and got out.

She stared at her brother's body. A halo of blood glistened around his head. His fingers were curled like claws into the dirt.

She didn't want to get closer. She wanted to run. But a hot, scratchy rope knotted around her heart, pulling her forward.

She had watched the argument.

Until the end, she'd been more afraid of Frankie than the policewoman. Even now, as he lay motionless on the pavement, Madeleine was certain he'd get up. He was dazed, or faking it. You couldn't kill Frankie that easily.

She took another step toward him. Rain began to splatter her clothes, soaking into the cheap green cotton of her patient scrubs.

She wanted to be back at the facility. She hated the security guard for springing her from her room, shuffling her without explanation to a service exit where Frankie had been waiting. Frankie had handed him a thick roll of cash, told him, *You didn't see anything,* then driven away with her.

She wasn't supposed to leave. The judge had said so. She hadn't been outside Stokes-McLean in four months.

"I'm going to show you something," Frankie told her. "I'm going to make you understand."

He wouldn't say where they were going. All she knew: This wasn't the way home.

He took a lazy route through the South Side, past dark fields and clapboard houses, store signs in Spanish, Hispanic men sitting in pools of yellow light outside cantinas. He seemed to be giving her a tour, going slow so she could memorize every storefront, every turn.

She wondered how much he'd heard from her counselors. She'd started talking about him in therapy. She hated him now, for the times he'd hit her, the things he'd said, the nights she'd awakened and found him sitting at the foot of her bed.

She knew now that Frankie had killed those women. She'd even toyed with the idea of talking to the police.

In art class, she'd made a clay sculpture of his face. The counselors said it would make her feel better if she smashed it, to get power over him. Most of the kids were younger than she. They'd all been sexually or physically abused before they did whatever violence got them committed. Their clay images were crude little voodoo dolls which they smashed with enthusiasm. But Madeleine was an artist. She made Frankie's clay bust with the same care as the blue self-portrait she'd drawn him for Christmas.

The bust looked just like him. Even the counselors said so. But she couldn't smash it. Every day they would encourage her to do so, but the clay hardened, drying in splotchy white patches like mold.

The counselors must've broken confidentiality to warn Frankie. They'd probably taken his money just like that son-of-a-bitch security guard.

Frankie turned onto Mission Road, a crumbling stretch of blacktop that led nowhere except into deeper darkness.

Then the cop pulled them over.

Frankie grabbed Madeleine and shoved her back against the door. "Not one sound. Whatever happens, you stay in this fucking car or I'll slap the shit out of you. Understand?"

Now, looking down at his body, she could still feel the electric charge of his rage, the promise of violence that made her skin tingle.

I'm going to make you understand.

She knelt. The policewoman's baton lay next to Frankie's motionless hand.

She thought about her classmate, the girl in the locker room who'd teased her about Frankie being a psychopath. Rumors were all around town, the girl said. Frankie raped women. He got off on strangling them. The girl asked if he'd tried anything with Madeleine.

Madeleine remembered picking up the nearest heavy object, a biology textbook. She remembered hitting the girl in the face, then slamming her to the floor, pummeling her, not realizing until her friends pulled her off that the girl wasn't fighting back.

She had done that to someone she barely knew, yet she couldn't touch a clay mask of Frankie's face.

She realized she should be doing something—running, calling the police. But she couldn't call the police. The police had done this.

Cicadas chirred in the woods. Water was trickling somewhere—a stream out in the fields. Far off in the direction the police car had gone, a single streetlight gleamed.

This was the place Frankie had killed those women. Madeleine was sure of it.

And he had brought her here, his own sister.

If the lady cop hadn't come . . .

The wound was just behind Frankie's ear. His hair was sticky with blood.

Madeleine felt no anger toward the policewoman. Instead, she felt a strange kind of awe. One quick strike . . . was that really all it took to stop him?

A siren wailed in the distance. Maybe another police car, maybe something else.

She didn't want the policewoman to get in trouble. Frankie had made a world of trouble for all those women he'd hurt. She didn't want Frankie to ever get up.

She tried to think of what to do. She couldn't go home. Her father would never believe Frankie had meant to hurt her. He would somehow turn this into her fault.

The hospital was just over those fields.

She would have to walk miles in the dark, but she could do it. The security guard would let her in. He'd keep quiet. What choice did he have? He couldn't say anything without getting himself in trouble. The counselors may have betrayed her, but Stokes-McLean was still the safest place she'd ever known. She would just have to be more careful. She couldn't talk about her family anymore. Nobody could help her but herself.

She'd leave Frankie, pretend she was never here. As long as he stayed motionless, as long as he couldn't hurt her any-more . . .

Then he groaned. Madeleine started to tremble when Frankie rolled onto his back.

His face was unmarred, his eyes—so like hers—were dazed, searching the sky. He didn't look exactly conscious, but he was trying to make a fist, like he was trying to grab hold of life, pull himself back.

In that instant, Madeleine knew what would happen. Frankie would live. He would get better. He would punish her. The lady cop, whoever she was, would die for daring to touch him, just like the other women had.

It wasn't fair.

She looked down at her brother's face, pale and perfectly sculpted, so much like the clay bust. She heard her counselor's voice: *Take control. You'll never be free of him otherwise.*

She picked up the policewoman's baton.

•   •   •

AFTERWARD, SHE RAN DEEP INTO THE woods. Cactus tore at her legs. Branches scraped her face.

She didn't look back.

She stumbled in a stream, dropped the baton in the water. She kept going, running from the sound of the police siren somewhere behind her, impossibly thin and weak, but growing steadily louder, like a lament from the other side of the world.

ABOUT THE AUTHOR

Rick Riordan is the author of six previous award-winning novels. He lives in San Antonio, Texas, with his wife and two sons, where he is at work on his next novel.